THE

WIREGRASS

THE

WIREGRASS

A NOVEL

PAM WEBBER

SHE WRITES PRESS

The Wiregrass is a work of fiction. Names, characters, businesses, organizations, places, events, and incidents are either the product of the author's imagination or used fictitiously.

Published 2015
Printed in the United States of America
ISBN: 978-1-63152-943-6
Library of Congress Control Number: 2015932138

For information, address:
She Writes Press
1563 Solano Ave #546
Berkeley, CA 94707

She Writes Press is a division of Spark Point Studio, LLC.

In memory of John David Campbell and
Sarah Nettie Campbell Bayliss

In honor of family: past, present, and future.
They are the inspiration and motivation for the storytelling.

Spring 1968

Mitchell leaned back against the old tree and studied the silhouettes of dozens of military helicopters blanketing Field 10. His heart quickened as the massive machines thundered to life and their blue-white lights began blinking in the dark. He felt the gentle breeze from their spinning rotors quickly increase to a sand-stinging wind that pushed him against the tree's rough bark. He loved everything about this part—the sound, the lights, the feel . . . the freedom.

Lifting off row by row and tails first, the helicopters headed north, back home to Mother Rucker. If he had counted the nights right, the training for this group of pilots and crews was coming to an end and they would be shipping out, most likely to Vietnam.

They know they might not come back, but they go anyway. Where does that kind of courage come from?

As the wave of lights and noise faded into the distance, the woods went dark and silent again. He hated everything about this part. He was alone again; his only comfort was knowing the helicopters would be back the next day with new pilots and crews.

With only smoky moonlight to see by, he hurried down the shadowy path through the woods. He had to get back to the shabby trailer that was his home before his pa and the others returned. If they caught him sneaking in again, there would be hell to pay, and he was afraid. He hated his fear most of all.

Chapter I

The overstuffed suitcase was too heavy to carry, so I bumped it down the stone steps and pushed it across the damp grass toward the driveway, placing it in line with the others being loaded into the trunk of the blue Oldsmobile. The sun would be up in a couple of hours to dry things out, but for now the damp, the dark, and the hum of hundreds of invisible crickets made me tingle with excitement. School was finally out, and we were leaving on vacation, or at least what my family called vacation. In just a little while we would begin the long drive south down Route 29, across Virginia, the Carolinas, part of Georgia, and finally deep into Alabama, where narrow roads were bordered by strips of red dirt, kudzu, and drop-offs that ended in deep, blackwater bogs. By late tonight we would arrive in the tiny South Alabama town of Crystal Springs, where my momma was born and raised and where she met and married my soldier daddy. Crystal Springs was also where I had spent every summer since I could remember remembering.

Impatience to leave began long before school was out. My summer clothes had been packed for weeks and unpacked almost daily as the weather warmed and I needed items in my limited wardrobe. But come June, that case was stuffed, snapped, and ready to go. If the trip went according to plan, we would stop just long enough to fill the car with gasoline, take a bathroom break, and grab a bite at one of the many country diners along the way.

Earlier, when the 4:00 a.m. alarm sounded, the smell of percolating coffee had reached the upstairs of our little house, which meant Momma and Daddy were already sipping their first cups. My fifteen-year-old sister, Cindy, who for some reason was nicknamed Sam, and my six-year-old brother, Carl, also known as Li'l Bit, and I had dressed quickly and headed to the kitchen for the inevitable prune juice. Momma, as did most of her Southern family, had a concerning preoccupation with the well-being of her bowels and the bowels of everyone around her. This preoccupation usually resulted in all of us getting a daily dose of prune juice so we would "stay reg'lar." The only time we didn't have to swallow the nasty stuff was in the summer, when we were staying with Ain't Pitty in Crystal Springs.

"Drink what you want when you're thirsty, and let nature take its course," she'd say.

Since this morning was special, Momma also let us have some coffee. Li'l Bit's had to be saucer cooled, but Sam and I were allowed a regular cup. Once we were dropped off in Crystal Springs for the summer, this would change, too. Ain't Pitty let us have coffee every day if we wanted it. The rules were just different down there.

With bed pillows in tow, we climbed in the car as Daddy slammed the trunk closed. Our travel ritual, or at least the one Momma and Daddy liked, was that Sam, Li'l Bit, and I would go back to sleep so they would have some undisturbed travel time before stopping for breakfast. For the most part their plan worked, except for me. My name is Nettie, and up to this point in my just-turned-fourteen years, summers in Crystal Springs were what I lived for, and I was not about to sleep through the drive to get there. So, as Sam and Li'l Bit settled down, I stuffed my pillow tight against the car window, said good-bye to my hometown of Amherst, and watched as the miles began to slip by and the stars grew dimmer in the lightening sky.

Thinking we were all asleep, Momma and Daddy began to

whisper about Crystal Springs, family members who lived there, those who did not, and those who would make the annual summer pilgrimage back. Momma was worried about the health of her mother, Susie "Granny" Campbell, and came close to whining about the weaknesses and irritating habits of her five sisters and two brothers and their assorted offspring. I figured these folks were probably whining about us the same way. Ain't Pitty said that's just what families do.

At the beginning of summer, when everyone arrived at the home place, it was obvious the adults loved each other. It was also just as obvious after a few days why most of them lived apart and why some came back just long enough to say hello and drop their kids off for the summer. This ritual would repeat when summer was over and it was time to pick us up.

As the sun climbed higher, I started counting the familiar landmarks signaling we were getting closer to Crystal Springs. By breakfast we would cross the little falls of the Dan River into the mountains of North Carolina. By early afternoon we would be in the flatlands of South Carolina and Georgia, places where you could look in all directions and see a whole lot of nothing. By late afternoon we would pass the gold dome of the Georgia capital, and by suppertime the green military vehicles from Fort Benning would fill the road and we would be crossing the painted rocks of the Chattahoochee River into Alabama.

For Li'l Bit and me, it was the military trucks we passed that were interesting, but for Sam, the jeeps filled with young soldiers were what had her sitting up higher and paying closer attention to what was outside her window. Sam didn't say a word about these easy-on-the-eyes fellows. She liked boys; so did I, just not the same way. To me they were ballplayers, friends, or annoying twits.

"Just wait," Sam warned. "That'll change."

As we rolled deeper into Alabama, cities gave way to scattered small towns and plowed fields that fit together like blocks on a quilt—some wide, some tall, some with tree-lined hedges, and some with rain-washed gullies separating them. In the distance, farm tractors followed by floating clouds of dirt moved back and forth across large fields that stretched to the sky. Some of the large fields gave way to smaller, hodgepodge ones belonging to dirt farmers and sharecroppers who did most of their plowing and picking by animal and by hand. Occasionally, we would see these folks sitting on crates and stumps under shade trees or taking a swim in nearby creeks, most likely trying to cool off after working long hours in the heat.

By day's end, the sun would be setting on dozens of small, pine-filled islands dotting Lake Eufaula and we could watch the water turn as red-yellow-orange as the sky, an impressive sight even for a fourteen-year-old. According to the billboard at the entrance, the lake was thirty miles long, had seven hundred miles of shoreline, and was the bass-fishing capital of the world. But more important, it marked our entry into the region of the Deep South known as the Wiregrass.

Chapter 2

The Wiregrass was like no other place in the South, at least according to Momma. Named for the spidery, razor blade-like grass that thrived in the hellishly hot summers, the region was known for the uniqueness of its water. Below ground was an enormous underground lake that supplied clear water to hundreds of creeks, lakes, and swimming holes. Aboveground, fierce thunderstorms frequently blanketed the region, flooding streets and pushing muddy water through crisscrossing rivers toward the Gulf of Mexico.

Pulling a tattered map from the glove compartment, Momma traced a smudged pencil line down the southeast side of Alabama, across the panhandle of Florida, and along the Suwannee River, back up into Georgia.

"This is the Wiregrass, and Crystal Springs is right here in the middle."

Momma said it was the hundreds of tiny, dots-on-the-map towns that defined the good and the not-so-good nature of the Wiregrass. Folks here were a mix of the rich (new and old money), the poor (little or no money), the good (believers and behavers), and the bad (nonbelievers and misbehavers). Most rich folks had good jobs, big houses with air-conditioning, and nice cars, while most poor folks lived in shabby trailers or houses sitting on trashy lots scattered with broken furniture and odds-and-ends car parts that if put all together would not make a whole vehicle, much less one that ran. Our folks were in the middle, richer than some, poorer than others, believers most of the time, and behavers, at least when folks were looking.

Momma loved the Wiregrass, but every summer she gave us the same warning.

"This is a place where angels and demons dance, so be careful whose toes you're steppin' on. Rich or poor, nonbelievin', misbehavin' folks are dangerous. Rich ones think the rules don't apply to them, and poor ones have nothin' to lose."

Finally reaching the Wiregrass was exciting for two reasons. The long trip would soon be over, and, more important, I knew the cussins would be waiting for us. Cussins was the name we had given ourselves years ago: a small band of Campbell cousins who spent summer vacations in Crystal Springs together and who had a habit of occasionally letting cuss words fly. After multiple mouth washings with bar soap, we learned to control the impulse in front of Granny and those ain'ts and uncles who viewed swearing as a going-to-hell type of sin, but among ourselves and the more tolerant, we let the words fly when no other words seemed to fit.

The same ain'ts and uncles who said we were going to hell for cussing also said "trouble followed us like gum on a shoe," which was not exactly true. We were seldom victims of trouble; we were the cause of it, at least the harmless kind. Trouble was the most entertaining part of our summer, and we were successful at it because we were fearless and had the ability to plan it, do it, and keep our mouths shut.

Once in Crystal Springs, the cussins would stay with Ain't Pitty and Uncle Ben. They were our favorites, mostly because without them summers in the Wiregrass would not be possible, but also because they liked to spend time with us. Ain't Pitty was always saying, "Let's go," and we would be off fishing, swimming, junking, or sitting at her kitchen table, playing marathon games of Aggravation on her homemade board.

Ain't Pitty and Uncle Ben had one son, Hank, who was in the military somewhere overseas and seldom made it home. Ten years earlier, when Hank left, Ain't Pitty said she missed having young folks around and invited the cussins to spend the summer with her and Uncle Ben. They must have enjoyed having us, because they had invited us back every summer since.

We enjoyed a level of freedom with Ain't Pitty and Uncle Ben that we did not have at home, but we also had responsibilities. Ain't Pitty expected us to help with meals, tend the garden, and take care of her chicken coop. She also expected us to watch out for one another and stay out of trouble, at least as she defined it. Failing in any of these responsibilities resulted in the loss of our freedom, at least for a day. So we learned quickly to take care of business and guard the boundary between chores and fun. As far as we were concerned, it was more than a fair trade.

Rolling through the dark, I could see the blinking lights of the helicopters, or choppers, as we called them, moving back and forth in the distance, indicating that we were getting close to Fort Rucker, the aviation center for the entire US Army. Local folks called the base Rucks, but Uncle Ben, who was a helicopter mechanic there, said the pilots and crews called it Mother Rucker because of its high, hot, and hell-of-a-lot training schedule. The main base was located near the small town of Enterprise, but Rucks had large training fields scattered all across the Wiregrass, including one near Crystal Springs, called Field 10. Located on Choctaw Road, Field 10 was hidden by thick forest and surrounded by a tall barbed-wire fence. If you did not know to look for it, the unmarked dirt road leading to the security gate was easy to miss. We'd found it by accident a couple of summers ago and made the mistake of telling Uncle Ben.

"Field 10 is off-limits to everybody except the military," he'd warned. "Those soldiers carry guns with live ammunition and don't take kindly to trespassers. Keep your distance."

We knew Uncle Ben was serious because he seldom ordered us to do or not to do anything. However, it was not his orders that stopped us from going back to Field 10; it was the gun-toting soldier with the growling German shepherd that convinced us. The kindly soldier, holding the dog back, had said, "Nothing but trouble for you here, kids. Be on your way."

Rucks and Field 10 were beehives of activity day and night, training chopper pilots and crews to be sent all over the world. Most were going to a place in Southeast Asia called Vietnam. I was not sure where that was, but according to Uncle Ben, it was on the other side of hell.

Crystal Springs folks had become so used to the heavy, thumping whirl of Rucks's low-flying choppers that they set their watches by the training runs going back and forth over their vibrating roofs day and night. Every morning precisely at ten, the sky would darken as a blanket of choppers of various shapes and sizes flew over, headed toward Field 10. Throughout the day, the pilots and crews practiced takeoffs, landings, and SERE—or survival, evasion, resistance, and escape training in the brutal climate. Then, at exactly 10:00 p.m., with a grand showing of lights and noise, the choppers would take off in precise formation and make their way back to Mother Rucker. This ritualistic passing over Crystal Springs marked the time most town folks could go to bed and not be disturbed again until the next morning.

Thanks to Uncle Ben, we knew most military choppers were simply modified Hueys but could still tell the difference between Chinooks, Choctaws, Shawnees, Army Mules, Slicks, and Dustoffs, whether they were on the ground or in the air. Tonight, even with the car windows rolled up, I could hear the choppers in the distance. They were heading home, which meant Field 10 was lit and busy.

Most of the lights around Crystal Springs were off when we pulled into Granny's driveway. Her weathered house had been standing long enough to be surrounded by tall trees, towering hydrangea bushes, and well-worn paths.

Before the car stopped, I could see the bright red glow of a cigarette burning on the low end of the front porch and watched as the glow arched out into the yard. The porch lamp gave just enough light for us to see the long legs of John David Campbell, or J.D., as we called him, jump the three steps to the ground and head toward the driveway. Close on his heels were his younger sister, Sandra, and even younger sister, Sharon.

"Hey! said J.D., lifting my momma off the ground with a bear hug. "I thought y'all'd never get here."

As J.D. set Momma down, she kissed his cheek and proceeded to tell him if she ever saw him with another cigarette, she was going to tell his momma and daddy. Then, putting her hand out, she demanded his stash.

"But, Ain't Saaraah!"

"Give 'em up now. Don't get any more. And I won't tell."

Winking at me, J.D. slid his hand into the pocket of his newly
cutoff jeans, pulled out a red, crinkled pack of Winstons, and
handed them over. Momma smoked and wished she didn't, so did
J.D.'s momma and daddy, but he knew better than to argue. We had
had this conversation with him before. There were not enough
smokers around during the summer for him to sneak a cigarette
from, and even if he had the money, he could not buy the little
white weeds in town without Granny and Ain't Pitty finding out,
which would cost him a lot more than a pack.

Getting his grin back, J.D. threw an arm around Momma's neck
and said, "What the hell—smokin' costs money I don't have!"

A dozen hands carried suitcases to the front porch, where
Granny Campbell was waiting. Standing beside her were Uncle Jim
and Ain't June, parents of J.D., Sandra, and Sharon. Uncle Jim was
tall, with dark hair and a ready smile, and Ain't June was tall and
slim, with honey-colored hair. Next to Ain't Pitty, she was one of
the nicest ain'ts we had. Uncle Jim and Ain't June owned a restau-
rant in Mobile that required daily attention, so their visits to Crystal
Springs were usually short and sweet.

Granny looked really small standing beside Uncle Jim. She was
short and round, with wire-rimmed glasses and mostly gray hair
pulled back in a bun.

"Y'all c'mon in! I've got fresh divinity waitin'."

Granny was famous for the cloud-like white candy that melted
in your mouth, and she knew how to use it as motivation to get us
to do just about anything she wanted.

Going through the front door put us in Granny's great room,
with the dining room on the left and the living room on the right.
Above the fireplace was a painting of a Saint Bernard dog lying
dangerously close to a steep cliff. Curled up next to him, asleep, was
a little girl in a dark blue velvet dress. For some reason, this picture
made me feel safe and I looked for it every time I came in the door.

Granny had lived by herself since Pa Campbell died, years ago.
Pa, or John D. Campbell, was buried at the edge of town up on

Hardshell Hill. Most of us had never met or barely remembered the tall, skinny man in Granny's pictures, but we knew exactly where his headstone was in that old cemetery and we knew J.D. was named after him. Now, Granny was head of the Crystal Springs Campbells, and she ruled them, or thought she did, with a firm but kind hand.

Once inside, we headed straight for the back bedrooms to get rid of suitcases. Rooms on the left were for parents, and the large room on the right, with its two big beds, was for us—one for girls and one for boys. We had slept in the same room every summer for as long as any of us could remember and saw no reason to change now, even though last summer some of the ain'ts started whispering that it was time to separate us.

The slanted ceiling in our bedroom was twelve feet tall at the highest point and about eight at the lowest. There were three large screened windows, which gave the room plenty of light, but it was the window at the back of the room we were most interested in. It was only three feet off the ground and had a wooden screen that was easy to pop in and out. Unlocking the window, J.D. raised and lowered it and gave us the thumbs-up sign. We did not spend many nights at Granny's during the summer, but when we did, it was nice to be able to come and go at night without her knowing.

"C'mon. Let's go outside," whispered J.D., as Li'l Bit and Sharon were being tucked into bed. Moving quietly past the adults visiting in the dining room, we made our way back to the front porch.

At fifteen, J.D. was our leader and the closest thing the Alabama Campbells had to a Huckleberry Finn. Tall and lanky, he had tanned skin, unkempt dirty-blond hair, brown eyes that sparkled with mischief, and a smile that was as contagious as yawning. He had led us in search of fun and adventure every summer since we were old enough to follow him; together we had explored every inch of Crystal Springs and most of Geneva County.

"When did y'all get here?" I asked.

"Last night."

"We almost didn't get to come!" piped in Sandra, grinning at her brother. "If J.D. hadn't passed algebra, he was gonna have to go to summer school."

Sandra, twelve, was a longtime tomboy and a smaller, pretty version of J.D. with big, brown eyes and honey-colored hair that hung in two loose pigtails. She was J.D.'s shadow, just as Sharon was hers. At six, Sharon was the baby in their family and a smaller version of Sandra, except she wore her hair in a ponytail.

"Yeah, it was a close call. That's what I get for skippin' class."

I tried to imagine what summer in Crystal Springs would be like if J.D. were not here.

It wouldn't be summer.

"When's Eric gettin' in?" asked Sam.

Eric, the last cussin to arrive, lived over an hour away, in Dothan.

"He and Ain't Rachel are comin' in the morning."

"Still no military school?"

"No . . . well, at least not yet. Ain't Rachel keeps threatenin' it, though. Apparently, Eric snuck outta the house a few weeks ago to meet some friends, and the police picked 'em up in a bad part of town. I'm not sure what they were doin', but Ain't Rachel had to go to the police station to get 'im. She took his allowance away and grounded him until school was out."

"Hmm," I said. "That means we'll have to be extra careful when we—"

"Shh!" hissed J.D. as the front door opened and we were summoned to bed.

The next morning, I woke to the smell of coffee and breakfast cooking. Slipping out of bed, I put on my summer uniform of cut-off blue jeans and a smiley-face t-shirt and padded barefoot to the kitchen. I wanted to watch Granny make the biscuits.

Her kitchen work was in full swing as I kissed her wrinkled cheek good morning. Momma was not there to say no, so I poured coffee into one of Granny's sea-mist Fiesta cups and lightened it with cream. Sitting down at the worn red Formica table, I looked around. Nothing had changed. The old electric stove was still there, with its always-ready-to-go cast-iron skillet sitting on top, the white Hoosier cabinet was still against the wall, and the ancient refrigerator was still humming in the corner. I knew the refrigerator held a never-empty pitcher of tea and another one of water. This kitchen served as a comfortable gathering spot for many of Granny's friends and neighbors, who made their way here to sip tea and table-talk.

"How's everything in Amherst, sug?"

"The same."

"Was your first year of high school a good one?"

"Good enough, I guess. I got moved up, but the best part is that it's over."

The past year had been rough. I'd had to change from my familiar old school to an unfamiliar and intimidating high school, and along the way my body had decided to start changing in ways that were too embarrassing to talk about. Seeing the look on my face, Granny smiled and changed the subject.

"I'm gonna get back up there one of these days. Those Blue Ridge mountains are beautiful, especially in the fall."

Going to the Hoosier cabinet, Granny pulled out a large tan-and-blue pottery bowl. This was her biscuit bowl, and its deep sides stayed lined with a mixture of freshly milled flour, baking powder, soda, salt, yeast, and finely cut-in lard. Not only were Granny's biscuits melt-in-your-mouth good, but the process she used to make them was what Momma called an art form. Twice a day, every day, Granny would pour fresh buttermilk into the middle of the bowl and then put the tips of her fingers gently into the flour mixture at the edge of the buttermilk. Moving her fingers around and around the bowl, she would blend just the right amount of flour and buttermilk to make a perfectly shaped biscuit. She would then place the dough in a seasoned baking pan and repeat the process until the pan was full. What amazed me was her fingers never got sticky or dough covered, and when she was finished, all the buttermilk would be gone from the bottom of the bowl and the remaining flour would be bone dry.

"How'd you learn to do that, Granny?"

"Practice, sug. Practice makes permanent."

Dusting the tips of her fingers on her apron, Granny put the biscuits in the oven, lowered the heat under the bubbling grits, and turned the sizzling hand-stuffed sausage links that I knew had come from our Uncle Red's farm.

It was not long before the rest of the cussins were up and making their way to the table. When everyone had a spot, Granny said a quick blessing and we began spreading sweet butter and homemade fig preserves on biscuits and eating fat sausages with our fingers, something that would not be allowed if the mommas were up.

As we ate, Granny walked over and draped an arm across J.D.'s shoulders. This was an unusual move for her, so it got our attention.

"I'm really glad y'all are here, and I want you to have a good time this summer, but at the same time I expect you to behave and be respectful of folks, just like I expect them to be respectful of you. And be careful. They're some mean-spirited folks around who'll cause problems just because they can. Stay away from them. Understood?"

Nodding, I glanced at J.D. I wasn't sure how much the family knew about our secret nighttime activities, but I suspected Ain't Pitty knew more than she let on, Uncle Ben knew bits and pieces, and Granny, I hadn't been sure about until now.

She's heard something.

Regardless, Granny was right—some town folks would complain whether we gave them a reason to or not—but the more they complained, the more likely the Sheriff would be to keep an eye on us, and that could cause problems.

As the mommas arrived in the kitchen, we gave up our seats and headed to the porch. The day was already heating up, but the crows and mockingbirds were still cawing and the air still smelled new. The far end of Granny's porch held a blue, three-seat glider and a variety of chairs and was bordered by a thin hedge that gave the illusion of privacy. Settling in, we watched Li'l Bit and Sharon head to the long, flat stone that served as the first step to the porch. It also served as a shelter for hundreds of little gray roly-polies. Snapping twigs from the hedge, the little ones began tickling the tiny gray critters as they trekked back and forth across the stone, causing them to curl up in a ball and roll off the step into the grass. Once on the ground, the roly-polies would uncurl and make their way back through the grass jungle to the protection of the stone.

"Look," said Sam. "There's Jessie."

Following her gaze across the street toward Miz Maddie Tucker's house, we saw a slightly stooped man with a thick middle and a short, military-style haircut kneeling in the front yard, working on an old lawn mower. Jessie was Miz Maddie's simpleminded grandson. His daddy had brought him to Crystal Springs when he was a little boy and left him. No one knew if that was okay with Jessie and Miz Maddie or not, but you could tell they loved each other. Jessie was well fed and had clean clothes and a job mowing grass. He mowed for Miz Maddie, Granny, and other folks in town who could not mow for themselves. He mowed every day except Sunday, even when the heat forced others into the shade, and during the fall and winter, when little, if anything, grew. Each day when his work was done, Jessie would clean his old mower and get it ready for the next day's work. Afterward, we would see him fishing at Geneva County Lake, gigging frogs at Pitcher Plant Bog, or just roaming the streets of town at all hours of the day and night. We were pretty sure Jessie knew about our secret nighttime activities. Now and then, we would see him watching us from the shadows. We would wave or whisper, but he never responded. Jessie did not talk to us—or anybody else, for that matter. Granny said he could talk, but since the day his daddy left him, he'd simply chosen not to. Ain't Pitty said that at this point it was probably a good thing.

"With all the traveling Jessie does around town at night, a lot of folks would likely be in trouble if he ever decided to open his mouth."

Miz Maddie was also the widowed head of her family, and she and Granny were good friends. Granny never said anything bad about Miz Maddie and her folks, but according to Ain't Pitty, Miz Maddie's husband, who had been a farmer by day, had made his money by running bootleg moonshine across the state line at night. He died under mysterious circumstances almost fifty years ago, leaving Miz Maddie to raise three boys and three girls by herself. Now, all of the children had moved away and it was just her and Jessie.

Miz Maddie's house had a wide, shaded porch, and in the middle of the driveway turnaround was one of the oldest oak trees in the county, believed to date back to the Civil War. The limbs were as big as grown men, and their base formed a hollowed-out chair where Jessie would sit sometimes, watching people and time come and go. Some folks said Jessie was creepy, but not us. He was neither friend nor foe—Jessie was just Jessie. He lived in his own world and simply moved around, mostly unnoticed, by folks in ours.

Hearing a motor, we saw a familiar car turning into Granny's driveway. Eric, the seventh and last cussin, had finally arrived. As he and Ain't Rachel got out of the car, I could see how much Eric had grown since last summer. He was almost as tall as J.D. but more handsome in a filled-out kind of way. Eric and J.D. were like brothers, but appearance-wise they were exact opposites. Eric had light olive skin, dark hair and eyes, and a shaggy Beatles haircut. He had scattered freckles across his nose and cheeks and a chipped tooth that flashed like a neon sign when he smiled, which he almost always did. He also talked in a slow Southern drawl, as opposed to J.D.'s lightning-fast one. Eric was our second in command, Tom Sawyer to J.D.'s Huckleberry Finn.

Eric's daddy had died when he was a baby, and now it was just him and his momma, and she worked hard just to keep them going. As they walked to the porch, it was obvious Ain't Rachel adored Eric and he adored her back, but they both looked a little relieved that summer vacation was finally here.

Like J.D., Eric had a knack for attracting trouble, so much so that for the last couple of years Ain't Rachel had been threatening to send him to military school if things didn't change. But either he hadn't been bad enough or she hadn't been able to bring herself to do it, because he was still home.

We gave Ain't Rachel a quick hug as she made her way up the steps and into the house and Eric plopped down on the glider.

"Boy! I thought summer never would get here."

"Long year?" I asked

"Hell of a long one!"

"J.D. said your momma still has military school in her head."

"Yep. Especially since the principal called the last day of school and told her I'd been caught drinkin' beer with a bunch of guys underneath the bleachers. He gave me after-school detention when school starts in the fall, but my grades were good, so I passed."

"Were you? Drinkin', I mean?" asked Sam.

"Yeah, kinda. We were celebratin' school bein' out, but it really upset Momma. She kept sayin' I was headed for the state penitentiary in Wetumpka, wherever that is. She also said she was gonna check out more military schools and if I gave her one more reason, she was gonna put me in one of 'em."

"I'm surprised Ain't Rachel didn't make you get a haircut," teased J.D.

"Oh, she was on me about that, too, but I told her I'd get it cut here."

We all knew there would be no haircut until Ain't Pitty insisted, and then she would be the one to do it. Ain't Pitty was a good barber, but she did not want to cut any head more than once a summer. So his hair would be short, very short.

By now another car was pulling into the driveway. It was a long white Oldsmobile, the same one we were all riding in last summer when Uncle Ben announced that the odometer was rolling over the two hundred thousand–mile mark. It was Ain't Pitty and Uncle Ben's car, and as old as it was, it still ran like a dream, thanks mostly to Uncle Ben's skill as a mechanic.

Uncle Ben was a head taller than J.D., stout, with dark hair and a deep tan on his face and forearms from working on helicopter engines in open fields. He was also a man of few words, quick to laugh, slow to get mad, and he adored Ain't Pitty.

Ain't Pitty's given name was Patricia, but it had quickly been shortened to Pitty Pat and then to Pitty by the time she started school. A little taller than Sam, she had short, salt-and-pepper hair, a round face, and brown eyes framed by black-and-silver horn-rimmed glasses. Dressed in her usual shorts and matching short-sleeved shirt, Ain't Pitty always managed to look cool despite the summer heat.

"Y'all ready to go to my house?"

"Yes, ma'am!"

"Well, Uncle Ben and I have some visitin' to do first." Heading into the house, she added, "Make sure your bags are ready to go when we are."

As the screen door slapped shut, we could hear a loud whupping sound approaching from the north.

"Here they come, y'all," shouted J.D.

Running into the front yard, we watched a cloud of Rucks's choppers roar overhead and waved to the young soldiers sitting in the open doors. Some waved back, others gave us the peace sign, and some just stared off into the distance. I couldn't help but wonder which of them would not make it back home. Last summer, Uncle Ben showed us a wall at Rucks where the names of pilots and crewmembers who had not made it home were written. There were a lot of names on that wall.

"It's ten o'clock," said J.D. after the last of the choppers had passed. "If we're gonna get to town before the streets get too hot, we better get movin'."

In a few weeks our feet would have some summer toughness, but until then we would need flip-flops, amazing pieces of rubber that provided air-conditioned protection for our feet and sound effects with each step. They would be our first purchase this morning at Wilkes's General Store, and if the price hadn't gone up, we'd get them for a quarter.

Making sure we had enough change in our pockets, we jumped the rain ditch onto Railroad Street and headed to town.

Chapter 3

Small towns around the Wiregrass were seldom planned. They just sprouted up wherever folks tended to gather, which was usually near road intersections, water, and shade. Crystal Springs had all three. There were several intersections surrounding the town, a natural springs pool, creeks, and an extraordinary number of shade trees, thanks to Mother Nature and the good ladies of the local Women's Guild.

Two county roads bordered Crystal Springs from the north, two bordered it from the south, and in between were the paved, white crushed-stone streets of the town. The most-traveled streets were set up like a tic-tac-toe board. Railroad Street and First Street ran north and south, and Magnolia Street and Pine Street ran east and west, with a smattering of smaller streets mixed in along the way. Crystal Springs proper was located at the intersection of First and Pine, on the southern end of town.

We knew the streets well, including the small, unnamed alleys and hidden paths that crisscrossed the town and surrounding woods. We did not know how all of the streets got their names, but we knew Railroad Street, or the Railroad, as we called it, got its name because there used to be a railway station at the southern end. But when farm produce started moving by trucks and folks started moving by cars, the railway station closed and eventually disintegrated into a pile of rotting lumber and partially dismantled tracks that were overgrown with weeds. However, the Railroad continued to be the major north–south street for the town, and we ran it daily, mostly because Granny lived on the northern end, Ain't Pitty lived in the middle, and the turnoff to town was at the southern end.

"The Railroad's already heatin' up, y'all. Don't be slowpokes," called J.D.

Picking up the pace, we ran from one patch of tree shade to another to keep our feet from burning. Where there were long sections of hot pavement without shade, we walked in the sandy dirt beside the road, pushing our feet under the top layer to the cooler dirt below.

By high summer, any attempt to walk barefooted on the pavement would result in frying-pan burns and blistered feet. Flip-flops would be our only protection, and staying in them took skill. If we were not careful, the melting, gooey street tar would suck them right off our feet, leaving us to hopscotch to the nearest tree shade or rain-filled pothole to relieve the burning until the captured flops could be recovered.

"C'mon, Sharon," said J.D., squatting down. "Hop on. The road's gettin' too hot for you to be walkin' on. Eric, you take Li'l Bit."

Eric scooped Li'l Bit up and swung him around to his back as easily as if he were picking up a kitten. Li'l Bit adored Eric and J.D. and did anything they told him to do.

"Momma said the *Farmers' Almanac* predicted a really hot summer with bad storms this year," said Eric.

"How's that any different from what it's normally like around here?" I asked.

"Beats me."

Everybody complained about the weather in the Wiregrass, but it was a love-hate relationship. Women loved what it did for their skin but hated what it did to their hair. Men loved what it did for their crops but hated having to work in the sweltering heat. As far as we were concerned, the weather was just part of summer.

Most of the houses along the Railroad were well equipped for the heat and rain. The newer ones had low-pitched white roofs and covered carports. Ain't Pitty's across-the-street neighbor, Miz Lettie, had one of these. She had built her house with money left to her by two dead accountant husbands. She lived there now with Accountant Husband Number Three, an unfortunate fellow Ain't Pitty called Mr. Lettie. I'm not sure what Ain't Pitty disliked most, Miz Lettie or her fancy, air-conditioned house.

Most other folks along the Railroad lived in older bonnet houses, which had steep roofs with flared bottoms. This design provided plenty of shade for porches and helped direct rainwater away from the houses and toward nearby trees, bushes, and sweet-smelling flowers, giving the Railroad a lush, almost tropical feel.

There was one exceptionally nice house on the street. Its single occupant was someone we had never met and hoped we would never cross paths with. It was Geneva County's one and only judge. Uncle Ben said the Judge was a stern, no-nonsense man, both inside and outside the courthouse. His stately home sat on top of the only hill on the Railroad and was one of the few two-story houses in the entire county. Covered with white stucco, it was surrounded on three sides by a columned portico and a host of trees and flowering bushes. One of the main attractions in the Judge's yard was his award-winning rose garden. Ain't Pitty said when the Judge's wife died, several years ago, he started growing roses and got so good at it that every summer, when the roses were in full bloom, he won the Women's Guild Garden of the Month award.

"Looks like the Judge is still up there," said J.D., eyeing the big house.

"Yep," agreed Eric. "All the years we've been coming here, and we've never seen 'im. Wonder why."

"Don't know, don't care," I said. "There are only two men in this town we really don't want to see: him and Sheriff Coker."

Whether we wanted the other neighbors to notice us or not, our first running of the Railroad was drawing attention. Some folks smiled and waved, some stared, some peeked out from behind curtains, and some paid no attention at all.

Our arrival each summer usually caused excitement among some and worry among others—excitement because we provided plenty of gossip fodder for the quiet little town, and worry because no one knew who was on this year's list. The list was rumored to include names of possible targets for our secret nighttime activities. While we had never been caught, we had been accused of things like toilet papering, or TP-in', front yards, washing car windshields with eggs and soap, tying full trash cans to car bumpers, setting off firecrackers and stink bombs underneath the windows of sleeping grumps, and raiding neighborhood clotheslines to steal his and her holey underwear to run up the two flagpoles in town. We had also been accused of breaking toothpicks off in the doorbells of the few houses in town that had them. The doorbells would keep ringing until the homeowners found the broken-off toothpicks and were able to tweezer them out. Perhaps the most lasting activity we had been accused of was stacking empty tin cans in open crawl spaces under houses and placing food scraps in the top one to attract jittery skunks. When the skunks attempted to get the food, the cans would collapse with such a loud, echoing racket, the terrified animals would attack the threatening tins with the only weapon they had. The effects of this battle usually lingered for weeks.

Over the years, Ain't Pitty had received complaints from folks, including Miz Lettie, that we had done this or that, but we would deny the accusations and offer a reasonable alibi, which we always prepared in advance, and Ain't Pitty would send the complainer away with her standard response: "If you have proof it was them, let me know. Otherwise, it could have been any of a dozen kids in town."

But late last summer, the complaining reached a new level. We were in Wilkes's General Store with Ain't Pitty one day, when a lady wearing a pillbox hat and a Women's Guild pin approached her.

"Pitty, you just have to stop these children from running wild around town at all hours of the night. They're getting older now, and who knows what shameful things they're up to?"

Ain't Pitty's eyes turned to slits, and her face darkened up like a storm cloud. Telling us to wait outside, she turned on the woman.

"How dare . . . shame on you . . . children . . . hypocrite . . ."

We did not have to hear all of Ain't Pitty's words to know their intent, and we were really glad all that fury was not aimed at us. It was not long before the Women's Guild lady came flying out of Wilkes's, holding tight to her hat. Ain't Pitty followed her out the door and watched as she squealed tires trying to get away.

We had been accused of a lot of things over the years, but what the pillbox-hat lady implied was different and we knew it.

Vacation ended last summer with no more complaints, but something had changed. Now, as we walked the Railroad for the first time this summer, something still felt off.

Chapter 4

Going single file, we made our way through the narrow alley separating the bank and Wilkes's General Store. Exiting on First Street, we could see cars and trucks pulling in and out of the slanted parking spaces in front of Booker's Feed and Seed.

"Looks like Willie Ray's still doing a boomin' business," said Eric.

"Yeah, Ain't Pitty said he's still a skirt-chasing, moonshine-drinking, evildoin' no-count and that she'll skin us alive if we ever go in there," replied J.D.

Willie Ray was one of the bad rich people Momma had warned us about. His family had owned the Feed and Seed store for more than fifty years and used what they called "friendly credit" to obtain many of Geneva County's most productive farms. They would give struggling farmers free credit at the store, and at the end of the growing season, if the farmers could not pay their bills in full, the Bookers foreclosed on their homes and land. Willie Ray was the latest and, according to Ain't Pitty, the meanest Booker ever to manage the store.

Willie Ray's wife, Annie, used to be Ain't Pitty's best friend, but after she and Willie Ray got married, he refused to let her see or talk with Ain't Pitty. Now, Annie was seldom, if ever, seen around town, not even at church on Sundays.

"Wonder if he's really sellin' illegal stuff out of the back of the store at night, like Ain't Pitty said," I mused.

We had staked out the loading dock at the Feed and Seed several times over the years but had never seen Willie Ray or anyone else doing anything that seemed illegal.

"I dunno, but we can watch 'em again this summer and see."

Wilkes's General Store was owned by brothers Digger and Short. If you saw them, it was easy to see how Mr. Short got his nickname, but it was different with Mr. Digger. According to Ain't Pitty, his name came from the New Testament and meant "to share," which Mr. Digger did a lot.

Their store was a dated, two-story clapboard building with a wide front porch and two large, wooden screen doors that squeaked when they opened and slapped loudly when they shut. On either side of the doors were tall windows with painted-on ads for Coca-Cola, Fresca, penny candy, and fresh meat. Under the window on the left was a long plank bench, and along the outside railings were a variety of crates. In the middle was a small barrel with a checkerboard painted on top. This sitting area served as the daily gathering place for the half dozen or so old, gray men who sat around chewing words, spitting chaw, and playing a never-ending game of checkers. These men, whom Ain't Pitty called the Porch Keepers, complained about the weather, which was always too hot, worried about the crops, which never seemed to be growing as they should, shook their heads over the latest gossip, and watched over the comings and goings of local folks. When the Porch Keepers were in session, their wives were usually across town at the senior center, quilting, planning their monthly dance, or putting together care packages for the Rucks pilots and crews who were being shipped out.

On the other side of the porch was a help-yourself bin, which was a large wooden box with a slanted lid. In the evenings when they closed the store, Mr. Digger would place jars of flour, oil, meat, and other edibles nearing the end of their usefulness in the bin. Any area folks who were in need could come and help themselves to whatever was in the box. The sign on the lid asked folks to take just what they needed so there would be some left for others. The next morning, Mr. Digger would sometimes find a note of thanks, a jar of fresh honey, or a basket of peanuts, and sometimes the bin was just empty.

The Porch Keepers watched as we made our way up the steps. Never one to be shy, J.D. suddenly turned toward the old men and, bending at his long waist, made a deep, arm-sweeping bow in their direction, which the rest of us immediately imitated, though not nearly as gracefully. Laughing, we hurried into the store, leaving the chuckling old men behind.

"Hi, kids! I was wonderin' when y'all'd get to town."

"Hey, Mr. Digger!"

In the center of the store was an old Ping-Pong table stacked so high with flip-flops in every size and color imaginable, they almost touched the six-blade fan hanging from the ceiling. By summer's end, most of these flip-flops would be long gone and the few remaining mismatches would go into the help-yourself bin.

Rooting through the pile, we selected the colors we wanted and the sizes we needed and headed over to the long oak counter. At the front end was an old National cash register, and at the far end were jars of pickled things that were fun to look at but that I would never eat. The counter's slanted glass front covered baskets overflowing with all kinds of penny candies, such as Mary Janes, Milk Maid caramels, Neapolitan coconuts, root beer barrels, bubble gum cigars, candy cigarettes, and saltwater taffy, but our favorite candy was not there.

"Mr. Digger, do you have any Fireballs?" asked J.D.

"Not today. But I'll have some in by Friday."

I watched as Mr. Digger put our second-choice candy in a bag. He was long, lean, and mostly bald and had on his usual black-and-white-striped apron, white shirt with rolled-up sleeves, and black pants. He always had a smile on his face and always asked about Ain't Pitty. By late August, when our candy money was low or gone, Mr. Digger would slip a few Fireballs into our bag regardless of what we had come to buy.

"Hey, kids! Welcome back!" called Mr. Short from the back of the store, where his butcher shop was housed.

Dressed just like his brother, he was putting a fresh coat of sweet-smelling mystery oil on his gigantic butcher block. Rumor had it that, in addition to walnut oil and beeswax, Mr. Short included a secret ingredient in his oil that kept folks coming back for more of his meat. Ain't Pitty said only the teetotalers called it a secret ingredient. Everyone else just called it Southern Comfort.

"Hey, Mr. Short! Good to be back!"

We watched as he began sharpening his knives on an old blue whetstone. His hands moved those knives so fast that it was hard to see the blades until they started to spark, which, according to Mr. Short, was when they were sharp enough to leave no usable meat behind. He had warned us many times not to touch his knives: "They'll cut you to the bone, and you'll never feel it."

Wilkes's backyard was also a center for business. It held a large cricket cage and a crawling mound of wormy compost, which was fed daily with Mr. Digger's culled vegetables. Folks would stop by the backyard to pick up their favorite fishing bait and pay for it by dropping pennies into the rusty flour sifter nailed to a nearby tree. The brothers let us have worms for free during the summer because we'd keep their compost pile turned.

Sitting on the store's back porch were Mr. Short's rocking chair and banjo. His bluegrass band played for the monthly senior center dances and for the Fourth of July and Labor Day picnics. At the end of the day or if the store was slow, we could hear his banjo echoing through the streets.

Slipping on our new flip-flops, we headed to the front door.

"Thanks, Mr. Digger! Bye, Mr. Short! We'll be back!"

This time, we ignored the Porch Keepers and jumped the steps to the ground.

"How bad do y'all want Fireballs?" asked J.D.

"Real bad!" said Li'l Bit, jumping up and down.

"Real bad, huh, little fella?"

J.D. glanced across the intersection at Crystal Springs' newer but less reputable store.

"To get 'em, we're gonna have to go over to Slater's."

"J.D., you know what Ain't Pitty said," I warned.

"I know, I know. But she didn't actually say for us not to go in."

"Well, we either go in or wait till Friday to get Fireballs," said Eric.

"We don't need to get into trouble on our first day," cautioned Sam.

"Well, we won't if Ain't Pitty doesn't find out," insisted J.D. "And if she does, she didn't tell us not to go in; she just said to watch out for Ol' Man Slater."

"Okay," said Eric, looking at Li'l Bit and Sharon. "But they need to know the rules."

"Right."

Squatting down, J.D. explained to the little ones that being a cussin meant you never, ever tattled, no matter what.

"Now swear," he added, holding his hand out, palm side down. Li'l Bit and Sharon stacked their hands on top, followed by me, Sandra, Sam, and Eric.

"Li'l Bit and Sharon, do y'all swear on all the graves on Hardshell Hill never to tell anybody anythin' about what we see, say, or do?"

With one big handshake, they swore and we headed across the intersection.

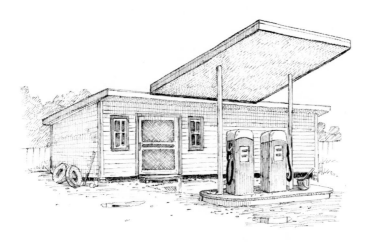

Slater's was newer than Wilkes's but was dirty and known for the trashy folks who hung around there, folks the Porch Keepers kept an eye on. But the store did a good business, since it sold two things the Wilkes brothers did not: beer and gasoline.

Slater's building was squat, with little windows, a screen door, and a shed-style tin roof that slanted upward over two gasoline pumps. When the afternoon thunderstorms came, the rainwater raced off the slanted tin like a waterfall and landed right in front of the store.

"What fool thought this was a good idea?" asked J.D., eyeing the roof and stepping over the permanent puddle guarding the screen door.

Inside, the store was dingy and smelled like the overflowing ashtray sitting on the counter. Teivel Slater, the owner, stood inside the door as we entered. He was taller than J.D., potbellied, and had thin, greasy hair. Miz Slater, who was behind the counter, was thin and plain and seldom smiled if her husband was around.

Mr. Slater stared at J.D. with narrowed eyes.

He probably heard the "fool" comment.

Cutting a wide circle around him, we hurried down the candy aisle and grabbed as many Fireballs as we could carry. Using my t-shirt to keep the candy from spilling, I turned toward the counter just as the screen door opened. Coming in was the prettiest boy I had ever seen—heart-stopping pretty. He had dark, almost black hair curling against his neck, tanned and smooth olive-colored skin, and big, deepwater-blue eyes set under long, dark lashes. He was so pretty, all I could do was stare and try to remember how to breathe, my legs wobbling like jelly.

"Nettie!" yelled J.D. "Watch what you're doin'!"

Jolted back to reality, I realized the Fireballs I was holding were falling to the floor.

Good grief!

Two grungy-looking men followed Pretty Boy into the store. Both were dirty and smelled like a sickening mixture of sweat, dirt, and kerosene.

"Well, well, who've we got here?" asked the taller, dirtier man, his eyes landing on Li'l Bit and me.

My face started to burn when I realized he was staring at my chest, his stinky smell stinging my nose and turning my stomach at the same time. Moving around him, I set my remaining Fireballs on the counter and pulled Li'l Bit beside me. The dirty man moved with us, standing so close that his arm touched my shoulder, making my skin crawl.

"Leave 'em alone," Pretty Boy said quietly from the door.

Glaring, the dirty man warned, "Now, Mitch, you ain't tellin' yer ol' man what to do, are ya?" Looking back at us, he added, "Besides, I'm just lookin' at the scenery."

The two men started laughing, revealing big gaps between the few teeth they had between them. Pushing past us, they headed toward the beer coolers at the back of the store, but Pretty Boy stayed where he was.

We paid for the candy and headed out the door, which Pretty Boy held open for us. I could not help but notice that he was as neat and clean as the two men were sloppy and dirty, and he smelled really good—fresh, like Zest, the same soap Ain't Pitty had in her shower and, as of that moment, my favorite soap.

Glancing at Pretty Boy as I passed, I tried to say thanks, but no sound came out.

"What's the matter with you, Nettie?" growled J.D. when we were out the door. "You were all fumble fingers in there!"

"Nothin's wrong with her," teased Sam. "She was just enjoyin' the scenery, too!"

"Hush up, Sam!"

I just stared at the street until the laughter died down.

"Let's go see Miz Tilly," suggested Eric.

Grateful the attention was off me, I followed the others toward Crystal Springs' only café, my breathing slowly returning to normal. Hoping to get one more look at Pretty Boy, I glanced over my shoulder. He was still standing in the doorway, watching us. Seeing me look, he flickered his hand in a little wave and smiled—a smile so warm and inviting it reeled me in like a fish with no fight. As I snapped back around, my breath left me in a flash and the heat in my face had nothing to do with the sun.

Miz Tilly's café was long and narrow, with a bright white counter, round metal stools with red vinyl seats, and picture windows across the front and sides. Tilly Jackson, the owner, said the windows were for light, but Granny said Miz Tilly liked to know what was going on around town and with those big windows, she did not miss much.

"Look," said J.D. "There she is."

We could see Miz Tilly standing at the counter. Tall, slim, and the color of lightly creamed coffee, she had salt-and-pepper hair, ageless skin, kind eyes, and a talent for country cooking. She had been preparing three meals a day, six days a week, for the better part of forty years and was known for her fried chicken, angel biscuits, turnip greens, and pecan pies.

The café's door burst open just as J.D. reached for the handle, and Willie Ray Booker came out, preceded by the smell of too much aftershave. Dressed in pressed khakis and a plaid shirt, he pushed his way roughly through the middle of us. I assumed he was headed back to the Feed and Seed, which was on the corner next to the café, its loading dock right behind Miz Tilly's.

"How rude," said Sam.

"Yeah," added Sharon. "And he's got on enough perfume to gag a maggot. Yuck!"

"Guys don't wear perfume, Sharon," laughed Eric. "They wear aftershave."

"What?" asked Li'l Bit.

"It's stuff guys put on their face to smell good."

"Well, it didn't work. He stinks!"

"In more ways than one," I added.

"Whadda y'all expect? It's Willie Ray. He could make roses smell bad," said J.D., pulling the café door open and causing the little bell at the top to ring.

"My, my! I was wonderin' when y'all were gonna make your way to my door!" said Miz Tilly, coming around the counter, wiping her hands on her neck-to-knees apron.

Giving each of us a wrapped-up hug, she commented on how much we had grown since last summer. Getting to me, she stepped back.

"Why, young'un! You's losin' your baby fat and growin' woman parts! Ooh-wee!" Fluffing my short hair, she added, "You's gettin' pretty like Sam with those big brown eyes and dark hair. You musta gotten your colorin' from your daddy, 'cause Sam and Li'l Bit are light-colored like your momma."

My face was in flames again as Miz Tilly headed back behind the counter and reached for a pitcher of lemonade. I felt Sam's hand in the middle of my back.

"Nobody heard that but you 'n' me," she whispered. "Keep movin'."

She was right. No one else seemed the least bit aware of my continuing humiliation, so I climbed on the closest stool and accepted the cold drink being pushed my way.

"So what's new, Miz Tilly?" asked J.D.

"Not much. Y'all musta done good in school for your mommas to let you come back."

"Well, maybe not good, but good enough," drawled Eric.

"I saw y'all comin' outta Slater's. Y'all need to stay away from over there."

"But they're the only ones with Fireballs, Miz Tilly!" squealed Li'l Bit.

"Yeah!" echoed Sandra, her fingers and tongue red from the one she kept taking in and out of her mouth to control the burn.

"That so? I 'magine Mr. Digger has somethin' better'n Fireballs in that big case of his."

"Please don't tell on us, Miz Tilly. Ain't Pitty'd have a fit if she knew," begged J.D.

"Your secret's safe with me. Just promise y'all won't go in there again."

"We promise. Right, y'all?"

I nodded but felt guilty doing it. It was unlikely we would keep this promise. We would just be careful not to let Miz Tilly see us next time.

"I'll bet Miz Susie's plumb tickled, bein' her family's home! You young'uns keep her young! She told me last week to stock up on lemonade 'cause y'all'd be here soon."

According to Granny, she and Miz Tilly had grown up on neighboring farms and used to climb trees, make mud pies, and pick berries together. But Miz Tilly's daddy had gotten behind on his bill at the Feed and Seed, and, as was their pattern, the Bookers had taken everything.

When her family lost their home, Miz Tilly went to work as a cook for Mary and Larue Murdock, the old couple who owned the Crystal Springs Café. Miz Tilly's cooking became so popular, and her relationship with the Murdocks so strong, they let her move into an adjacent apartment and open and close the café. Within a year, Miz Tilly was running the entire business and the Murdocks retired to Panama City. Miz Tilly visited them twice a year to deliver a check and let them know how the café and Crystal Springs were doing. When the Murdocks eventually died, they left the building to Miz Tilly, much to the chagrin of their seldom-seen children. Since then, Miz Tilly had expanded the café and started a carry-out service so folks could stop by and pick up a meal to take home. According to Ain't Pitty, Miz Tilly ran a better business than most men.

"We ran into Willie Ray comin' in," said J.D. "He still eatin' here all the time, Miz Tilly?"

"Breakfast, lunch, and sometimes supper."

"How much have you collected from him so far?" asked Sam.

"A fair amount, sug," she replied with a wink. "A fair amount."

Miz Tilly served Willie Ray just like everybody else who came into the café, but she'd told Granny a long time ago she was going to get back what the Bookers had taken from her family, even if she had to do it one coin at a time. So every time Willie Ray paid his bill, Miz Tilly put the money in a big coffee can. When the can was full, she put the money in a savings account at the bank. According to Granny, she'd already saved more than the Bookers made foreclosing on her family's farm, and one day she was going to buy the Feed and Seed, tear it down, and build her own farm-supply store where the old railway station used to be. One that has a payment plan for folks who need it.

Setting a plate of butter cookies on the counter, Miz Tilly said, "It's best if y'all just stay away from Willie Ray, ya hear? He's trouble."

The Wiregrass is a place where angels and demons dance, just like Momma said, and we know which one Willie Ray is.

"Mr. Eli still churning butter, Miz Tilly?" asked Sandra.

"All day, every day, 'cept Sunday."

Years ago, Miz Tilly had married Eli Jackson, a hardworking man who kept her and most folks in Crystal Springs supplied with home-churned butter. They would come by his barn with bowls, jars, and crocks to buy scoops of the creamy spread. Mr. Eli had rigged up a system in his barn that allowed him to churn four barrels of butter at a time, using a small windmill and pulley to raise and lower the handles. He also had an old hand churn Miz Tilly insisted he use when making butter for her café. We could not tell the difference, but she could.

Miz Tilly and Mr. Eli had raised several children, all of whom had grown up and moved away. One of their grandsons, Luke, lived with them for a while and helped out in the café and butter barn after school. When we were in town, Miz Tilly let him go swimming and exploring with us if the café was not busy. But several years ago Luke had disappeared on his way home from school. The Sheriff and his deputies looked for him for weeks but never found him or a clue as to what had happened. Folks around town said Luke probably ran away, but Miz Tilly insisted her grandbaby would never have run away from his grandmomma like that. Regardless, after a while folks gave up and quit looking for the little boy. We even stopped asking for news about Luke, because every time we did, Miz Tilly teared up and sadness wrapped around her like a blanket.

We were finishing the cookies when the café door opened and

a group of folks made their way in. Downing the last of our lemonade, we hustled around the counter, washed our glasses, and turned them upside down on the drying rack.

"Thanks, Miz Tilly! We'll see you later!"

"Y'all stay together, ya hear? There've been drifters around town lately."

"Yes, ma'am. We will."

Uncle Ben always said most drifters were just good folks who were down on their luck. But he also cautioned us about the ones who moved in and out of the shadows around town at night. "They're lookin' to steal what they can't swindle, so be careful."

Bad, poor men—they don't have anything to lose.

According to Uncle Ben, some drifters would even steal corn right out of the fields to grind into moonshine. They kept their stills hidden in low-lying swamps around the county, places that had a good water supply but were hard to find. The Sheriff and his deputies searched for these stills all the time, but as soon as they found and destroyed one, the cagey moonshiners would build another one somewhere else.

"If y'all ever find one of their stills while you're out and about, leave it alone," Uncle Ben said. "Moonshiners take their business seriously, and they'll hurt anyone who gets in their way."

Leaving the café, we headed north. At the edge of town, where First Street intersected with Magnolia, was an outdoor community gathering place called the Crossing. It held a large gazebo, benches, and a flagpole complete with spotlight. There was even a little storage house toward the back where the Women's Guild kept seasonal and holiday decorations.

The little house was a great place to hide and watch what was going on around town at night. We had been warned by the Women's Guild, via Miz Lettie, to stay away from the house, and as far as she knew, we did. However, several years ago, we found the key to the door hidden under the front step, so we would sometimes sneak in at night, just because we could. We were also careful to leave everything as we found it so the good ladies would not change the hiding place for the key.

Memorial Day decorations were still up at the Crossing when we got there. The gazebo was draped in red, white, and blue buntings, and there was a miniature red, white, and blue cannon and a small stack of fake cannonballs sitting in front of the flagpole.

Crystal Springs always honored its military dead. Granny's oldest son, our uncle Jack, had been killed during World War II in France. We never had a chance to know him, but Granny still talked about how handsome he was, his service to his country, and his sacrifice. We also knew other families in Crystal Springs and Amherst whose sons had died in places like Korea and Vietnam, so we knew better than to mess with the Crossing on this holiday.

Li'l Bit and Sharon went to play with the cannon while the rest of us sat down on the steps of the little house, grateful to be in the shade.

"Key's still here," said J.D., running his fingers under the first plank.

"Remember how we almost got caught in here last summer?" laughed Eric.

"Yeah! We were damn lucky."

"Really!" I added. "I don't know how that couple didn't see us."

"They were concentrating on other things, I imagine." J.D. grinned.

Late last summer, we'd been roaming around town in the middle of the night and had gone into the little house to take a break and escape the mosquitoes. We had not been in there very long when we heard voices and saw a couple hurrying up the path toward the house. We did not recognize the man, but the woman was the Women's Guild lady with the pillbox hat who had accused Ain't Pitty of letting us run wild and do shameful things in the middle of the night.

When the couple reached the steps, they started searching for the key, which J.D. still had in his pocket. Luckily, we managed to sneak out the back door and into the woods as they realized the front door was unlocked and came in. After hiding for what seemed like hours, we saw the couple finally leave, each going off in a different direction. When J.D. was sure they were long gone, he locked both doors and put the key back under the step.

At the time, I had an idea about what the couple was doing in the little house but didn't know enough to say anything. Now, I had more information. Momma had given me the mortifying "birds and bees" talk last fall. Plus, I had seen and heard a lot of things in the halls of the high school over the past few months.

What in the world was God thinking when he thought all this stuff up? There's gotta be an easier way to get babies into this world!

"J.D., do you think those two will be back this summer?" asked Sam.

"I don't know," he chuckled. "But I bet they never said a word to Miz Lettie or any other Women's Guild members about the key bein' missin'."

Ain't Pitty was not a member of the Women's Guild. We were not sure if this was her idea or theirs, but she called their meetings "hen sessions" and said most members went just to keep from being the one roasted on the spit that day. According to Ain't Pitty, when it came to gossiping, the Women's Guild made the Porch Keepers look like amateurs.

Reaching Church Street, we stopped in front of the town's high school. The building was on the same block as Granny's house, and the football field bordered her backyard. School was out for the summer, and there were no cars in the parking lot.

"Wanna go inside?" I asked.

"Not now. It's too hot."

We had been inside the building many times, mostly at night, because it had bathrooms and water fountains and was a safe hiding place when we needed one. Access was easy, since the window in the ground-level maintenance room had a broken lock that no one had bothered to fix in years.

Turning from Church Street onto the Railroad, we headed back to Granny's. It was time to move our suitcases to Ain't Pitty's and get settled in for the summer.

Ain't Pitty and Uncle Ben's house was originally built by old Doc Anderson as a combined home and doctor's office. They'd bought it from young Doc Anderson thirty years earlier, when he'd decided to move his practice to a larger building in nearby Samson.

I'd always thought it fitting that Ain't Pitty lived in a doctor's house, because she was a healer of sorts. She had a kitchen full of healing plants, such as aloe vera for scraped knees and sunburns, echinacea for sore throats, ginger for upset stomachs, and chamomile for restless nights. She also used fresh lime juice to help us get rid of pimples and made a paste out of witch hazel and baking soda to stop the itching caused by mosquito and fire-ant bites. Ain't Pitty could even get rid of warts. Last summer, I'd found a small string of them on my finger. So Ain't Pitty soaked a chicken bone in vinegar until it was soft, scraped off the outer layer, and rubbed the remaining bone over the warts. Then I had to go outside and throw the chicken bone over my shoulder. When I woke up the next morning, the warts were gone and never came back.

Ain't Pitty and Uncle Ben converted the large examination room at the front of the house into a guest bedroom with a big feather bed, which was where Sam, Sandra, and I usually slept, lying sideways because the bed was longer than it was wide. Eric and J.D. slept on army bunks Uncle Ben brought home from Rucks and placed against the bedroom wall. Li'l Bit and Sharon slept in the back bedroom, near Ain't Pitty and Uncle Ben.

Ain't Pitty had strict rules if you were going to sleep in one of her beds. You had to bathe with soap and wash your hair, and when everyone was finished, the bathroom had to look as good as when we'd started. Over the years, we had perfected our nighttime ritual to the point where each of us could be in and out of the shower in under two minutes, which allowed all of us to have a little bit of warm water if we wanted it. Sam, Sandra, and I would go first, followed by Eric and J.D.; then we would take turns cleaning up.

Connecting the bedroom to the rest of the house was a narrow pantry-passageway leading to the dining room. Ain't Pitty said this was where both Doc Andersons kept their medicines, but now it was filled with dishes and whatnots. The passageway gave the bedroom an air of secrecy and warned us when someone was coming our way.

The bedroom also had a separate door leading to the front porch, which Ain't Pitty kept locked most of the time. But she kept the key in an old-fashioned water pitcher that sat on the dresser so it was easy for us to slip in and out at night unnoticed.

We stowed our suitcases under the beds, checked to make sure the key was in the pitcher, and headed to the kitchen to help Ain't Pitty fix lunch. We were just about to eat, when there was a knock at the front door.

"Y'all stay put," said Ain't Pitty.

We let her get to the front door before we peeked through the dining room to see who had knocked.

Damn! It's the Sheriff!

Geneva County's longtime peacekeeper, Sheriff Coker, was standing in the doorway. He was an older fellow with sandy-gray hair, a broad-rimmed hat, and a big belly.

"Pitty, I've already gotten a phone call this morning from one of your neighbors saying your nieces and nephews are back in town and there's gonna be trouble. I really need you and Ben to keep a closer eye on them this summer. My deputies and I just don't have time to deal with complaining neighbors again. We've got more important things to do."

"Sheriff, the children are growing up, and I'm sure they will be well behaved, as usual. Tell Lettie to relax."

Sheriff Coker looked surprised that Ain't Pitty pinpointed Miz Lettie as the complainer, but he continued with his mission.

"Please, Pitty, try to keep 'em out of trouble and away from the neighbors. I really meant it when I said we're too busy for this kind of nonsense. Plus, it's unsafe for them to be running around alone at night." Putting his hat back on, he nodded and turned to leave. "Have a nice day."

"You too, Sheriff."

I heard her mumble, "Jackass" as the door clicked shut.

We scurried back to the table and sat down just as Ain't Pitty came through the door.

"When I tell y'all to stay put, I mean stay put."

"Yes, ma'am."

"Sheriff Coker want anythin' in particular, Ain't Pitty?" probed J.D.

"Just the usual. Lettie's bein' Lettie, that's all."

I caught J.D.'s eye.

This isn't usual. This is trouble. Sheriff Coker has never come to the house before.

By Saturday, our parents were headed home and we had completed most of the early-summer chores, such as pumping up our inner tubes, cleaning Ain't Pitty's outdoor kitchen, re-restringing the fishing poles and adjusting the weights and bobbers, sharpening the points on the frog giggers, and reacquainting ourselves with the chickens in the coop and the weeds in the garden.

After supper, we had just settled into the rockers on Ain't Pitty's front porch, when her fancies begin to tinkle. Fancies were what we called the hundreds of delicate miniature cups, saucers, tea sets, figurines, and other pieces of petite glass and china that sat on the dozen or so little tables, curios, and wall shelves in Ain't Pitty's dining room and living room. Whenever anyone walked across the hardwood floors in these rooms, the fancies vibrated, making tinkling, almost musical sounds that echoed up the twelve-foot walls and out onto the front porch. The tinkling served as another early-warning system for us that someone was coming. We had also figured out that if we walked close to the walls, the fancies stayed quiet—a fact that served us well if we needed to move around the house at night undetected.

As the tinkling stopped, Ain't Pitty pushed the screen door open, walked to the steps, and looked up and down the Railroad.

"If Li'l Bit and Sharon are going to be spendin' time with y'all this summer, you need to be more careful than usual. They're too young to go most places by themselves, so I expect y'all to stay with them. No gallivantin' off and leavin' them behind. Understood?"

"Yes, ma'am."

Ain't Pitty looked like she wanted to say more but turned for the door instead.

"Don't stay up too late."

"Yes, ma'am."

When the door closed, J.D. whispered, "That was strange. She sounded like Miz Tilly."

"Yeah," added Eric. "She knows we'd never leave the little ones alone. Wonder what's up."

"I don't know, but seems like somethin's got folks a little spooked."

Chapter 5

Most days, four o'clock was fishing time. The worst of the day's heat was over, and the bream would be surfacing to eat the bugs flitting across the water at Geneva County Lake.

Ain't Pitty's skill at fishing was legendary. From selecting the right bait to cleaning and cooking them, no one did it better. She also knew the best time to have the lines in the water, so if we weren't ready to go when she was, we got left behind, which seldom happened. Fishing was one of our favorite summer pastimes. It was also one of the ways we earned our summer keep. Thanks to Ain't Pitty, we could gig frogs and catch, clean, debone, and fry fish by the first grade.

Ain't Pitty's transportation to and from her favorite fishing spots was also infamous. For the past decade she had driven a black-turned-light-gray, rusty, four-door 1948 Plymouth named Jigger. The old car had suicide back doors, rotting cushions, scratchy upholstery, and Swiss cheese–like floorboards that allowed us to see pavement whizzing by underneath our feet. Jigger had a boat trailer hitch welded onto her back bumper and two wooden brackets bolted to her roof that held fishing poles and frog giggers. The old car had a six-cylinder engine with a three-speed transmission that allowed her to really move in 1948, but now her top running speed was about thirty miles per hour. As with the Oldsmobile, the only reason Jigger was still running was because of Uncle Ben's skill as a mechanic. Every evening after supper he would go out to check on the "old girl," jiggling this and that around her engine to make sure she kept running smoothly. Ain't Pitty told him any car needing that much jiggling deserved a name, and Jigger was born.

"I call shotgun," yelled J.D.

"No!" snapped Eric, taking off after him. "You always sit up front."

"That's 'cause my legs are longer."

"That's bullshit and you know it, J.D.!"

"Yeah, I know, but it works."

"Yeah? Well, paybacks are hell."

Sharon and Li'l Bit climbed in the front seat next to J.D. while the rest of us slid into the backseat with the cricket cage, a bucket of wormy compost, fishing nets, a jar of eucalyptus oil, fish stringers, a bucket for the fish, and a gas can. All of these combined to give Jigger a rather earthy scent that would have nauseated the unseasoned rider, especially when we added the smell of fresh fish.

To make matters worse, years ago someone left the lid off the cricket cage and dozens of desperate crickets had made their way out and down into the nooks and crannies of Jigger's upholstery. It had not taken long for the fertile little jumpers to turn Jigger into a cricket hotel. When we arrived in June, all we had to do to catch the restless insects was wait until they jumped on us, which they did by the dozens. By August, we would have to dig between the seat cushions and behind the lining of the doors and ceiling to find them.

Riding in Jigger was windy and loud, mostly because her windows had quit rolling up years ago and everyone had to shout to be heard.

"C'mon, Ain't Pitty, let me drive," yelled J.D. "I can do it. You know I can."

"Not with everybody in the car."

"How about with them out of the car?"

"Patience, J.D."

"Let me sit on your lap, J.D. I can't see," yelled Li'l Bit.

"Me too!" added Sharon.

J.D. winced and moaned as little elbows and heels dug into his legs and chest.

"How's the front seat working out for ya now, J.D.?" quipped Eric.

"Still beat you, didn't I?"

On the outskirts of town, Ain't Pitty pulled into Sallie's Gas Station to get fuel for her three-seat fishing boat. Watching Mr. Sallie fill the can, I wondered why his parents gave him such a sissy name. He must have been teased something awful as a boy, but as an old man he seemed proud of it. He even had the name SALLIE'S embroidered in big letters on the front of his shirt and across his hat.

"Takes a brave man to do that," whispered J.D.

"Mighty brave," added Eric.

"Ain't Pitty, are we lake fishin', bridge fishin', or swamp fishin' today?" I asked.

"Lake, unless y'all wanna go swampin'."

"Lake!" everyone yelled.

I breathed a sigh of relief. Bridge fishing was fun, but if swimmers were there, the fish were not. Swamp fishing was great for catching big-mouth bass, and it was also an easy type of fishing to do—all you had to do was lay your pole on the water within reach and wait for the fish to bite. But no one except Ain't Pitty and J.D. actually liked wading waist deep into the thick, coffee-colored swamp with just shorts and t-shirts on. The muck at the bottom sucked at your feet, and the black water prevented you from seeing what was around and under you. Plus, we had to deal with bloody leeches when we waded out. Those little suckers had a knack for getting into places that hurt like hell when you pulled them off.

Any of us could have chosen not to go swamp fishing, but there was more at stake than fish. None of us wanted to be left behind or say we were afraid to wade into the brackish water. So we lived with the mosquito bites, the leeches, and the creepy-crawly things slithering around and between our legs and prayed the snakes had better things to do and the gators had not made it this far north. The payoff for this misery was continued respect and fearless bragging rights around those relatives too afraid to go.

Geneva County Lake was small by most standards but large enough to serve this part of the Wiregrass well. The water and the road surrounding it were bordered by tall longleaf pines, a thick pine-needle-and-sand carpet, and scattered low-lying brush. Cutting across the middle of the lake was a one-lane dirt-road dam that led to two partially hidden boat ramps. Fishing folks used the ramps during the day, but, according to Ain't Pitty, teenagers used them at night.

"Many of Crystal Springs' finest citizens got their start on those ramps," she laughed.

Ain't Pitty's favorite fishing spot was a quarter mile down Lake Road. It had a picnic table, a covered, T-shaped fishing dock, and a nearby boat ramp with an incline low enough that Jigger could get her boat and its rickety trailer in and out of the water. Most of the time Ain't Pitty left the boat turned upside down on the bank by the lake. No one ever bothered it, or anyone who did always capped off the gas tank and put the boat back where it belonged.

Ain't Pitty had several fishing rules: No one fished alone, and to go with her in the boat you had to be at least six and prove you could dog-paddle for ten minutes. She also allowed only three of us in the boat at a time.

"Any more, and you'll catch more than fish."

Another rule was that talkers were walkers, meaning anyone making too much noise walked home, and since no one was allowed to walk home alone, we all had to walk. As a result, this rule was seldom broken.

No other four o'clockers were in sight as Jigger eased through the pines toward the dock. Stuffing the crickets we could catch into our pockets, we grabbed buckets, nets, and stringers, claimed our poles, and headed for the water. One of Ain't Pitty's "rules of necessity" was that the fishing hooks stayed stuck in our poles until we had bait in hand and our target in the lake identified. She had grown tired of digging fishing hooks out of our butts whenever J.D. decided to see if he could snag someone's cutoffs without getting skin.

Ain't Pitty, Li'l Bit, Sam, and Sharon headed for the boat while the rest of us flip-flopped down the dock. Sandra and I headed to the opposite ends of the T, and J.D. and Eric took their usual places along the middle. Pulling unsuspecting crickets out of our pockets, we stuck them on our hooks and hoped they would stay there long enough to sacrifice themselves for our supper. One by one, our lines hit the water, sending layered ripples gliding across the surface to merge with those caused by fish beginning to feed.

"First one to catch the last fish has to clean 'em all," whispered J.D.

"Like hell," drawled Eric. "I fell for that once, and I'm not doin' it again. Last time you just cut your line so you wouldn't have the last fish."

"You remembered that, huh?"

"Yeah, I remember! You didn't tell anybody what you'd done until I'd cleaned every one of those damn fish."

Across the lake, I could see light blue dragonflies and yellow something-or-others flitting just above the water, fish snapping at them from below and kingfishers snapping at them from above.

"Those have to be the stupidest bugs in the world. You'd think they'd figure out not to come near the water. It's dangerous. They're at the bottom of the food chain out there."

"It's like bug Russian roulette," said J.D., swatting at one of the bees living in the T's rafters.

"What's that?"

"It's like when you double-dare somebody six times and they can't win more than five. At some point, they're gonna lose."

"My point exactly. Why be out there at all?"

"Because they're doin' what they have to do to survive."

The fish were biting fast, and we had a baker's dozen of hand-size sunfish on the stringer when we heard the growl of a motor behind us. Headed toward the boat ramp was an old Ford pickup truck pulling a boat trailer. In the back was a familiar face. It was Pretty Boy. My heart started pounding as I watched him jump over the side and begin unhooking the boat from the trailer. Using a hand crank, he lowered the boat into the water and pulled it over to the bank. Surely God had never made a finer-looking boy in all the ages.

Breathe, Nettie.

"Looks like we've got company," said J.D.

The truck pulled into the pines, and two men climbed out of the cab. They were the same two we had seen with Pretty Boy at Slater's. One of them grabbed a brown jug from the cab, while the other one started talking to Pretty Boy and pointing in our direction.

Oh, gosh! He's sending Pretty Boy over here!

Finally, both men stepped into the boat, pulled the motor to life, and began skimming across the lake.

Pretty Boy picked up his gear and started walking along the water's edge toward the dock. The closer he got, the faster my heart raced and the more aware I was that any benefits from last night's shower were long gone. Now I was just hot, sweaty, and downright dirty.

I smell like Jigger.

"Hey," said J.D., as Pretty Boy made his way down to the T.

"Hey. Okay if I join y'all?"

His voice was soft and landed like silk in my ears.

"It's a free country," muttered Eric, glancing at Pretty Boy and eyeing the men in the boat.

Shooting Eric a "behave yourself" look, J.D. asked, "What's your name?"

"Mitchell. Mitchell Ames."

Pretty Boy has a pretty name: Mitchell.

"I'm J.D., this is Eric, Sandra's down there, and that's Nettie over there."

My heart jumped clear into my throat as Mitchell turned in my direction.

Good grief, Nettie! Get a grip!

"Hey."

Just like at Slater's, I tried to speak, but no sound came out. I turned back toward the water, painfully aware that Mitchell had stepped between J.D. and me to cast his line.

Glancing out of the corner of my eye, I could see he was wearing an old but clean gray t-shirt, cutoff jeans, and sneakers without socks. Unlike the rest of us, the smell coming from him was again fresh and Zesty.

Wonder what it is about this boy and that soap.

As Mitchell teased his line through the water, I noticed that his hands, like his face, looked soft and his nails were clean and trimmed.

I've got dirt and cricket guts under my fingernails.

"Who are they?" asked Eric, nodding toward the men in the boat.

"One's my pa, and the other's a neighbor. Those folks with y'all?" asked Mitchell, nodding toward the speck that was Ain't Pitty's boat.

"Yeah," answered Eric. "You live around here?"

"Uh-huh. We have a trailer farther down Choctaw Road. We moved back here last month."

"Back? You mean you lived here before?"

"Yeah. A couple of years ago."

"Your parents divorced?"

"No. My momma died the last year we were here."

"Oh. Sorry."

"I heard your pa call you Mitch the other day. You go by that?"

"No. I go by Mitchell. It was my momma's last name."

"Where did you—"

"Oh, for gosh sakes, Eric!" growled J.D. "Enough with the twenty questions! Let 'im be!"

"Sorry."

"I don't mind. It's natural to wanna know."

"Then it's your turn to ask somethin'," said J.D., shooting another warning look at Eric.

"Ol' Man Slater said y'all were visitin' Miz Campbell for the summer."

"Yeah. She's our grandmother, but we stay with our Ain't Pitty—uh, Miz Miller—most of the time. She's out there with Sharon, Li'l Bit, and Sam—she's a girl."

"I know Miz Miller. She's a nice lady."

"She sure is," agreed Eric. "How do you know her?"

"My momma went to school with her son Hank."

After a pause, Mitchell asked, "Where are y'all from?"

"Sandra, Sharon, and I are from Mobile," said J.D.

"Dothan," said Eric.

There was a lull, as Mitchell looked at me.

"How about you?"

"Virginia," I squeaked.

"That's a long trip."

"Yeah. Long trip," I echoed, my skin tingling as if the wispy blossoms on Ain't Pitty's mimosa tree were tickling me.

Hearing the buzz of a boat, we saw Ain't Pitty heading back toward the dock.

"She's quittin' early," said J.D. "Musta caught her fill."

Pulling our lines in, we watched as Ain't Pitty motored closer.

"Hey, Mitchell, do us a favor. Don't say anythin' in front of Ain't Pitty about us bein' in Slater's yesterday, okay? She'd have a hissy fit if she knew we were in there."

"Sure. I understand. Slater's is a rough place." Looking over at me, Mitchell winked, "But what's summer without Fireballs?"

Ugh!

My klutziness in Slater's had not gone unnoticed, but at the same time, Pretty Boy Mitchell had just winked at me.

As Ain't Pitty nosed the boat onshore, Sam jumped out and stilled the rocking so the others could climb out. Together, they pulled the boat under the trees, tucked the motor inside, and turned it over.

Slapping at the mosquitoes swarming her ankles, Ain't Pitty turned to those from the boat.

"Y'all get your gear and head on up to Jigger."

Sharon and Li'l Bit scampered up the hill, and Sam followed, eyeing Mitchell and grinning at me as she went.

Ain't Pitty made her way down to the T and pulled our stringer out of the water.

"Good work."

From underneath the brim of her big straw hat, she looked at Mitchell and glanced out at the other boat.

"Hey, Mitchell. Haven't seen you 'round lately. Where've you been?"

"Hey, Miz Miller. We were livin' up near Opp. Pa was workin' at the warehouse there. But now he's drivin' the delivery truck for Booker's Feed and Seed."

"Were you able to finish the school year up there?"

"Yes, ma'am."

"Good. Who's out yonder with your pa?"

Mitchell looked toward the boat and then down at his feet.

"His name's Otis Pierce, Miz Miller. His trailer's parked near ours."

"Thought so."

"You know 'im, Miz Miller?"

"I know of him, Mitchell, which isn't the same thing. You'd be wise to steer clear of him. Your momma wouldn't be happy knowin' you were around that kinda trash."

"Yes, ma'am," replied Mitchell, a funny look on his face.

Heading to the bank, Ain't Pitty called over her shoulder, "When you're in town, c'mon by the house. These kids are better suited for you to be around."

"Thanks, Miz Miller."

Thank you, Ain't Pitty!

Ain't Pitty never had to tell us to follow her. We knew better than not to, so we quickly gathered our gear.

"Take it easy, Mitchell," drawled Eric, his tone warming.

"We're headed to the Crystal Springs pool tomorrow," said J.D. "Why don't you meet us there?"

A spark lit in Mitchell's eyes but then faded a little.

"I gotta work, but if I can get off early, I'll be there."

Making our way up the bank, we loaded the fishing gear on top of and into Jigger and climbed in. I glanced back at the dock and saw Mitchell watching us, just like that day at Slater's. He smiled and flickered his hand in a little wave, and once again my face went up in flames.

"Better watch out, Nettie," giggled Sam. "Your face is going to stay that color."

"Mind your own business, nosy."

"Why? Yours is a lot more fun to watch."

Ain't Pitty's last fishing rule was "you catch 'em, you clean 'em"— including hers. While it wasn't our favorite part of fishing, it was a small price to pay for being able to go in the first place, and over the years we had streamlined the process. Heading to Ain't Pitty's bricks-sunk-in-sand patio and makeshift, outdoor kitchen, we lined up next to the long, shallow sink and adjacent weathered farm table. Pouring the bucket of fish in the sink, J.D. and Eric began scraping scales, cutting off heads, and gutting what would become our supper. As they finished each fish, Sam or I deboned and rinsed it, and Sandra patted it dry, dipped it in buttermilk, and placed it in a bag containing cornmeal, salt, and pepper. When there were at least three fish in the bag, Li'l Bit or Sharon shook it and stacked the fish on a plate near Ain't Pitty's big camping stove.

While we were prepping the fish, Ain't Pitty lit the stove, covered the bottom of two oversize frying pans with peanut oil, and placed them over the low flames.

"Ain't Pitty, it's okay if Mitchell comes to the pool with us tomorrow, isn't it?" I asked.

"Sure. Y'all can spend all the time you want with Mitchell. But stay away from his pa and Otis Pierce, ya hear? I don't want y'all anywhere near those men."

"Why?" asked J.D.

"Because they're trouble."

"Mitchell seems nice enough."

"That's 'cause he takes after his momma. She was a good person and a friend of mine."

"How'd she die?" I asked.

"She was . . . I don't really know what happened to 'er."

Ain't Pitty looked sad as she began stirring chopped onions and hot peppers into a batter of cornmeal and buttermilk.

She does know. She's just not saying.

"If Otis Pierce is bad, why does Mitchell's pa let him come around?"

Ain't Pitty stopped stirring.

"I don't know, Nettie. Mitchell's pa may have been a half-decent man at one time, but he got mixed up with the wrong people a long time ago and started drinkin' heavy. Once he got hooked on moonshine, it didn't take long for any good left in 'im to disappear."

And Mitchell has to live with what's left.

Ain't Pitty placed the prepped fish in one pan of bubbling oil and dropped hush puppy batter by the spoonful into the other one. Then she filled a deep pot with water and put it on the stove.

"After y'all bury the fish guts in the garden, see if there's any early corn ready to pick. While you're down there, get some tomatoes, and pick some field peas and snaps to slow-cook for tomorrow."

"We'll get the tomatoes," yelled Li'l Bit and Sharon, running for the garden.

"Eric and I'll get the corn," called J.D.

"I hate picking field peas and snaps," moaned Sam.

"I'd rather pick them than shuck corn," I said. "You never know if those ol' green corn worms are gonna be in there."

"You don't seem to mind putting worms on your fishin' line."

"Corn worms are different. They have faces. Ugly ones."

"That's right. You like pretty faces, don't you, Nettie? Pretty ones like Mitch—"

"Hush up and start pickin', or we'll be here all night."

Sometimes I really don't like her very much.

Having finally emptied a row, we carried the basket back to the patio.

Next to the sink was an open pull-chain shower that we used to rinse off the day's dirt and fish scales, clothes and all. Then, while drip-drying, we sliced tomatoes, blanched the corn, and set the picnic table with Ain't Pitty's outdoor dishes, which were really just chipped or cracked indoor dishes, coupled with mismatched silverware and glasses. Sam brought out a pitcher of iced tea, and Sandra followed with a crock of butter and tin shakers full of salt, pepper, and sugar.

"Make sure the shakers have plenty of dry rice in them," said Ain't Pitty. "I don't want everything clumpin' up." Giving J.D. an "I dare you" look, she added, "And make sure the lids are on tight."

J.D. was famous for loosening the caps on the tins, causing their contents to fill the plate of the unsuspecting shaker. The last one to have been caught was Ain't Pitty, and she had failed to see the humor. She'd made J.D. eat every bite of the ruined food and do the dishes by himself.

Ain't Pitty's picnic table sat in the shade of a tall oak tree growing between the patio and a gray barn-board lean-to. The front of the lean-to, which faced the Railroad, served as a carport of sorts for Jigger and the Oldsmobile; the back was a storage shed that faced the patio. The shed had a low, back-slanted roof that provided a great place for us to eavesdrop when folks on the patio did not want us listening.

Uncle Ben pulled into the driveway as Ain't Pitty set the fish and hush puppies on the table.

Settling into our usual spots, we held hands, bowed our heads, and offered our traditional summer grace.

"God is great, God is good, and we thank Him for our food. By His hands shall we be fed. Give us, Lord, our daily bread . . . and fish. Amen."

Chapter 6

Ain't Pitty's chicken coop was actually a retired five-window 1939 school bus that she and Uncle Ben had rescued and parked in the trees on the back of their property. The back door of the bus opened into a shaded pen that was surrounded on the top, bottom, and sides with chicken wire. While not overly attractive, the bus made a good home for Ain't Pitty's chickens.

As part of our chores, we gathered eggs twice a day, and in the evenings we would also clean and restraw the nests, give the birds fresh water and feed, and check the wire to make sure no chicken-eating predators could get in. All of this made for happy chickens and lots of big brown eggs that Ain't Pitty would use in her own kitchen, give to folks she liked, or sell to those she didn't.

The school bus–chicken coop was a touchy subject between Ain't Pitty and Miz Lettie, who also happened to be president of the Women's Guild and a very prim-and-proper lady. She had repeatedly told Ain't Pitty, and anybody else in town who would listen, how dreadful it was to have a chicken coop in the neighborhood, much less one in a old school bus. Ain't Pitty just scoffed and ask Miz Lettie if she would like to buy some fresh eggs.

Not everyone in Miz Lettie's house hated chickens living close by. Her big, mean-spirited cat loved it. He had tried many times to go over, under, and through the chicken wire but failed, so he started hiding in the weeds near the coop's door, just waiting for someone to make a mistake. Last summer, despite repeated warnings from Ain't Pitty, we had done exactly that. After gathering the morning eggs, we left the coop's door ajar just enough for the cat to squeeze in and cause pure panic in the henhouse. Hearing what was happening, we raced back to the coop and, in a flurry of flying feathers, battled the cat to save the hens and avoid the wrath of Ain't Pitty. Unfortunately, despite dozens of scratches and bites, we were unable to accomplish either. The cat managed to kill one of the small hens before J.D. finally caught him by the tail and threw him out of the bus, getting badly clawed in the process. When Ain't Pitty found out, she cleaned our wounds with pure rubbing alcohol and made us scrub the bus clean, spread fresh straw, and readjust the door to make sure it closed completely.

Following this battle, J.D. dubbed Miz Lettie's cat Satan and began planning a gruesome reckoning that "damn cat" would never see coming. Unfortunately, vacation had ended before the reckoning could be delivered, so it was on J.D.'s agenda this summer.

When the evening chores were done, Li'l Bit and Sharon ran for the swing, while the rest of us headed for the rocking chairs. The air was sweet with the smell of magnolia blossoms, and the steady hum of crickets and tree frogs was growing louder. It was a great night for rocking, but we still had work to do. Sitting in front of the first rocker was the basket of field peas and snaps we had picked earlier. Whoever sat here was responsible for snapping the ends off and passing the pods to the second rocker, who would do the stringing and pass them to the third rocker, who would hull them into a colander held by the fourth rocker, who would pick out any bugs and debris that made it that far. Lastly, the fifth rocker would take the full colander to the kitchen, wash the contents, and set them to soak.

"Look!" yelled Li'l Bit, scampering off the swing and pointing toward the back wall of the porch. "It's Wilbur!"

We could see the familiar little green lizard with his exceptionally large head, big eyes, and wide, funny-looking feet scurrying along the edge of the house. Wilbur had kept us company on the porch for as long as we could remember. He made his home in nearby flowering shrubs and sought shelter among Ain't Pitty's potted plants and hanging ferns when it was too hot or when enemies were around.

"Glad to see he made it through the winter," said Eric.

"No thanks to Satan, I bet," added J.D. "He's been trying to catch Wilbur forever."

One of the ways we knew Wilbur was Wilbur was that the tip of his long green tail was bent at a right angle, something we assumed Satan or some other lizard-loving critter was responsible for. It would take a few days for Wilbur to get comfortable with us again, but when he did he would cruise the porch at will, munching on pieces of dead crickets we tossed down for him. If we forgot to feed him, Wilbur would run in front of the rockers to remind us he was hungry and then wait in the corner for us to deliver his supper. Tonight his bent tail just disappeared over the edge of the porch.

From the back of the house, Ain't Pitty called Li'l Bit and Sharon.

"Go on, you guys," urged J.D.

"But I wanna stay up with y'all," whined Li'l Bit.

"You know the rules. What Ain't Pitty says goes."

"It's not fair," grumbled Sharon.

"Fuss about it, and you won't get to stay with us in the daytime, either."

With the little ones in the house, the remainder of the evening was ours and we could do what we wanted, as long as we were quiet. But for now, we just needed to talk.

"It's a shame Mitchell's pa's a drinker," said Sam.

"Yeah. And it's a shame Mitchell has to be around that stinky Otis Pierce," I added.

"Well, Ain't Pitty likes Mitchell, so I guess he's okay," said Eric.

"Apparently, she likes him better than you do! I can't believe you hounded that boy with all those questions today," chided J.D. "You were bein' way too nosy."

"Yeah, well, you know . . . Momma says you can't be too careful about some folks. Anyway, he was with those smelly men at Slater's," Eric said.

"You can't pick your family," I added.

"Yeah, but Eric can pick your nose-y," laughed J.D., jumping up to avoid his cussin's kick.

"Hey, look," said Sandra. "There goes Jessie."

"Wonder where he's headed."

"He's probably checkin' to see if we're up to anythin'."

"Naw," said Sam. "He doesn't care what we're doin'. He's probably goin' to get a Coke from the machine outside Slater's."

"Don't kid yourself, Sam," said J.D. "He knows and he cares."

J.D. called out, but, as usual, Jessie never looked up. He just kept on walking.

"Wanna follow 'im?" asked Sandra.

"No. He's not botherin' anybody. Leave 'im alone."

J.D. had a soft spot in his heart for Jessie. When he was little, Jessie had saved him when he slipped and almost fell out of one of Granny's tall pecan trees. Barely hanging on, J.D. was yelling for help, but none of us were big enough to do anything except yell with him. Jessie was mowing grass nearby and got there just in time to catch J.D. as he dropped. Shaking like a leaf, J.D. thanked Jessie over and over again, but Jessie never said a word. He just set J.D. on the ground and went back to his mowing. We never did figure out how Jessie knew J.D. was in trouble. With the mower running, he would have had a hard time hearing us yelling, and the tree was so full of leaves he could not see what was happening, but somehow he knew. Since that day, Jessie had had a friend, whether he knew it or not.

"I hope Mitchell makes it to the pool tomorrow," said Sam. "Don't you, Nettie?"

I could hear the teasing in her voice but did not take the bait.

"I hope he comes," said Eric. "I wanna find out more about his pa and Otis Pierce, especially if they're gonna be around here all summer."

"Leave 'im be, Eric," yawned J.D. "Whatever it is, Mitchell must be free of it, or Ain't Pitty wouldn't let him come around."

Please, Lord, let him be there.

Chapter 7

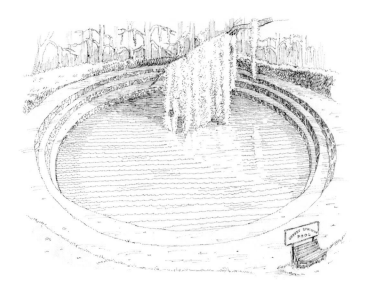

Bathing suits. The only part of vacation I was dreading. Since last summer, I had developed what Momma called breast buds, which stuck out on my chest like half lemons. Plus, now there was a curve between my waist and hips that made it impossible for my cutoffs to fit right. But the crowning glory of all of these humiliating changes was the day Momma dragged me to Leggett's Department Store in Lynchburg and had the old, gray-haired salesladies measure me for what they called a training bra. I wasn't sure what needed training, but having those old ladies looking at and touching me around my half lemons, pushing in on the small of my back, telling me to "stand up straight" so they could assess my "figa," made for the worst day of my life.

"Well, she's no Barbie doll, but she'd be real cute if she didn't dress like such a tomboy."

I didn't give a fat rat's ass about looking like a Barbie doll, but I cared a lot that the mess of lace, hooks, and straps they wrapped me up in was uncomfortable as hell and served as a painful reminder that I was changing and there was no stopping it.

"Momma, please! Their hands are freezing!"

"Hold still, Nettie. They're almost done."

"Get me outta this thing. I can't stand it!"

I could not reach the hooks, so I pulled the blasted thing over my head and tossed it in the corner. Putting my t-shirt back on, I folded my arms across my half lemons and backed against the wall. Momma did not make me put the torture device back on, but she did make me apologize to the old ladies and sentenced me to a week of washing supper dishes.

Girls at school who wore bras, or "over-the-shoulder boulder holders," as the boys called them, got teased. Now I was one of them, and there was no hiding it. Even Scott Phillips, who sat next to me in English class, stared at my chest and asked if I would like to go to the movies with him. Part of me was disgusted, but another part was curious about what it would be like. The disgusted part won, and I told Scott to go suck an egg.

Before we left for Alabama, I hid the over-the-shoulder boulder holder under my mattress and hoped Momma would think I'd packed it. Whatever training my half lemons needed could wait until after summer vacation.

Now, in front of God and everybody, I had to put this distorted body in a bathing suit. Sam had tried to get me to buy a two-piece suit like hers. She already had lemons and a waist and was not bothered by them at all.

"You have a waist now—show it off."

Show it off? Hell's fire! She's out of her mind.

Unfortunately, finding a more tolerable bathing suit proved to be almost impossible. If I found one that covered the half lemons, the back plunged down to my butt. If I found one that covered my butt, the front showed too much of the half lemons. Finally, I picked a one-piece black suit, not because I liked it but because it covered most of what I wanted to cover, at least in the front.

Now, looking in the full-length mirror on the back of Ain't Pitty's bathroom door, I was in a panic. No matter how I twisted and pulled—up, down, or sideways—the half lemons and hips were still obvious and the back of the suit dipped so low it showed the curve of my butt.

I'd be better off going naked.

Running my fingers through my Twiggy-like haircut, I debated what to do.

I'll wear something over the top of it!

Grabbing yesterday's t-shirt from the dirty-clothes basket, I pulled it on and headed for the door.

It's gonna be hot as hell, but there's no other way.

Flip-flopping down the steps to the patio, I watched the faces of those sitting around waiting for me, especially the boys, and was grateful not to see any funny looks.

"What the hell took you so long?" growled J.D., as he and the others got up, grabbed their towels, and headed for the lean-to. "We're wastin' daylight!"

With our inner tubes strapped to her roof, we climbed in Jigger and headed toward the pool, which was about a half mile northeast of town.

Geneva County had lots of creeks, ponds, and swimming holes, but the most popular place by far was the Crystal Springs pool, which was a cold-water lagoon formed by a cluster of natural springs bubbling up from the underground lake. The pool was tucked into a secluded grove of trees, and lush undergrowth surrounded it on three sides, keeping the water shaded. The fourth side served as both a parking lot and a beach.

Decades ago, Pa Campbell and others had built a knee-high, two-level stone wall around the springs with three wide steps leading down into the pool. The top wall was high enough for diving, and the low wall provided a place to sit and dangle our feet in the water. The sides were moss covered, which tinted the water blue green, but the bubbling springs were still visible at the bottom in a dark, wavy kind of way. The pool was about sixty feet wide, five feet deep at the wall, and twelve feet deep at the springs. On days that were so hot you felt as if your skin was going to melt right off your bones, this pool was a gift from God.

A common ritual among arriving swimmers was to dive down to the springs, grab a handful of sand, and ride the bubbles back to the surface, where they would show off the sand and prove their worthiness. All of us, except Li'l Bit and Sharon, would make the dive this time. Maybe by summer's end we would let them try, but for now they were too little and could not hold their breath long enough to get down there and back.

At the back of the pool, tree branches, vines, and Spanish moss hung down like a green veil, forming a hidden room. Ain't Pitty told us to stay away if we heard whispers and giggles coming from behind the veil. "You might see something you shouldn't."

Turning off the road, Ain't Pitty eased Jigger onto the beach. No one else was around as we untied our tubes, threw our towels into nearby bushes, and slid out of our flip-flops.

"Ain't Pitty," yelled Li'l Bit, "can Sharon 'n' me skinny-dip?"

"Nope. Y'all are gettin' too old. Besides, nowadays there are folks watchin' who have no business being around kids with no clothes. Y'all be home by supper."

"Yes, ma'am. Bye!"

From that moment, it was a race to see who would hit the water first, but we knew it would be J.D.—it always was. Eric, who was stronger, would give J.D. a run for his money, but ultimately he was no match for J.D.'s longer legs. The rest of us followed in mixed order, with Li'l Bit and Sharon bringing up the rear.

Li'l Bit stopped at the top of the wall, knees bent and arms swinging back and forth, as if getting up his courage to hit the cold water. Then, upside down and with arms and legs flailing, he dove in, hitting the water with his eyes closed and his mouth open. Quickly popping to the surface, he spit, sputtered, and dog-paddled his way back to the wall, ready to do it all over again. Sharon required much less fanfare. She just held her nose and jumped.

Once the sand-grabbing ritual was complete, J.D. and Eric headed to the wall to practice dives and cannonballs, and the rest of us climbed into the tubes to float around and offer unsolicited comments on their diving skill and the quality of their splashes. After lunch, we tried to see who could go the longest lying upside down against the pool wall. With knees bent over the low wall, we held our noses and pushed down and back into the water until we were hanging upside down. The last one to float up without holding his or her nose was considered the champ.

It was a hot day, so none of us was surprised when another car pulled up on the beach, but we were disappointed to see it was Lucilla Hines and John Thomas Barnett.

We had known Lucilla for years, and since her house was just down the Railroad from Granny's, we saw her during the summer whether we wanted to or not. Cilly, as we called her, was an attention-needing crybaby who enjoyed tattling even when there was nothing to tattle about. But last summer, Cilly had changed. She'd become more interested in flirting with J.D. than in tattling on him, and whenever he was around she'd primp—pulling a hide-a-brush out of one pocket to comb her long, blond, flipped-up hair and taking a small mirror out of the other pocket to check for zits. If one was visible, she would pull out a tube of Clearasil and rub it in, making her face redder than when she'd started. All of this was bad enough, but when she tried to kiss J.D. in the middle of town, we started going out of our way to avoid her. Even when the local ain'ts pushed us to play with "pretty little Lucilla," we would wait until they were out of sight and earshot and then split up and run in different directions. Cilly always followed J.D., even though she didn't have a snowball's chance in hell of catching him. I guess she thought one day he would stop and wait for her, but that day had not arrived, and unless I'd missed my guess, it never would. When we were sure Cilly had given up the chase, we would meet at the clearing in the woods behind the Crossing. Cilly would go home crying to her momma, Effie, who would call Granny and Ain't Pitty to complain that we were being mean to her little girl. Granny just let her grumble, but Ain't Pitty suggested Cilly might be happier playing with older children. Effie did not appreciate the advice.

It was hard for us to take Effie Hines seriously—not because she was a tall, hefty woman, but because she had more black and gray hairs on her chin and upper lip than most old men and we could not stop staring at them. Granny said this was because Effie had a hormone problem, but J.D. said he thought God just could not make up his mind about whether she was supposed to be a man or a woman.

"Y'all just wait and see—Cilly's gonna end up looking just like her hairy man-momma."

Cilly climbed out of John Thomas's car, wearing a two-piece bathing suit with whole lemons spilling over the tiny top, and she was making no effort to cover them up.

"Well, would you look at that," said Eric. "Cilly's got herself some boobies."

"Yeah. Well, I wonder if she's shavin' her chin like her momma yet," hissed J.D.

I started giggling so hard I had to go underwater to stop. When I surfaced again, Cilly and John Thomas were coming down the steps.

"Hey, J.D.," drawled Cilly with a sly smile, noticeably hoping he would look her way and like what he saw, but when he did neither, she turned her disappointment toward the rest of us.

"Sheriff Coker know you hoodlums are back in town?"

"Know him well, do you, Cilly?" yelled J.D. over his shoulder.

"Smart-ass!"

"Hey, John Thomas," said Eric.

"Hey," he replied, pushing off the steps and diving toward the springs.

John Thomas was not unattractive—average height, stocky, and with a mild case of acne, he was a star football player for the Crystal Springs Bucks. His daddy owned an insurance company in Samson, and they lived outside of town in a fancy house. John Thomas was also one of the few boys around with a car that ran and was not a composite of junkyard parts.

As John Thomas surfaced and let go of his handful of sand, he smirked and breaststroked toward my sister.

"Hey, Sam. I hope you got my letter. I don't need you following me around like a lovesick puppy like you did last year."

Sam had been sweet on John Thomas last summer. He had showered her with attention and had even tried to kiss her, but he'd closed his eyes before finding Sam's mouth and kissed her nose instead. Ain't Pitty had witnessed the pitiful attempt and sent John Thomas packing before he could refocus.

"He was sucking my nose like a straw," Sam had laughed.

John Thomas and Sam had exchanged letters for a while after we left, but over the winter he'd decided he liked the taste of the local girls better and sent Sam a "Dear Jane" letter. At the time, Sam had been okay with it. "Out of sight, out of mind," she'd said.

But now, with John Thomas right in front of her, Sam was obviously not okay. She was turning red, and I could see crocodile tears welling up.

Sam and I did not always get along, but she was my sister and needed help, so I frantically searched my brain for something, anything, to help her fight back.

Do something, Nettie!

Staring at John Thomas, I saw a big red pimple on the side of his nose.

"Hey, Cilly! Share some of your Clearasil with John Thomas? He needs some for that red blob on his nose."

"Touché, Nettie!" said J.D., as he grabbed the side of Sam's inner tube.

"Hey, Sam, didn't you tell me John Thomas had really bad body odor?"

Sam's mouth fell open as Eric joined in: "Yeah! And didn't you say he got spit all over your face when he tried to kiss you?"

Sam's giggle garbled as J.D. spun her inner tube around so fast, water flowed over her head. Regaining her breath and her composure, Sam turned to John Thomas.

"I sure hope you bought some good soap and learned how to do a proper kiss, John Thomas. Cilly shouldn't have to hold her nose or have lipstick smeared all over her face when she's with you." Spinning around, she winked at me and added, "And really, John Thomas, do somethin' about that big ol' pimple. It's gonna take over your face."

Our laughter echoed across the pool as Cilly and John Thomas shot us the bird and splashed toward the green veil.

When they were out of earshot, Eric looked at Sam. "You wanna go?"

"Oh, hell no! We're not gonna be run off by Stinky and Hairy."

"Good for you, Sam," laughed J.D. "That's the way to bounce back."

"Thank you," said Sam, kicking my foot as she floated by.

Wish I knew how to bounce back like that.

Hearing a rattling noise coming from the beach, I saw Mitchell riding toward us on an old bicycle, a faded towel around his neck. My heart started racing, but I did not look away—he was too pretty not to watch.

Mitchell laid his bike down in the sand, tossed his towel on top, and pulled his t-shirt off. His shoulders and chest were tanned and smooth, and his cutoffs were riding so low on his hips that I could see a tan line on his low back. I also thought I saw the shadow of a bruise, a big one.

"Glad you could make it, Mitchell," yelled J.D.

"Me too!" he replied, diving into the water. Making the required pilgrimage to the springs, he resurfaced and made his way back to the steps. "Gosh, that felt good!"

Glancing over, he caught me watching him and smiled. By the grace of God Almighty, I did not faint and even managed to send a quick smile back his way.

Atta girl! If Sam can pull it together, so can you.

"Did you say you worked at Booker's Feed and Seed?" asked Eric.

"Yep. I work on the loadin' dock."

"Every day?"

"Most of 'em."

"You make good money?"

"Dammit, Eric!" snapped J.D. "That's none of your business!"

"I don't mind," laughed Mitchell. "I'm not sure how good the money is. It goes to my pa."

"What?" asked Eric. "You don't get to keep the money you earn?"

"Nope."

"Damn! Somethin's just not right about that. Your pa do anythin' other than drive the delivery truck?"

I figured Eric was thinking about his momma working two jobs to support them.

"Not really."

"Again! Enough with the twenty questions, Eric," said J.D. "Mitchell just got here. Cut 'im a break."

"Sorry, Mitchell."

"No problem. Like I said, it's natural to wanna know. What's your pa do, Eric?"

"He died in a car wreck when I was a baby."

"Gosh. I'm sorry to hear that."

"It's okay. I don't remember him."

I thought I heard Mitchell whisper, "Lucky" just as Cilly and

John Thomas splashed out from behind the green veil, their hair messed up and lipstick smudged across their faces. As usual, Cilly looked to see if J.D. was watching and pouted when he was not.

We had been swimming and visiting with Mitchell for about an hour when two more carloads of teenagers arrived and began cannonballing their way toward the center of the pool. Included in the group was a big girl who landed right in front of Cilly and John Thomas, hitting them full force with her splash. The resulting shrieks and cursing seemed to go on forever, but when no sympathy came their way, John Thomas and Cilly yelled insults at the girl and exited the pool in a huff.

"Good riddance!" said Eric, giving them a one-finger salute as they drove away.

"We gotta go, too, y'all," said J.D. "Sun's past the tree line."

Reluctantly, we climbed out of the pool, slid our wrinkled toes into sandy flip-flops, and, with Mitchell walking alongside, began rolling our tubes toward Ain't Pitty's. We were just turning onto the Railroad when a familiar old truck pulled alongside us. It was the same truck we had seen at the lake, and Mitchell's pa was driving. When he was younger, he might have been considered good looking, but now he was just stooped, beady eyed, and dirty.

"Hey, Mitch. Whose yer buddies?"

"Friends," replied Mitchell, lifting his bike onto the back of the truck and climbing into the cab.

"Introduce me."

"They've gotta go. Leave 'em alone."

His pa whirled around with his fist in the air.

"Mouth off to me again, boy, and you'll wish you hadn't!"

Mitchell had both hands up to ward off the blow.

"Please. Just leave 'em alone."

Mitchell's pa glared at him and then spit tobacco juice out the window and pulled off. Looking out the back glass at us, Mitchell looked relieved.

"What the hell was that about?" asked Eric.

"I dunno," answered J.D., staring after the truck, "but I bet Ain't Pitty's right: that ol' man's trouble."

"Mitchell sure didn't want his pa around us," I said.

"He gives me the creeps," added Sandra.

"Nettie, why was he gonna hit Mitchell?" asked Sharon.

"Because he's bigger and could, I guess."

"He's scary," said Li'l Bit, taking my hand.

"Yeah, sugar. He is."

Reaching Ain't Pitty's driveway, we hung our tubes on wooden pegs in the lean-to and rinsed our feet under the outdoor shower.

The day had not ended well, and even the smell of Ain't Pitty's fried chicken coming from the kitchen did little to lift our mood.

"Nettie, did you see Mitchell's back?" whispered Sam as we headed inside.

"Yeah. I saw it."

Chapter 8

A soft breeze was blowing across the porch by the time we reached the rockers, causing nearby leaves to quiver as if they were nervous. Lights were popping on around the neighborhood, and Wilbur was snacking on cricket parts the little ones had put in his corner.

"Lights are on at Miz Lettie's, but I haven't seen her since we got to town," said Sam.

"She knows we're here," I said.

"She and everybody else on God's green earth," chuckled Eric.

"She probably thought havin' Sheriff Coker visit Ain't Pitty would scare us off," said J.D. "Reckon we oughta visit her tonight. She's at the top of the list again this year."

"I was wondering when we'd get started," I said. "Supplies are in their normal spot."

"Who else is on the list this time?" asked Sam.

"What list?" echoed Sharon.

"What are y'all talkin' about?" asked Li'l Bit.

"Nothin' you two need to worry about," snapped J.D., sending us a "be quiet" look.

"I'm not worried," pouted Sharon. "I just wanna know what it is I'm not worried about."

"When you're old enough to know, you'll know. Until then, remember—no talkin'!"

"But we don't know what we're not 'sposed to talk about."

"Then not talkin' about it will be easy, won't it?"

"Shh," I hissed, as tinkling fancies announced that Ain't Pitty was headed our way. As she came through the door, I could tell she wasn't happy.

"Li'l Bit and Sharon said y'all were talkin' with Mitchell's pa today. What did he want?"

I saw J.D. shoot the little ones a dirty look. They'd talked.

"He wanted Mitchell to 'troduce us!" yelled Li'l Bit.

"What?"

"He wanted Mitchell to tell him who we were," I interpreted.

"And!" added Sharon. "When Mitchell wouldn't do it, his pa almost hit him in the face!"

"I see," said Ain't Pitty, putting her hands on her hips. "I told y'all to stay away from that man, and I meant it. If he or Otis Pierce comes around, I expect to hear about it immediately." Pointing at the concrete floor, she added, "And if y'all can't do that, then plan on spending the summer right here. Understood?"

"Yes, ma'am."

I knew it would do no good to explain how we'd ended up with Mitchell's pa today. The problem was, we had not been the ones to tell her.

"Ain't Pitty, Sam and I saw a big bruise on Mitchell's back today at the pool. Do you think his pa could've done it?"

"Did Mitchell say his pa hit him?"

"No, ma'am."

"That's the problem—he never does," mumbled Ain't Pitty. "If Mitchell ever tells you his pa or anyone else hurt him, let me or Uncle Ben know."

"Yes, ma'am."

Ain't Pitty held her hand out to the little ones. "C'mon, you two. The rest of y'all stay close."

As the tinkling faded, J.D. whispered, "I'm glad you mentioned the bruise, Nettie. Eric and I saw it, too."

"I should've asked Mitchell how he got it."

"I did ask him," said Eric. "He said he fell off his bike. But after seeing what his pa did this afternoon, I'm not so sure."

"Ain't Pitty is as serious about us stayin' away from Mitchell's pa as I've seen her about anythin'," added Sam.

"If he keeps comin' around, do you think she'll make us stay away from Mitchell, too?" I asked.

"Maybe," replied J.D. "We'll just have to figure out a way to include Mitchell in stuff without crossin' paths with his ol' man.

"Yeah, and we need to make sure Li'l Bit and Sharon keep their mouths shut."

"Well, one thing's for sure: if they can't, we have a big problem," added Eric. "Plus, we're gonna have to be more careful about what we say when they're around."

"Yeah, you're right. I'll talk with them again in the morning," replied J.D.

"Who else is on the list besides Miz Lettie?" asked Sam.

"The Crossing is second and the Judge is third," answered J.D.

"The Judge?" we echoed in pitched-up voices.

"Keep it down! Y'all want the whole neighborhood to hear?"

Moving to the edge of our rockers, we all started whispering at the same time. I loved pulling pranks on folks in the middle of the night and watching their reactions the next day, but pranking the Crossing and the Judge was much more public and potentially dangerous. There would be hell to pay if we got caught at either place.

"Will y'all please shut up and listen for a cotton-pickin' minute!"

"Shh, y'all. Let J.D. have his say," said Eric.

"Uncle Ben told me Ain't Pitty got stopped by one of Sheriff Coker's deputies because Jigger didn't have an inspection sticker. He gave her a warnin' and told her to take care of it as soon as she could, but she got caught without it again and had to go to court. The Judge told her laws were made for a reason and should not be ignored. He fined her and said she couldn't drive Jigger anywhere except to get it inspected. It took Uncle Ben a week to get Jigger ready to pass a not-so-close inspection, and, needless to say, Ain't Pitty wasn't happy. That's when the Judge got added to the list."

"Well," I said, "Miz Lettie will be the one hollerin' loudest about the Crossing, since she's president of the Women's Guild and they're the ones who take care of it. The Judge will probably just blame it on the neighborhood kids 'cause he doesn't even know us."

Getting up, Eric walked to the end of the porch, his hands deep in his pockets.

"I don't know, y'all. There's no wiggle room with the Judge. If we get caught, Momma will send me to military school for sure."

"Well, we just won't get caught," said J.D. "We'll practice on Miz Lettie's and the Crossing and scope out the Judge's place really carefully—what time his lights go out, what his neighbors can and can't see, and how much traffic there is around his house at night."

"Or maybe Eric could just sit this one out," Sam suggested.

"Like hell! If y'all go, I go," said Eric. "We'll just have to be really careful, that's all."

"Well, we don't have to decide about the Judge now," I said. "Let's see how the other TP-in's go and then decide."

"J.D., why's the Crossing on the list?" asked Sam.

"Because Miz Lettie and the Women's Guild have been givin' Ain't Pitty grief about the chicken coop again."

"Hmm," I mused, "so Miz Lettie's gettin' a double dose this summer."

"Well, she deserves it. Ain't Pitty's never done anythin' to that woman, but Miz Lettie keeps causin' her problems."

"Wait a minute, J.D. We've TP'ed Miz Lettie's yard every summer since I can remember, so somebody started somethin' sometime. Maybe if we left her alone, she'd leave Ain't Pitty alone."

"Yeah. And maybe rocks grow."

"Nettie, do you really think stoppin' the TP-in' would end all this?" asked Eric. "Ain't Pitty and Miz Lettie have been at each other for years."

"I know, but it's gotta end sometime."

"Yeah? Well, it's not endin' tonight," snapped J.D.

Every summer when we arrived at Ain't Pitty's, a pyramid of toilet paper would be stacked in the front bedroom closet with a list of names stuck in the top roll. Without ever being told, we knew what we were supposed to do: TP the yards of those on the list. J.D. picked the nights and led the planning for each TP-in', the goal being to cover as much of the targeted yards in the least amount of time, without getting caught. We scouted each yard at least twice before the actual TP-in' to identify good hiding spots, in case somebody in the house woke up or a car happened by. If we were lucky, right after we finished the job it would rain, soaking the thin paper and making it harder to clean up.

Miz Lettie was always the first TP-in' of the summer, and the next day, she and Husband Number Whatever would usually march across the Railroad to complain and insist we clean up their yard. Ain't Pitty would demand proof of our guilt, which they never had, and then she would offer to sell them some fresh eggs.

Darkness had settled in and the lightning bugs were putting on an impressive show by the time the 10:00 p.m. choppers appeared with their own blinking lights. We watched the windows up and down the Railroad go dark as the thumping tide disappeared northward. When all was quiet, we changed into our dark clothes and collected rolls of TP from the closet, stringing them on pieces of clothesline with big knots on one end. Wrapping the unknotted end around a hand allowed us to carry multiple rolls and work at the same time.

Once back on the porch, we waited another half hour to make sure Miz Lettie and her husband were asleep and then moved into the shadows along the Railroad. J.D. and Eric crossed the street first, running down Miz Lettie's white concrete driveway, and began covering the shrubs closest to the house. After a minute, when no lights had come on, Sam, Sandra, and I crossed over and began covering the bushes in the yard, carefully weaving the TP in and out of the leaves and branches so it would be harder to remove. Finally, Eric and J.D. tossed the last of their rolls up and over the top of the dogwood tree near the carport. As they finished, a light breeze began to blow, causing the long white streamers to dance.

When we were safely back on Ain't Pitty's porch, J.D. gathered our lines to take inside while the rest of us settled down to admire our handiwork. As he returned, lightning flashed in the distance.

"Great timing," said Sam, counting Mississippis until we heard thunder.

"Dammit!" snapped J.D., staring at Miz Lettie's house. "Look. We forgot to do the stupid carport!"

"Aw, just leave it," Eric said, yawning. "They have plenty of TP to pick up. Besides, I saw—"

"Never leave a job half done," interrupted J.D.

Slipping back into the bedroom, he came out with another roll of TP, jumped the steps, and snuck back across the Railroad.

For a while we could see shadowy movements as J.D. strung TP around the carport railings and car, but when he reached the back, it was too dark to see.

Suddenly, the quiet night was shattered by the ear-piercing scream of a cat in pain, followed by the loud crash-bang of tin trash cans getting knocked over and kicked around. Above the racket we heard J.D. yell out a string of four-letter words that would have gotten his mouth washed out with soap every day for a month if Granny had heard them.

By now lights were popping on all over Miz Lettie's house and J.D. was nowhere to be seen. According to our plan, if anyone got caught, we were on our own, the logic being that one person could be forgiven more easily than five. So, leaving J.D. to fend for himself, we ran for the safety of the dark bedroom, tripping over each other as we tried to get in and shut the door. Stacking one on top of the other, we peeked out the front window, straining to see if J.D. had been caught. But the only thing we could see was Miz Lettie and her husband marching around outside in their matching bathrobes, their hands planted firmly on their hips.

Wide eyed, we watched and waited. After inspecting their yard and carport, Miz Lettie and her husband went back inside, leaving the front door open and the lights on. J.D. was still nowhere to be seen.

"There's gonna be big trouble this time," Eric whispered over our heads.

We waited and watched as the lightning and thunder closed in and the first drops of rain began to hit the window. Our hearts sank as headlights lit up the Railroad and Sheriff Coker's car pulled up in front of Miz Lettie's. About the same time, we heard a rustling sound coming from the passageway, and J.D. stumbled into the room, looking dazed and in pain.

Wiping his face and arms with what looked like the kitchen dishrag, he peeked out the front window and hissed, "Quick! Get your pajamas on and get in bed! We've gotta make 'em believe we were sleepin', or we're all in deep shit!"

Flip-flops flew as we tried to find our pajamas in the dark. Shoving clothes under the beds, we jumped into our sleeping spots and pulled the sheets up to our quivering chins. Not a minute later, there was a loud knock on Ain't Pitty's front door.

The fancies were going crazy as heavy footsteps crossed the dining room and entered the passageway. When the overhead light clicked on, we pretended to stir and saw Uncle Ben and Sheriff Coker standing in the doorway.

"Kids, wake up."

"Where've y'all been tonight?" boomed Sheriff Coker, his eyes scanning our faces.

Eric rose up on an elbow and faked a yawn.

"Whaddaya mean, Sheriff? We've been here, sleepin'."

What a cool liar you are.

"In a pig's eye!" snapped the Sheriff. "Y'all get up. You're goin' over to Miz Lettie's and pick up every bit of that toilet paper."

Ain't Pitty came through the passageway, tightening her robe and sliding her glasses up her nose.

"Now, Sheriff, these kids are stayin' right where they are. I was with them on the porch earlier tonight, and I heard them come inside for bed right after the choppers passed, so they didn't have time to do anythin' to anybody."

"They most certainly did have time, Miz Pitty. And they could've snuck out right there," replied Sheriff Coker, pointing at the door leading to the porch.

"They could've, but they didn't."

"And just how do you know that?"

"Because I keep that door locked and the key hidden."

Sheriff Coker walked over to the door and turned the knob. Sure enough, it was locked tight. Turning around, he stared at us and then at Ain't Pitty.

"Well, they could've used the front door."

"Ben and I would've heard 'em if they had," countered Ain't Pitty. "One person can't walk across the livin' room without makin' all that glass clatter, much less five!"

"Miz Pitty, I don't know how they did it, but they did it, and you know they did it! They do it every summer. And this time they almost killed Miz Lettie's cat in the process! Now that damn cat's up on her roof and I have to find a ladder, climb up there in the rain, and try to get 'im down. It's gotta stop, Miz Pitty. I'm too old to be chasin' cats and too tired to listen to Miz Lettie go on and on 'bout this. She's gonna make my life a misery 'cause she has to spend the next two days pickin' up toilet paper again."

We could see Uncle Ben trying to stifle a grin, but Ain't Pitty never wavered.

"I'm real sorry, Sheriff. I know Lettie can be a challenge at times . . . bless her little heart."

As Sheriff Coker lost steam, his face took on a look of reluctant surrender. Shaking his head, he turned to leave but stopped at J.D.'s bunk.

"Son, I've got more important things to take care of in the middle of the night than toilet paper and cats. Keep your nose clean from now on, and make sure they keep theirs clean, because if you don't, when I catch you—and I *will* catch you—I'm gonna take you before the Judge, and he'll send every one of you to the juvenile detention center in Dothan. That place isn't fit for anybody, much less young boys and girls." Turning toward the passageway, he added, "Pitty, Ben, I mean it. We're trying to keep folks safe around here, these children included. Help us out."

The Sheriff headed back to the front door amid louder-than-usual tinkling.

He's really gonna be on the lookout for us now!

When a combative Satan had been rescued from Miz Lettie's roof and the back of Ain't Pitty's house had gone quiet again, we turned on the light and looked at J.D. He was gingerly pulling his t-shirt over his head. His arms and chest were covered with long, wicked-looking scratches, welts, and gouges, some still oozing blood.

"Oh, jeez!" said Sam. "That's gotta hurt!"

"No shit!" moaned J.D.

"Hang on," I said, scrambling off the bed and digging through my suitcase. "Momma sent a big bottle of Bactine spray with us to use on Li'l Bit's scraped knees. We can use it on you."

Wiping the blood off J.D.'s broken skin with the dishrag, I began spraying the jagged red lines with the antiseptic. J.D. bit his lip as the stinging intensified. As he turned, we could see even more scratches and bleeding across his shoulders and down his back.

"Was it Satan?" asked Sandra.

"Are you kiddin'? Of course it was!"

"Well," said Eric, "I tried to tell ya I saw Satan hidin' in the bushes next to the carport as we were TP-in' the dogwood tree."

"What the hell? You knew that damn cat was there and didn't tell me?"

"I tried! But you took off before I could finish."

"You coulda come over there and told me!"

"Well . . . I . . . I didn't think about that at the time."

"What was Satan doin' outside, anyway?" asked Sam. "Miz Lettie usually takes him in at night."

"Well, he sure as hell wasn't inside tonight, was he? That damn cat 'bout tore me to pieces! It was like he was in three places at once. I went to string TP from the side door, and when I put my foot on the stoop, I musta stepped on his tail. I shoulda kept it there, too, 'cause when he got loose, he jumped on my chest and clawed his way around my shoulders and down my back all at the same time. I think I even have one of his stupid claws stuck in my butt!"

"I'll check for you," offered Eric.

"Like hell you will!" hissed J.D., spinning his butt toward the wall. "Ain't no one lookin' at my butt but me! I'll check it in the mornin'."

"Yeah, but you need to spray it tonight," I insisted, handing him the Bactine.

Taking the bottle, J.D. backed into the closet, sprayed as best he could, and sat down gingerly on his bunk.

"I can't believe in the hottest part of the summer I've gotta wear a long-sleeved t-shirt until these scratches heal. If anybody sees 'em, I'll get a one-way ticket to the detention center Sheriff Coker was talkin' about."

"It's a good thing we opened the rollout window in the kitchen, and it's a really good thing we remembered to lock this door. That's good plannin'!" bragged Sandra.

"Well, it didn't keep us from forgettin' the stupid carport in the first place, now, did it?"

"Well, you've got a point."

Moaning, J.D. laid back, lifted his long legs onto the bunk, and closed his eyes.

"I just wish we'd anticipated that damn cat!"

"Don't forget, tomorrow's Sunday," said Sam, turning out the light. "Granny's gonna be expectin' us at church, and considerin' what happened tonight, we'd best show up."

"Holy hell and damnation!" came J.D.'s voice out of the dark. "You mean I've gotta sit through Pastor Flemming's long-winded preachin' while I'm in pain, in a long-sleeved shirt, in a hot-as-hell church, with a cat's claw in my butt?"

There was silence as the rest of us choked back giggles. None of us had a solution to offer, even if we could have managed not to laugh.

"Well," chuckled Eric, "we've gotta go; otherwise, it's gonna look suspicious. J.D., you're just gonna have to suck it up and act natural."

"I know! I know!" whined J.D. "Maybe I can get some aspirin before we go."

"I guess Satan's gruesome reckoning just got worse."

"Damn right it did!"

Chapter 9

While many regions across the South claimed to be the "buckle" of the Bible Belt, the Wiregrass did not. According to Ain't Pitty, folks here seemed to require more Monday-through-Saturday forgiving than the rest of the stretched-out Belt, and you did not have to look far to find the sort of things they needed to be forgiven for. From the gambling shacks, cathouses, and sneaky he-in' and she-in' to the thieving, bootlegging, and more serious devilry, the Wiregrass was a hotbed of sinners.

In an attempt to save these sinful souls, there were Jesus-believing churches everywhere, hundreds of them, in every size, style, and denomination. Folks could choose from the holier-than-thou Methodists; the let's-call-a-meetin' Presbyterians; the primitive, don't-have-any-fun hard-shell Baptists; the Bible-thumpin' Southern Baptists; and the you've-gotta-be-kiddin', snake-handlin' Holy Roller Pentecostals. There were not many Catholic churches in the Wiregrass, though. Ain't Pitty said this was because Catholics not only have to believe, they have to be good, do good, and make the priests happy in order to get into heaven, and if everybody in the Wiregrass had to do that, they were all doomed to hell.

There were two churches in Crystal Springs: a Methodist church, where Miz Lettie and Husbands One, Two, and Three went, and a Baptist church, where our folks went, except for Ain't Pitty. She was a Jesus believer but only went to church for weddings and funerals. When asked why, she said, "It's hard to see folks in church on Sunday and watch what they do the rest of the week."

"Then why do you make us go?" I asked.

"Because it's easier than explainin' to your momma and granny why I didn't."

So, whether we wanted to or not, every Sunday we were stuffed into our best clothes and sent to the Baptist church for a long, hot morning of preaching.

According to Granny, our church was started by primitive Baptists in a one-room building just outside of town on Hardshell Hill. Twenty years ago, the congregation had boarded up the old church and built a new brick one on the north side of town. However, they continued to lay their folks to rest on Hardshell Hill. Every summer Granny would take us on a pilgrimage there to pay our respects to all of the Campbells who had passed over.

"It's important to know these folks. Without them, you wouldn't be here and you wouldn't know where you're goin' when you leave here."

I didn't mind visiting Hardshell Hill; none of us did. Dozens of birds, butterflies, and bunnies called this quiet hill home, and it was surrounded by large shade trees and wildflowers. It was a peaceful sort of place, not scary, like some folks made cemeteries out to be.

During our visit, Granny would pull weeds and talk with the occupants enclosed in the Campbell plot. Pa Campbell was there, along with two little boys and one little girl he and Granny had buried as babies. The names and dates on the little graves were fascinating to us: John, James, and Laura Will. If these babies had lived, we would have had two more uncles, another ain't, and more cousins. In my mind, it was nice to know Pa Campbell was with them in heaven.

"Wonder who's winnin'," Eric said, as we passed the church parking lot.

"Looks like a tie to me," said Sam, eyeing the parking lot of the Methodist church down the block. "That'll have the ain'ts' lips flappin' this afternoon."

Every Sunday morning, the good Christian folks of both churches would count the cars in each other's parking lots, hoping to claim the greater number of Christians at the next meeting of the Women's Guild.

Like most churches in the South, ours had a steeple with a cross, an altar and pulpit, and incredibly uncomfortable wooden pews that got harder the longer you sat on them. There was also a baptism pool where Pastor Flemming would occasionally lay somebody down in the water and preach about being saved. We weren't sure how taking a dip with your clothes on saved people from the devil, but we envied their being cool.

The only ventilation in the church came from the windows and the well-worn cardboard fans donated by Bell's Funeral Home over in Samson. The message on one side of the fan said, COOL OR HOT, WE'VE GOT YOU COVERED WHEN THE TIME COMES. The other side said, GET YOUR ANGEL'S WINGS AT BELL'S. Unfortunately, fans were of little help when it was a hundred degrees and the pews were packed.

There had been a variety of preachers in the pulpit of the Baptist church, but several years ago the congregation had called a young fellow named Jim Flemming to shepherd them. Pastor Flemming was a big man with sandy-colored hair and happy brown eyes. He was quick to smile, quick to offer his hand, and quick to hug those who needed hugging, by their idea or his. He was also a handy fellow to have around. If things around the church broke, he could fix them. He would even go to folks' homes to fix things, if needed. He never accepted money for this work; he just asked folks to help the next person in need and to remember the church when the offering plate was passed on Sunday.

Pastor Flemming had a woodworking shop in his garage where he built furniture, mostly rocking chairs, the mission kind. Ain't Pitty had several on her front porch that the Pastor had built for her at costs. But she did not like being "beholden" to anyone, so she made a donation to the church when each rocker was delivered.

"Miz Pitty, one of these days I'm going to look out and see your smiling face in church on Sunday," Pastor Flemming had told her.

"Don't hold your breath waitin' for me, Pastor, but I'll pray while I'm rockin'."

Pastor Flemming took the care of his flock seriously, but he was not above downing a beer or two on a hot day and was known to cut a pretty good rug at the monthly senior center dances. In some Baptist circles, this would have gotten a brother in trouble, but he seemed to be a good fit for the Crystal Springs Baptists, who seemed to like their shepherding reins a little loose.

"There she is," said Sam, pointing at Granny, who was waiting for us in front of the church.

"You cold, J.D.?" asked Granny, looking skeptically at his long-sleeved shirt and sweaty brow.

"No, ma'am. Just thought I'd show some respect, bein' it's Sunday an' all."

"Uh-huh."

Following Granny into the church, we made our way down the aisle toward her regular front-row pew while turning heads and whispers followed us like a wave at Panama City.

According to Ain't Pitty, you could tell a lot about folks by where they sat in church. "Sittin' in the left front means one of three things: they can't hear, believe they're the best Christians in the place, or know they're the worst."

We assumed Granny had a hearing problem.

Pastor Flemming was grinning and his eyes sparkled as he watched Granny sit down and pull J.D. down beside her. When the rest of us had settled into the pew, Pastor Flemming stood and in a full-throated voice welcomed sinners, saints, and seekers alike.

Gonna be a long morning.

Being in the left front row was a problem for two reasons. First, there were never enough fans, because there was no pew in front of us with pockets to store them in, and second, we were right in front of the Pastor and had no choice but to behave. Luckily, I was sitting by an open window and could occupy myself with whatever was going on outside and maybe catch a rare breeze. For the most part, my attention weaved in and out as Pastor Flemming talked about the usual—sin, grace, and salvation. But today he was also talking about a man named John the Baptist. This John fellow was a hellfire-and-brimstone kind of soul saver, which, combined with the fact that he wore camel hair and ate locust on purpose, made me think he'd be pretty good at getting folks to pay attention.

When the sermon ended, we put what was left of our allowance in the offering plate under Granny's watchful eye.

"We've all got to help keep the lights on, and the Pastor has to eat," she'd say.

As we walked back to Granny's house after the service, J.D. looked puzzled.

"Granny, that John the Baptist fella knew those people were gonna kill 'im if he didn't shut up, but he kept on preachin'. Why?"

"Savin' souls is not the same thing as savin' bodies," said Granny. "It took a lot of courage for him and others in the Bible to do the right thing for the right reason, especially when they knew the price they were gonna pay."

"Still, I can't believe they cut off his head," said Eric.

"I can't believe he ate locust," I added, feeling the sensation of insect legs going down my throat.

Every Sunday after church, Granny hosted a potluck dinner. Family who lived close by were expected to come, and those who could not were prayed for when Granny said her usual "cover all the bases" grace, thanking the Lord for the food and everything good, and asking for forgiveness of all Campbell sins, known and unknown. I did not understand the unknown-sins part, but Granny included it every time, so I figured it was important.

We filled our plates and then escaped to the steps of the back porch, where we had a bird's-eye view of the high school football field. The team would soon begin Sunday-afternoon workouts in preparation for twice-a-day practices beginning in August. Sam and John Thomas had spotted each other during one of these workouts last summer. She'd watched him practice, and he'd showed off his football skills for her. Now she just stared at the empty field.

"Stop mopin' around after Stinky," said J.D. between mouthfuls.

"I'm not mopin'. I'm just wonderin' what Cilly has that I don't."

"Lemons! Big ones!" I blurted out.

"Lemons?" asked Sandra.

"Not real lemons," laughed Sam. "She means boobs."

"Oh," replied Sandra, looking down at her chest, as if hoping to see something.

"I don't think it's the fact Cilly has them that makes the difference," said Eric. "I think it's what she does with them."

"Oh, gross!" I snapped.

"Careful," said Sam, nodding toward Li'l Bit and Sharon.

"Nettie, Mitchell's coming to the pool this afternoon, isn't he?" asked J.D.

"You know he is."

"Yep. I just wanted to watch you turn red."

"Jackass."

Mitchell had been meeting us after work and on the weekends whenever he could, and while I was getting more comfortable around him, I still blushed when his name came up, especially in relation to me.

"He sure seems to like being around you," teased Eric.

"Us. He likes being around us."

"Right."

"Let's go, y'all," said J.D. "I've gotta get outta these long sleeves."

"You did a good job sittin' still in church today," teased Eric. "I know you had to be hurtin'."

"No thanks to you."

"Hey, don't be mad. I really did try to warn ya."

"Yeah? Well, you didn't, did you?" Then, with a sly smile, J.D. added, "I hear paybacks are hell."

Chapter 10

The Fourth of July was a big deal around the Wiregrass. Crops were growing in the fields, and most folks were not as preoccupied as they had been during planting season or would be during picking season. They came from miles around for the community-wide celebration, which included good food, music, and a fireworks show.

The festivities were held at Geneva County Lake, in part because there were plenty of picnic tables and parking spaces, but also because the fireworks could be launched from the dirt-road dam in the middle of the lake. This location enhanced the effects of the fireworks and reduced the likelihood of burns if the fireworks malfunctioned, as they often did.

Ain't Pitty and Uncle Ben dropped us off early so we could visit the booths that were set up near the parking area. Community groups sponsored most of these booths as part of their fund-raising activities and sold things like cold drinks, popcorn balls, funnel cakes, snow cones, firecrackers, and sparklers. Even the Women's Guild was there, selling rhinestone flag pins for women, matching tie tacks for men, and red, white, and blue candy for the kids.

Nearby was a kissing booth sponsored by the fire department. It was divided into a pink side for girl kissers and a blue side for boy kissers. Local football players and cheerleaders had been asked to sell ten-second, on-the-mouth kisses for a dollar, and folks were already lining up to see who was kissing whom.

There were also carnival-type booths where you could win prizes for things like throwing darts at balloons, shooting plastic ducks, and tossing beanbags through a hole. We accomplished little at these booths except losing most of our allowance.

Booker's Feed and Seed sponsored the last booth and was selling ant and bee spray, charcoal and lighter fluid, and Coca-Colas out of the front and something in little Dixie cups out of the back when Willie Ray thought no one was looking. Knowing better than to stop, we decided to circle Lake Road to see who had arrived.

The first picnickers we passed were the bearded Miz Hines and her extended hairy family—sisters, brothers, and others—all with an extraordinary amount of hair in unusual places. The only one sitting at their table who was not hairy was Mr. Hines; he was completely bald.

Spotting us, Miz Hines stood up, crossed her hairy arms, and stared. Cilly and John Thomas were nowhere around, which was a good thing. It would be best if we could avoid their kind of trouble on a day like today, at least while Cilly's man-momma was around.

Perched on Lake Road's only hill was a group of older folks we did not know. They had the only sheltered table and were positioned so they could see most of the other tables on this side of the lake. One older gentleman, with round, wire-rimmed glasses, a salt-and-pepper beard, and thinning hair, was leaning back against the picnic table, smoking a pipe, and watching us go by. He didn't smile, frown, or wave. He just watched until we were out of sight.

"That was kinda creepy. Wonder who he is," said J.D., looking over his shoulder.

"Nobody we want to know," I replied.

Farther down the road, at a table back in the trees, were Mitchell's pa, Otis Pierce, and a lady with twisted-up blond hair, bright red lipstick, and a wrinkled face with a cigarette hanging from the corner of her mouth. She was wearing a tank top and shorts that were too small for what she had squeezed into them, and her expression was hard.

"Eww," Eric whispered. "She could haunt a house all by herself."

"Yeah. She's scary, all right," I added, relieved that Mitchell was not with them.

On the picnic table in front of the three were a brown jug and scattered food wrappings. I could feel Ol' Man Ames watching as we walked by. Glancing up, I caught his black-eyed stare and felt cold shivers run up my spine. Pulling Li'l Bit with me, I moved to the far side of the road.

"What's wrong?" asked J.D., looking toward the men.

"Nothin'. They're just givin' me the creeps, that's all."

"Just keep movin', y'all," said Sam. "Remember what Ain't Pitty said."

Otis Pierce spit what looked like tobacco juice out of the corner of his mouth, reached for the brown jug, and yelled, "Y'all wanna taste somethin' good?" Wobbling toward us, he held out the jug. "C'mon, it ain't gonna hurt ya. It'll make ya feel real good."

"No," snapped J.D., giving him a hard look. "We gotta go."

Ignoring J.D., Otis Pierce took another step toward us and asked, "How 'bout it, li'l ladies? Wanna taste?"

Sam and Sandra turned their heads and kept walking. I followed, pulling Li'l Bit with me.

"Aww! C'mon! Don't ya wanna try just a li'l taste?" yelled Otis Pierce, stumbling after us and laughing.

"Walk faster, y'all," urged Eric.

But J.D. had stopped and was staring at Otis Pierce with clenched fists.

Coming back to stand with him, Eric whispered, "C'mon, J.D., you don't wanna blow the entire summer over the likes of him."

J.D. hesitated for a moment, as if trying to decide whether to take a swing at the wobbling drunk.

"He's not worth it, J.D.," whispered Eric. "Let's go."

"Asshole," mumbled J.D., as he unclenched his fists and turned away.

Otis Pierce snorted, took a swig from the jug, and stumbled his way back to the picnic table.

Once we were around the next bend, we slowed our pace.

"Are we gonna tell Ain't Pitty bout this?" I asked.

"Of course we're gonna tell her," said Sam.

"Maybe not," said J.D., glancing at me. "Ain't Pitty's already nervous about those men hanging around; she may really tighten the reins on us if she finds out about this. She may even say Mitchell can't come around anymore."

"Well, it's not like we went lookin' for 'em," offered Eric. "All we were doing was walkin' by, so maybe it doesn't count."

"I bet Ain't Pitty would say it counted," warned Sam. "We have to tell her. It'll be a lot worse if we don't and she finds out."

Stopping in the middle of the road, J.D. grinned.

"Sam's right. We have to tell her. But I'll be the one to do it." Squatting down in front of Li'l Bit and Sharon, J.D. asked, "Do you two hear what I'm sayin'? I'm gonna tell Ain't Pitty about those men, not you. If you say anythin' to her, anythin' at all, you can't go 'round with us anymore. Got it?"

Nodding, Li'l Bit and Sharon agreed and took off running ahead of us.

"Okay, J.D., what are you up to?" asked Eric. "What are you gonna tell Ain't Pitty?"

"It's more about what I'm not gonna tell her than what I am. All Ain't Pitty asked us to do was to let her know if we saw those men again, and that's exactly what I'm gonna tell her. Nothin' more, nothin' less."

I could not help but wonder if telling part of the truth was as bad as telling a lie, but I was also relieved. Mitchell had become an important part of my summer, and I didn't want anything messing that up.

Continuing our walk around Lake Road, we passed by Mr. Digger and Mr. Short, who were with some folks dressed like Sunday. Mr. Digger offered us free Fireballs from an overflowing basket.

"You kids have a good time, but be careful. All kinds of folks out here today."

"Yes, sir. We will. Thanks for the candy."

"Sounds like he knows Ames and Pierce are out here," said Eric when we were out of earshot.

A little farther up the road, Li'l Bit ran up to a big, knothole-covered tree that had part of its root ball showing. Storm-water runoff had washed away much of the soil on one side, and the roots were hanging down the bank like thick spaghetti.

Peeking underneath, Li'l Bit yelled, "Hey, look, y'all! There's a cave in here!"

He and Sharon climbed in and sat down in the hidden space.

"Hmm, I wonder what critters live in there," teased J.D. "Skunks? Possums? Snakes?"

"There's no snakes in here," yelled Li'l Bit, as he and Sharon scrambled out the other side of the root cave and started running. In their panic they bumped right into Jessie, who was standing in the road, watching them. He had a fishing pole in one hand, an empty stringer in the other, and the pocket of his shirt was wiggling, which meant it was full of crickets or fishing worms.

"Hey, Jessie," said J.D. "How ya doin'?"

The rest of us echoed with "heys" and "hi's," but, as usual, Jessie didn't say a word. He just started walking down the road.

"I wonder if Otis Pierce and the others will bother him," I said, watching Jessie disappear around the bend.

"I doubt it," said J.D.

"I dunno. Jessie's pretty trustin'."

"Drunk doesn't mean stupid, Nettie. If those ol' men messed with Jessie, everybody in town would go after 'em, especially Miz Maddie."

"Yeah, but how would they know? Jessie's not gonna tell 'em."

"Gosh, you're right. I hadn't thought about that. Y'all wait here."

J.D. turned and ran down the road after Jessie, reappearing a few minutes later.

"Jessie's okay. Those creeps called him a bunch of ugly names, but he just kept on walkin'."

We had planned to meet Mitchell at the Bait and Tackle Shop when he got off work, so when Lake Road ended we hurried over to see if he had arrived. Just as J.D. reached for the knob, the door opened and he was nose to chin with Sheriff Coker. We all froze as the Sheriff pushed his hat to the back of his head, put his hands on his hips, and stared. After a minute of dead silence, we backed down the steps, silently deciding we could wait for Mitchell outside in the heat just as easily as we could inside the nice, air-conditioned shop. We had just sat down in some tree shade, when Sheriff Coker called J.D. and Eric.

"You two come back here."

"Oh, shit," whispered J.D.

"Lord, help us," mumbled Eric.

The two tried to look fearless as they headed back to the porch and the grim-faced officer. The rest of us could only watch as Sheriff Coker talked and shook his finger, occasionally pointing in our direction. J.D. and Eric, their eyes fixed on the Sheriff's face, were nodding as if in full agreement with whatever he was saying. Finally, the Sheriff let them go and they sprinted back to us, arriving about the same time as Mitchell.

"What was that all about?" asked Mitchell, easing down into the grass next to me.

"I'm not sure."

Sensing his closeness and smelling Zest, I felt warm all over.

"Well?" asked Sam. "What did Sheriff Coker want?"

Glancing sideways at Eric, J.D. answered, "He just told us to stay out of trouble and other stuff."

"What kind of other stuff?"

"Same stuff as the other night."

"Hmm. Are you sure about that? That's all he wanted?"

"Yeah, pretty much."

J.D. tilted his head toward the little ones as if to say, *Not here and not now.*

"Ha!" laughed Eric. "Look who's in the kissin' booth!"

Following his gaze, we saw Cilly and John Thomas entering the back of the booth, getting in line with others to sell their kisses.

"You'd think those two would be tired of kissin'," Sam sniped.

"Naw," muttered Eric. "They're just tired of kissin' each other."

Suddenly, J.D. laughed and jumped to his feet.

"Give me any money you've got."

Obediently, we dug around in our pockets and handed over what we had.

"What are you gonna do, J.D.?" asked Sam.

"You'll see. Just stay put!" he yelled, heading off through the crowd.

"Sheriff Coker's still over there. J.D. better not pull anythin'!"

"Yeah," replied Eric. "J.D. knows he's there."

By now Mr. Short's bluegrass band was playing on the make-shift stage in the dell between the Bait and Tackle Shop and the lake. Listening to the lively music, we scanned the crowd, waiting for J.D. to return. Finally, he slipped back in behind us and sat down.

"Okay, what are you up to?" asked Eric.

Smiling wickedly, J.D. nodded toward the kissing booth.

"Watch."

Looking up, we saw Jessie making his way through the crowd toward the pink side of the booth just as Cilly stepped up to take her turn at the counter. He laid down a handful of change, grabbed Cilly's startled face, and planted a big, flat-lipped kiss right on her surprised mouth. At the same time, the big girl John Thomas had given a hard time at the Crystal Springs pool walked up to the blue side of the booth. Tossing her money down, she threw an arm around John Thomas's neck and planted a sloppy kiss right on his lips.

The stunned silence of the crowd gave way to squeals of laughter as Jessie and the girl walked away, getting pats on the back from those they passed.

The shocked looks on Cilly's and John Thomas's faces changed to disgust as they started rubbing their mouths, hocking, spitting, and dry heaving. After washing their mouths with every cup of water they could find, they left the booth in a huff.

Our laughter was louder and lasted far longer than that of anyone else who witnessed the kissing ambush. Even Cilly and John Thomas started looking our way, but we kept on laughing, rolling around in the grass until our stomachs hurt and our tear ducts dried up.

Weak, but finally able to catch his breath, Eric warned, "Y'all realize we're gonna pay for that. Somewhere, somehow, we're gonna pay."

"Yeah, but it sure was worth it," giggled Sam, lying limp in the grass.

"That's somethin' Cilly and John Thomas will never forget," laughed J.D.

"How'd you get Jessie to do it?" asked Eric.

"I just asked him," replied J.D., shrugging. "He didn't say a word. He just took the money and did it. I think he understands a lot more than most folks give him credit for."

"I feel sorry for Jessie and that girl," said Sharon. "Now they've got Stinky and Hairy's cooties all over their faces, and everybody was laughin' at 'em."

Sharon had a point, not about the cooties but about Jessie and the girl. J.D. had used them to play a prank on Cilly and John Thomas, and now I wasn't sure who was being laughed at.

The wrong people may have been hurt.

"Gosh, you're right, Sharon," added Sam.

"Well," countered J.D., "they didn't have to do it if they didn't want to. Besides, I told Jessie I'd fill his lawn mower up with gas tomorrow, and the girl—whose name is Noni, by the way—wanted just one thing."

"What's that?" I asked.

"She wants to meet Eric. She thinks he's really cute!" Punching

Eric in the arm, J.D. grinned and added, "She'll catch up with us later today."

Eric smacked J.D. upside the head, which started another round of grass-rolling laughter.

Ain't Pitty and Uncle Ben were taking the last of the hamburgers and hot dogs off the smoking grill when we arrived, so we loaded our buns, added deviled eggs, homemade potato chips, and baked beans with extra mustard, brown sugar, and onions to our plates, and settled around the table. Mitchell sat down next to me, his plate filled to overflowing.

I wonder if his pa ever feeds him or if he has to make do for himself.

When our plates were empty, Ain't Pitty made us leave the picnic table to eat the watermelon slices she'd brought for desert. She knew there would be a seed-spitting contest and that very few of the seeds would make it into the paper cups we were supposed to be aiming for.

When the watermelon was gone, we headed to the lake to wash up.

"Hey, look at the size of those minnows," said J.D., squatting at the water's edge.

"I'll get the net and bucket," said Eric. "Dead or alive, they'll make good bait for tomorrow's fishin'."

Uh-oh! Ain't Pitty likes to use minnows for swamp fishing.

I shivered, feeling the leeches crawling on me already.

Get a grip, Nettie! If they can do it, you can.

The boys netted dozens of minnows, putting them in a bucket of lake water and setting them on Jigger's back floorboard.

By now, the sun was setting and folks were packing up their picnic baskets and picking spots along the lake's edge to watch the fireworks. Making our way down to the dock T, we placed Li'l Bit and Sharon on the middle railing and settled in beside them. After the fireworks show, we would set off the firecrackers and sparklers Uncle Ben had given us, but we had to be on our feet and off the dock when they were lit.

As the last remnant of sun disappeared, the crickets and tree frogs began singing and the crowd circling the lake grew quiet, as if enjoying the moment.

"I really like this time of day," I whispered to Mitchell.

"Me too." Pausing for a second, he added, "Nettie, I'm really glad you're here."

"Me too."

Gosh, this is a whole new kind of happy.

When it was completely dark, the fireworks started and the oohs and aahs began echoing across the water. For thirty minutes or so we watched as sparkling red, white, and blue lights streaked across the sky, the effect doubled by their reflection in the lake. Judging by the cheers that erupted when the finale began, this Fourth of July celebration was a success. But just as the fireworks peaked, I saw a match flare to life where J.D. was sitting and watched as the flickering light moved to where Eric was balanced on the railing and looking up.

"What the hell? J.D.! What are you doin'?" yelled Eric, straining to look over his shoulder. He was grabbing at his back pocket and trying not to fall backward off the railing when the first firecracker went off.

"Damn you, J.D.! If you burn my good cut—"

The loud, rapid-fire popping of firecrackers coming from Eric's backside drowned out the rest of what he was trying to say. Struggling to keep his balance, he half-fell, half-climbed off the railing and started running up the dock, grabbing at his butt and trying to unbutton his cutoffs at the same time. As he reached the bank, the sparklers that were in the same back pocket ignited, causing a cascade of thousands of dancing lights to trail him up the hill.

The dancing light show ended when Ain't Pitty yelled for Eric to jump in the lake, clothes and all. Afterward, Uncle Ben fished him out of the water, helped peel the scorched jeans off his tender backside, and wrapped him in Ain't Pitty's red-checked tablecloth. Giving J.D. a look that could have melted metal, Eric climbed into the front seat of the Oldsmobile and, with arms folded, stared straight ahead.

The ride from the lake was quiet and a lot less crowded, since J.D. and Eric rode in separate cars. Sam, Mitchell, and I were in Jigger's backseat, and as we turned onto Choctaw Road, Mitchell found my hand in the dark and squeezed it. It was the first time a boy had ever held my hand for something other than a game, and it felt nice.

It didn't take long for us to reach the small, shabby trailer Mitchell called home. The place was dark and eerie and looked deserted.

Mitchell squeezed my hand again and climbed out.

"Bye, y'all! See ya soon."

"Bye, Mitchell."

Uncle Ben helped him untie his bicycle from Jigger's roof and lift it down.

"Thanks, Mr. Miller. I appreciate the ride."

"You're welcome, son. We'll wait here until you're inside."

Uncle Ben kept Jigger's headlights on the front door until Mitchell opened it and waved.

"I'm sure Pitty has told y'all to stay away from here. She means it, and so do I. You're not to come near this place unless one of us is with you."

"Yes, sir."

Watching Uncle Ben stare at the dilapidated trailer, I knew he was upset and I knew why. He did not want to leave Mitchell behind in that awful place. When we got home, I heard him complain to Ain't Pitty.

"It's a damn shame that boy's father doesn't take care of him. Mitchell's tryin' to raise himself."

"It's a good thing he has as much of his mother in him as he does," replied Ain't Pitty. "It's his only hope."

Chapter 11

Ain't Pitty took Eric to the bathroom to apply aloe vera goo to his backside while Uncle Ben took J.D. to the storage shed to deliver his accountability. The rest of us headed to the porch to wait, not envying either one. Eventually, Li'l Bit and Sharon were called in and Eric and J.D. came out, both opting to stand and not speak. We knew better than to interfere; the issue was between them, and they had to work it out. So we waited and listened to firecrackers popping up and down the Railroad and watched the occasional skyrocket shoot up and explode. Finally, Eric broke the silence.

"I can't believe you caught my good cutoffs on fire as payback for Miz Lettie's damn cat attacking you! Especially after I tried to tell you not to go back over there. You 'bout burned me up and scared the shit outta me at the same time!"

"Yeah, well, I did go back over there, didn't I?" snapped J.D. "And I got to dig a cat's claw out of my butt for the effort! All because you didn't bother to tell me Satan was out! As far as I'm concerned, you had it comin'! One sore tail deserves another."

Eric looked like he wanted to snap back but ended up chuckling instead.

"You really did look funny after Satan got ahold of you!"

"Yeah? Well, you were an absolute hoot flying up the bank with your ass on fire!"

"Okay, we're even. Deal?"

"Deal."

It was good to see our leaders make peace.

"Okay, J.D., what did Sheriff Coker want with y'all this afternoon?" I asked.

He and Eric exchanged somber glances.

"He said we'd best be mindin' our p's and q's, because he was watching us. He also warned us to be careful about runnin' around town after dark. He said there were some really mean folks prowlin' around in the shadows who wouldn't think twice about hurting us."

A few nights later, we were on the porch, listening to J.D. try unsuccessfully to pick out a tune on Uncle Ben's old harmonica.

"Enough already!" complained Eric. "My ears are hurting."

"Huh. You couldn't do any better."

"Well, I sure as hell couldn't do any worse."

Putting the harmonica in his pocket, J.D. said, "Listen, y'all, we're almost halfway through summer, so if we're gonna TP the Crossing, we'd better get to it. We don't want the last two jobs too close together—it'd be too risky."

After the near disaster at Miz Lettie's, I was surprised we were going again.

"Do you think we should? Remember what Sheriff Coker said."

"I remember. But I don't think we need to give up our entire TP-in' plans for the rest of the summer, especially since we've stopped the other types of pranks."

"Okay," whined Eric, touching his backside, "but I still can't move too fast."

"Oh, hush. You've gotten worse sunburns at Panama City. Besides, if we do the Crossing tonight, the TP will mix with the leftover Fourth of July decorations and the good ol' ladies of the Women's Guild will have a hell of a mess to clean up."

"Ha!" laughed Sam. "I bet—"

"Oh no!" Sandra cried. "Look at Wilbur!"

The little lizard was trying to make his way across the back of the porch, not at his usual fast clip but much more slowly, his right leg limp and dragging behind him.

As we surrounded him, Wilbur stopped moving, his big eyes looking around at us while his head stayed still. I knew it was impossible to tell what a lizard was thinking, but Wilbur's eyes were sad. Moving past us, he continued his slow, leg-dragging walk to the edge of the porch and disappeared over the side.

"He's in trouble," said J.D.

"Big trouble," added Eric. "Especially if Satan spots him. Wilbur can't outrun 'im now."

"Hell, Satan probably did it."

"We have to help him!" insisted Sandra, close to tears.

"There's not much we can do, Sandra. Even if we could catch Wilbur, which I doubt, we can't splint his leg. Plus, we don't know where he goes when he's down there in the bushes. 'Bout the only thing we can do is try to keep Satan away and hope Wilbur's leg heals fast."

"Well, don't tell Li'l Bit and Sharon he's hurt," cautioned Sam. "It'll break their hearts."

"Poor thing," I whispered. "It must be scary knowin' somethin's out there, just waitin' to hurt you. Wilbur must be so afraid."

"Wilbur *should* be afraid," said J.D., a hard edge in his voice. "Satan doesn't want to hurt him; he wants to eat him! Fear is what keeps Wilbur alive."

As that somber thought settled in, the choppers from Field 10 started their noisy passover. Soon after, the Railroad went dark and we went inside to change and gather supplies.

Using the moon's hazy glow for light, we tiptoed across the patio and hurried past the garden and the chicken coop to the dirt path leading to Pine Street. At the end of the block was a deserted lot that faced the Crossing. Squatting in the weeds, we did a last assessment of the target.

The spotlight at the base of the flagpole shone upward toward the Stars and Stripes hanging limply at the top, but its light spread across the entire corner.

"Dammit!" snapped J.D. "We forgot to bring the cover for the stupid spotlight. We're slippin', y'all, and that's not good. Wait here. I'll be right back."

After a few minutes, J.D. reappeared with an empty bait bucket from Wilkes's backyard.

"I'll cover the spotlight with this. When the corner goes dark, y'all come over. We'll do the TP-in' and then hightail it back here. I'll grab the bucket when we're done and take it back to Wilkes's. Remember, if we need a hidin' spot on this side of the street, we'll use the hedge over there next to the post office. If we need to hide on the Crossing side, we'll head to the clearin' in the woods. Got it?"

Without waiting for a reply, J.D. took off, and few seconds later the Crossing went dark, except for a small ring of light shining around the bottom rim of the bucket. The rest of us scooted across the street and began TP-in' everything in sight. J.D. and Eric did the bushes, small trees, and lower branches of the tall ones. Sam and Sandra worked on the gazebo, wrapping the support columns and hanging TP streamers. I did the same to the porch of the little storage house and even made a TP bow for the door.

"Y'all know this isn't gonna stop Miz Lettie and the others from complainin' about the chicken coop," I whispered, as we ran back to the vacant lot.

"Yeah," muttered Eric, "but it might make 'em think twice about how they do their complainin'."

Kneeling in the weeds, we watched as J.D. reached to retrieve the bucket covering the floodlight. Suddenly, the bucket went flying and J.D. launched into yet another string of cuss words that would have sent Granny running for the soap.

"Damnation, son of a bit—! That sucker's hot!" yelled J.D., doing a high-step dance and shaking his hands to cool them off.

Worried someone would hear the commotion, we looked up and down the street, but all stayed dark and quiet.

With the Crossing lit up again, J.D. quickly pulled off his t-shirt and used it to scoop up the hot bucket. Dashing toward the vacant lot, he reached us about the same time we heard the heavy rattle of an old motor coming up First Street. Running, we dove into the scraggly hedge separating the deserted lot from the post office. From between the scratchy branches, leaves, and vines, we watched as Mitchell's pa pulled up in front of Wilkes's, bringing his old truck to a hard stop. It looked like there were two other people in the cab: Otis Pierce and somebody shorter in the middle. The hair was too light to be Mitchell's, and it didn't look like the piled-up hair of the haunt-a-house lady.

Mitchell's pa stumbled out of the truck and up Wilkes's steps. Opening the help-yourself bin, he took out whatever was there and slammed the lid. Then he opened the screen and rattled the door-knob. Finding it locked, he half-fell down the steps and climbed back into the truck. As the old Ford made a sloppy U-turn, we saw the shadow of another man in the back—a really big shadow.

It was dumb luck, drunkenness, or angels that kept those in the truck from seeing our sweaty white faces in the hedge as the headlights passed over us. The last thing we needed was another face-to-face meeting with the likes of them, especially at this time of night.

"Did y'all see that monster man in the back of the truck?" asked Eric, climbing out of the hedge and brushing himself off.

"Yeah! He was huge," I replied, pulling leaves out of my hair.

"Hey, y'all," whispered J.D., "I need help."

Going back to the hedge, we could see that J.D. was tangled up in sticker vines and every time he moved, they were scratching and drawing more blood.

"Damnation! First the stupid bucket burns the daylights outta me, and now I'm playin' pincushion to these damn sticker vines! What else can go wrong?"

"Hey!" snapped Eric. "No pity parties allowed! Hold still."

"All right, all right! I'm just feelin' snakebit, that's all."

Sticker by sticker, Eric and I separated J.D.'s red and welting skin from the hedge.

"Looks like another Bactine night," said Sam.

"I can't win for losin'!" J.D. whined when he was finally free.

"Well, at least we didn't get caught! Be happy about that!"

"We've gotta figure out who that was in the back of the truck," said Eric. "He was huge!"

"No, we don't," replied Sam. "Whoever he is, he's nobody we should be messin' with."

I hope Mitchell doesn't have to be around him.

"Wonder who was in the front seat with Mitchell's pa and Otis Pierce," I said.

"I dunno," replied J.D. "I couldn't even tell if it was a him or a her."

"Me either."

"Did y'all see Ol' Man Ames tryin' to get into Wilkes's?" asked Sandra. "That greedy sucker took all the free stuff and still wanted more."

"At least Mitchell will have somethin' to eat."

"If he gets any of it," replied Sandra. "Where's Sheriff Coker when you need him? Mitchell's pa was drunk as a skunk, and I bet the others were, too."

"Let me get this straight," said Eric. "We just TP'ed the Crossing, and you want Sheriff Coker to show up? Are you nuts?"

"Oh. Sorry. Didn't think about that."

J.D. returned the cooled bucket to Wilkes's, and we headed back to Ain't Pitty's. Glancing over my shoulder, I saw Mr. Digger standing in the upstairs window of his store, watching us.

No sense worrying everybody else. I don't think Mr. Digger will tell on us. Plus, maybe he saw the men in the truck.

Coming around the corner of Ain't Pitty's house, we stopped dead in our tracks. Satan was coming down the porch steps, and clenched in his teeth was a small green lizard, limp and unmoving, its right leg dangling.

"Dammit!" yelled J.D., taking off after the cat. "He's got Wilbur!"

Satan glared at us with glowing, demon-like eyes, then sprinted down the sidewalk and across the Railroad, heading for Miz Lettie's backyard. By the time we got there, Satan was at the edge of the woods, waiting for us, his evil eyes smirking and a still-motionless Wilbur dangling from his mouth. With a tilt of his head, Satan turned and disappeared into the thick, dark brush. We started to follow, but J.D. stopped us.

"It's too late. Wilbur's done for."

"We've gotta try!" begged Sandra.

"No, Sis. We'll never find them in those woods, as dark as it is, and somebody's liable to get hurt if we try."

Just then, a light came on inside Miz Lettie's house, followed by another and another. We were already in a dead run by the time the second light came on and just made it into the shadows of Ain't Pitty's mimosa tree when Miz Lettie's front door opened.

Standing perfectly still in a tight ring around the tree's large trunk, our heads and arms nestled among the low-hanging branches, we watched as Miz Lettie and Husband Number Three searched their yard. The old mimosa's long, fernlike branches cast dark shadows all around its drip line, providing us with the perfect cover. Most of the time, I loved the tree's sweet, peachy smell and the wispy feel of its blossoms against my skin, but tonight they offered no comfort. Satan had killed Wilbur, and nothing was going to make me feel better.

Finding everything in order, Miz Lettie and her husband went back inside and began turning off lights. When all was dark, we unfroze and made our way back to the now-lizardless porch.

"Poor Wilbur. He must have been hurting so bad," sniffled Sandra. "If we'd been here, he'd still be alive."

"Maybe. Maybe not," said J.D. "We didn't know Satan was around."

"Yeah, but—"

"Look, I know it's sad, but that damned cat had already gotten to Wilber twice without us knowing, so all he had to do was sit in the shadows and wait for the right time."

Wilbur's presence during our porch time had come to mean a lot. The loss we felt and the chilling way Satan had taken him cinched the decision for all of us. We didn't know when, where, or how, but Satan's day of reckoning was at hand. He had gone too far.

Chapter 12

At breakfast, we stayed mum about Wilbur. We were too sad to talk and didn't want Li'l Bit and Sharon to know what had happened, at least not yet. We also figured Miz Lettie, as president of the Women's Guild, would be getting a call about the Crossing anytime now, and she in turn would call Sheriff Coker. Luckily, Ain't Pitty had planned a junking trip for today, which gave us a good excuse to be out of town until these folks got distracted with other things.

We packed a picnic lunch of leftover fried chicken, biscuits, and peanuts, filled blue mason jars with tea, and headed for Jigger. As we pulled out of the driveway, neither Miz Lettie nor the Sheriff was anywhere in sight.

That's good. I just hope they're not waiting for us when we get home.

Ain't Pitty's definition of junking was to snoop around old, abandoned houses and barns to see what valuables she could scavenge. During the winter, as she and Uncle Ben made their way around the Wiregrass, she would identify potential junking sites, and during the summer, we would investigate them. In the past, junking had proven to be quite profitable. We'd found an old egg basket, which Ain't Pitty had added to her collection, an antique lamp table Ain't Pitty had cleaned with oil soap and put in her living room to hold more fancies, and two porcelain door handles that were now on Ain't Pitty's front door. We'd even found two walnut-size, glass marbles with green centers that looked like three-leaf clovers. Ain't Pitty had given the marbles to Li'l Bit and Sharon.

"Hang on to them," she said. "They'll bring you good luck."

"Isn't it the four-leaf clover that brings good luck?" I pointed out.

"Finding two big marbles exactly alike in the same place at the same time seems pretty lucky to me."

Once, when crossing a low-water bridge, we saw an old steamer trunk caught in the brush along the edge of a creek. Cutting a path down the bank, we fished the trunk out of the water and found children's clothing and old toys inside, but everything was soaked with mud and unusable. Even the trunk came apart as we tried to pull it up the bank.

"Why would somebody throw perfectly good stuff into the creek?" Sandra asked.

Ain't Pitty just shook her head, but the look on her face was sad.

Today, we were going to a deserted house on the road between Samson and Opp. Pulling into a long dirt driveway, we could see an abandoned clapboard house set back in the middle of a grove of old, neglected pecan trees. Never tolerant of waste, Ain't Pitty gave each of us a used flour sack from Jigger's trunk.

"It's not the right time to pick pecans, but we still might find some good ones. Remember, as long as the husks are opened just a little, they're good."

Eric and J.D. climbed into the closest trees and began shaking branches. The rest of us started sorting through the falling nuts. When our sacks were full, we loaded them into the trunk and went to explore the house.

The front door was missing, which made getting in easy but also reduced our chances of finding anything. Other junkers had already been here and taken the door and anything else of value. The house was in such bad shape, we had to be careful where we stepped; otherwise, we would end up in the crawl space below. Roaming from room to room, we searched for any good junk that might have been left but found nothing. Even the backyard was bare, except for another grizzled pecan tree and a dilapidated shed that we decided to investigate. Leading the way, Li'l Bit stubbed his toe on something sticking out of the ground and squatted down to see what it was.

"Hey, Ain't Pitty, come look. There's somethin' pink down here."

Brushing away the dirt, Ain't Pitty uncovered an old pink drinking glass.

"This is good depression glass."

"Here's another one," announced Sam, brushing at another small mound of dirt.

"I found one, too!" shouted Sharon, squatting down near Li'l Bit.

"Why would someone bury good glasses in the dirt like this?" I asked.

"Don't know, but I'm glad they did, or this junkin' trip would've been a waste," replied J.D.

Before long, we had dug up a dozen pink glasses and Sandra was trying to clean one with spit and the hem of her t-shirt .

"Ain't Pitty, I'm not sure we're gonna be able to get these clean. They must've been in the ground a long time to get this dirty."

Ain't Pitty suddenly stood up and stared at the ground, her face ghost white.

"Ain't Pitty, what's the matter?" asked J.D.

"*That's* the matter!"

As we stood up and looked down, it was obvious what she had seen. The pink glasses had been buried in a perfect rectangle and appeared to be outlining a grave.

"Oh, shit!" yelled J.D., jumping back. "We're gonna get cursed for grave robbin'!"

"Oh, hush!" snapped Ain't Pitty. "And watch your mouth. We're not gonna get cursed! But we *are* gonna put these glasses back where they came from, and we're gonna do it right now!"

Faster than the pink glasses had come out of the dirt, they went back in, placed as close to their original spots as we could get them. Once they were all back, we respectfully smoothed dirt over the top of the grave and hightailed it to the front of the house, pushing and piling into Jigger like a human ball. Ain't Pitty offered a quick prayer about being real sorry for disturbing the dead and then hit Jigger's gas pedal so hard, the old car's back wheels produced a rooster-shaped cloud of dust that followed us all the way back to the main road. Ain't Pitty barely slowed down coming out of the driveway, pushing Jigger at a faster-than-normal speed as we headed south.

Shortly after we'd gotten back on the hard surface road, we heard a police siren coming up behind us. Sirens were rare around these parts, so Ain't Pitty pulled over and waved the police car around. But instead of passing us, it pulled up behind Jigger and stopped.

"Good grief!" muttered Ain't Pitty, looking in the rearview mirror. "What now? Jigger can't speed, and all of those dagum stickers the county wanted on are on, so what does this whipper-snapper want with me?"

The rest of us swallowed really hard. We had a pretty good idea who they were after and why.

A young, barely shaving deputy walked to the driver's window and looked in at Ain't Pitty and the others sitting in the front seat. When he glanced into the backseat, his eyes stopped when he saw Sam.

"Well, son," asked Ain't Pitty, getting agitated, "did you pull me over me for a reason, or did you just want to stare into my backseat?"

Embarrassed, the deputy cleared his throat, "Uh . . . yes, ma'am. Were y'all just at the pecan grove, back down the road a ways?"

I watched Ain't Pitty's face in the mirror as she weighted her options.

"You mean the deserted place back yonder?"

"Yes, ma'am. But it's not deserted. The owner lives across the road, and when he saw y'all shakin' his trees, he called us. He said y'all were trespassin'."

"Well, now, that's a surprise. I thought that ol' place was abandoned, it bein' in such bad shape and all."

I could tell Ain't Pitty was mad, and I knew why. All the owner of the house had to do was tell us to leave and we would have, but he'd decided to be mean instead.

"No, ma'am. It's private property. Now, if you're willing to take the nuts back to the owner, I'll let you off with a warning," he offered, stealing another glance at Sam, who by now had pinked up and was looking back. When Ain't Pitty hesitated too long, he added, "Otherwise, I'll have to give you a ticket for trespassin' and take you in for stealin'."

"Oh, all right."

Ain't Pitty mumbled under her hat all the way back to the pecan grove. Coming to a stop in front of a redbrick house, we climbed out of Jigger and pulled the overflowing sacks of pecans out of the trunk. Answering the bell was an unsmiling, pudgy Elmer Fudd look-alike, who stood in the doorway with his hairy arms crossed over a big, bare belly.

Ain't Pitty swallowed hard and then led the apologies for everyone. She told Elmer Fudd we were sorry for trespassing and taking the pecans, explaining that she thought the house was abandoned—"it being in such bad shape and all."

She just couldn't help herself.

Having delivered the apology and the parting shot, Ain't Pitty asked for a basket to put the returned pecans in.

"No," snapped Elmer Fudd, in a surprisingly squeaky voice. "Just carry them around to the carport and leave 'em in the sacks."

"No," countered Ain't Pitty. "I'm not leavin' my flour sacks. Just give me somethin' to put the nuts in, and we'll be on our way."

"I don't have to give you nothin', lady," chided Elmer Fudd. "You were stealin' from me, and if you don't leave those nuts and get off my property, this deputy's gonna take you and these no-count brats to jail!"

Elmer Fudd had just made a big mistake. Ain't Pitty would take a good bit of guff from folks, but no one messed with her family, especially us. Her face clouded up like a summer thunderhead, and she stood up as tall as her short bones would let her.

Through gritted teeth, she hissed, "Noo . . . he's . . . not. He told us if we brought the nuts back, all we'd get was a warnin'. Right, Deputy?"

The now-wide-eyed young lawman stuttered as he realized he was in the middle of a mess.

"That's . . . right."

"Good!" declared Ain't Pitty, turning triumphantly back to Elmer Fudd. "It seems to me you have two choices: give us somethin' to put these nuts in, or we'll dump 'em right here on your porch. Either way, we got our warnin' and you get your . . . uh . . . nuts back."

With that, Ain't Pitty dropped her gaze down past Elmer Fudd's potbelly to his low-hanging shorts, her dark eyes shooting sparks and her body language daring him to say another word.

The standoff between Ain't Pitty and Elmer Fudd did not end for another fifteen minutes, and it stopped then only because the young deputy managed to find a bag in the trunk of his car that he donated in the name of peace.

Escorting us back to Jigger, he managed to walk next to Sam.

"Nice to meet you, Miz Miller, you and . . . uh . . . your family. You're right about the property across the road not being posted for trespassin'. I'll ask the Sheriff to send him a letter."

"That would be nice, uh . . ."

"Danny, ma'am. My name's Danny Grimes."

"Thanks, Danny. Don't forget to check out that grave over yonder," she urged, pointing toward the abandoned house. "Somethin's just not right about that."

"Yes, ma'am. I will."

As we were pulling away, J.D. leaned out the window and yelled, "Hey, Danny, her name is Sam, and she'll be at the Crystal Springs pool Saturday afternoon. C'mon by!"

Sam slid down the backseat, ready to both kill and kiss J.D. at the same time.

By now the day was heating up, so we decided to eat our picnic lunch at the Sandy Bottom Creek boat landing and take a swim. Ain't Pitty drove down the access road and across the sunbaked sand, stopping in the shadow of the bridge. By suppertime folks would be stopping here to cool off, but now it was deserted. Stretching an old bedspread out in the shade, we settled down to eat.

"Ain't Pitty, I thought you were gonna bop that man right in the nose," said Sandra.

"Me too," added Sharon. "I was wishin' you would! He was nasty."

"Well, I was tempted, but I didn't want to end up in jail," laughed Ain't Pitty. "He's just an unhappy person, and sometimes unhappy people think the only way to be happy is to make someone else unhappy."

"That's sad," said Sam.

"But true."

I wonder if that's why Mitchell's pa is so mean.

After lunch, we cracked peanuts and listened to the echoes of cars crossing the bridge. Sandra finally broke the silence by singing "Found a Peanut," which killed any remaining interest we had in eating them.

Lying back, Ain't Pitty said, "Y'all can go swim and explore if you want to. I'm gonna take a nap." Pulling the brim of her hat across her eyes, she added, "Don't be gone long, and wake me when you get back."

We followed J.D. single file along the shallow edge of the creek, searching for the best place to swim. After a while, we reached a long, narrow beach and made our way into the shade at the edge of the woods to take a break.

"I bet there are some great hiding places back in there," said J.D. "We should check 'em out while we're here."

"C'mon, Sharon," urged Li'l Bit. "Let's go look."

As the little ones pushed into the brush, Eric waded into the middle of the creek to check its depth while J.D. made his way farther along the beach and into a field of tall grass to conduct some personal business.

"Water's plenty deep in the middle, and the current's not bad if y'all wanna swim."

"In a bit," mumbled Sam, who had lain back in the shade and was dozing.

"Hey, y'all!" yelled Li'l Bit from the woods. "We found honeysuckle—lots of it!"

Following their voices, we found the little ones partially hidden in a thick patch of the sweet-smelling vines. They were picking the trumpet-shaped flowers, pinching the caps off the bottom, and slowly pulling out the white stems. If they were lucky, the flared end would hold a drop of clear, sweet nectar they could catch on their tongues.

Using the bottoms of our t-shirts as baskets, we pulled dozens of blossoms from the vines and headed back to the beach to open them. Coming out of the woods, we saw J.D. studying something in the sand near the edge of the field.

"Hey, y'all! Come look."

Dumping the honeysuckle in a pile, we crossed to where J.D. was fingering a boot print. There were more prints leading in and out of the grass.

"Wonder whose they are," Eric said, looking up and down the beach for more.

"I haven't got a clue, but look at the size of 'em."

J.D.'s extra-large flip-flopped foot fit well within the borders of the print, with inches to spare.

"All the storms we've had the past few days woulda washed old prints away, so these have to be pretty fresh. C'mon, let's see where they go."

Entering the waist-high grass, we followed a narrow path leading across the field toward a grove of trees. As we got closer, we could see an old, partially hidden wooden building. It had a stone foundation, no windows, and a crumbling shingled roof layered in leaves, sticks, and Spanish moss.

As we came around the corner of the building, we saw that the path ended abruptly in front of a large, weatherworn door. Weeds had been cleared from the entrance, as well as along a second path leading to an overgrown but used driveway.

J.D. lifted the door's metal latch, which moved easily, considering the amount of rust on it. As he pulled the creaking door open, we could see the doorframe and walls were a least a foot thick. Inside, the air was damp and filled with the nauseating smell of dirt, sawdust, and kerosene.

"You know," said J.D., "I remember Uncle Ben sayin' that when the railroad was runnin', a company up near Montgomery would ship big blocks of ice down here. Local men would cut 'em up and sell the smaller blocks to folks for their iceboxes—ones like Granny and Pa Campbell used before they got electricity. I bet this is where the ice was stored. These thick walls would keep it from meltin' too fast."

As our eyes adjusted to the low light, we could see a dirt floor, wooden walls with sawdust flaking out from between the planks, and exposed rafters in the ceiling. There was an old cot with a thin, filthy mattress pushed against the back wall and a worn straight-back chair with a torn cane seat sitting next to it. Nearby was a dirty, two-toned brown jug lying on its side. Moving farther in, we spotted a dirty rope hanging from a broken pulley in the rafters. The lower part of the rope was frayed and smudged with something black.

"Strange place for a rope. Wonder what it's for," said J.D., giving it a hard tug.

The rope didn't fall, but it left big, dark smudges on J.D.'s hands.

"Smells like soot."

"Maybe they were usin' it to hold this," Eric suggested, reaching for a rusty oil lamp that was hanging on the wall. Lifting the dirty globe, he pulled out a box of matches.

"There's a picture of the new Miracle Strip roller coaster on this box, so it hasn't been here long."

The Miracle Strip was an amusement park near Wayside Beach in Panama City. Ain't Pitty took us there at least once a summer.

Walking over to the wall, J.D. pulled one of two large iron hooks out of the wood and rubbed his finger along the tip.

"Damn! This thing could hurt somebody."

"I bet they used them to pick up blocks of ice."

"It's surprising nobody's junked this place before," said Sam. "I wonder if Ain't Pitty knows it's here."

"It looks like somebody's been here recently, so we better not take anythin'," I warned.

Slapping the hook back into the wall, J.D. continued walking around the room. All four walls had rotted or missing ladder-like rungs going up into the rafters. At the top of the back ladder, I could see the outline of a jug.

They're hidin' their liquor up there.

"I bet they used this old rope and pulley to stack the ice blocks and then used the wall ladders and hooks to bring 'em down," said J.D.

"I wonder who's been in here," said Sam, kicking at a pile of rags lying in the dirt. "There's not enough stuff for anybody to actually live here, but somebody's sure been around."

"Yeah," agreed Eric. "And not too long ago."

"Maybe it's a drifter," J.D. proposed.

"Gosh! This thing stinks," said Sharon, looking at the dirty, stained mattress on the cot. "Who'd wanna sleep on that?"

Squatting, J.D. picked up the old jug that was lying nearby, sniffed the top, and then quickly tossed it back down.

"Guess if you're a moonshine drunk, you don't care where you sleep."

Mimicking J.D., Li'l Bit picked up the jug with both hands and took a big sniff.

"Yuck! That really stinks!"

Tossing the jug down just like J.D. had, Li'l Bit picked up one of the rags and held it to his chest. It looked like a small t-shirt.

"Hey! This would fit me."

"Li'l Bit! Put that down right now!" I snapped, grabbing the shirt. "No tellin' what that dirty thing has on it." I threw the t-shirt on the cot, grabbed Li'l Bit's hand, and headed for the door. "What would a little kid be doin' in this nasty place, anyway? Let's get outta here."

"C'mon, y'all," said Sam. "Nettie's right. Let's go."

Shading our eyes, we stepped back into the sunlight and pushed the heavy door closed.

"Sure smells better out here."

"No wonder we never noticed this place before. It's really overgrown," said J.D. "But someone's been drivin' in and outta here—look at the tire tracks and footprints. These big ones match the prints we saw on the beach."

"I think you're right about this being the old ice house," said Eric, pointing at some railroad tracks that led into the woods. Some of the steel rails were missing, and most of the crossties were gone or rotted.

Continuing around the bend in the driveway, we heard the echo of a car crossing a bridge.

"Look, that's Choctaw Road in front of us, and that's Sandy Bottom Bridge way down there. We can go back this way," said Sandra.

"I don't think so," said J.D. "If we take the road back, Ain't Pitty's gonna want to know why and how, and I don't think we want her to know about the ice house, at least not yet." Looking at Li'l Bit and Sharon, he added, "Did y'all hear what I said? Nobody tells Ain't Pitty about this place, especially y'all."

Having been threatened with removal from the group, Li'l Bit and Sharon had gotten much better about keeping their mouths closed.

"Yep," replied Li'l Bit.

"Okay," added Sharon.

"Good. We'd better get goin', or we're gonna be late gettin' back to Ain't Pitty."

The little ones ran ahead of us past the ice house and down the path to the creek.

"It's a real shame this place feels like the wrong kind of trouble. Cleaned up and aired out, it woulda made a great hideout," grumbled J.D.

Wading along the edge of the creek, we followed Li'l Bit and Sharon back to the boat landing.

"I wonder if we're gonna hear about the Crossing when we get back to town," whispered Eric.

"Probably," replied J.D. "The question is, who are we gonna hear about it from? I'm hoping it's just Miz Lettie. And remember, if anybody asks, we don't know anythin' about it."

The thought of facing the consequences for our most recent TP-in' dampened our mood.

"Why are we still doing it if we're worried about gettin' in trouble?" I asked.

"Because it's what we do," said J.D. "It wouldn't be summer if we didn't."

Yeah, but it feels different this summer.

Ain't Pitty was up, shaking sand and crumbs off the bedspread, when we waded ashore.

"Y'all have a nice swim?" she asked, glancing at our mostly dry clothes.

"Yes, ma'am."

"Did you have a nice nap, Ain't Pitty?" I asked.

"Yep," she replied, bending over to rub the red spots popping up on her leg. "That is, until the fire ants decided they were hungry."

To delay going home a little longer, we talked Ain't Pitty into stopping at the Pitcher Plant Bog to catch a mess of fish for dinner. Smearing ourselves with eucalyptus oil to keep the giant mosquitoes from carrying us away, we stood on the berms and used the minnows we'd netted last night to catch a bucket full of perch and bigmouths.

Unfortunately, the delayed arrival did not help. Sheriff Coker's car was sitting in front of Ain't Pitty's house when we turned onto the Railroad, and he was standing on the front porch, talking with Uncle Ben.

"Guess that answers that," I whispered.

Coming to a stop in the lean-to, Ain't Pitty said, "Sam, Sandra, you two take Li'l Bit and Sharon and go to the garden. The rest of you, go get my linens off Miz Sadie's clothesline and fold 'em. Nobody comes around front unless I call you."

"Yes, ma'am."

Ain't Pitty took a deep breath, raised herself up just like she had done with Elmer Fudd, and headed to the front porch.

Miz Sadie, who was Ain't Pitty's widowed neighbor, had a big clothesline in her backyard near the storage shed. She let us use it in the summer because Ain't Pitty's line was too small to hold the wash of nine people. In exchange, Miz Sadie got fresh eggs all year long.

"Do you think the Sheriff's here because of the Crossing or the nut man?" I asked.

"I don't know," replied J.D. "But both are trouble."

"Do you s'pose they've cleaned up the Crossing yet?" asked Sandra.

"Yeah," replied Sam. "I bet those prissy ladies had that TP cleaned up before the post office opened."

We were folding the last of the linens when the Sheriff's car pulled away. A minute later, Ain't Pitty called to us from the kitchen window.

"We're gonna eat inside tonight, y'all. Bring the fish and vege-tables in after they're cleaned."

We were dying to know what Sheriff Coker wanted, but we didn't know if Uncle Ben knew we were responsible for the TP-in'. We also did not know if Ain't Pitty was going to tell him about the nut man, so we needed to stay quiet until she was alone.

At supper, both Ain't Pitty and Uncle Ben appeared to be pre-occupied. Afterward, Uncle Ben excused himself and headed out to jiggle Jigger's things.

As soon as he was out the door, J.D. asked, "Ain't Pitty, what did Sheriff Coker want?"

"Huh? What?"

J.D. repeated his question, but Ain't Pitty still looked distracted.

"Nothin' y'all need to be concerned about." Getting to her feet, she added, "Better get started on the eggs."

Knowing better than to push, we headed to the chicken coop.

"Somethin's up," declared J.D.

"You're right," I replied. "And I bet it does concern us."

Chapter 13

We've gotta figure out what the hell's goin' on, y'all," said J.D. as we sat in the dark and watched the lights go out along the Railroad. "Not a word about the Crossing from anybody, and the Sheriff comes here and we still don't know why? Somethin's up, and it's gonna drive me nuts until we figure out what it is."

"I agree," said Eric. "But Ain't Pitty and Uncle Ben aren't talkin', and there's no one else to ask."

"We need to lie low for a while and see what floats up," I said.

"Nettie's right," agreed Sam. "Somebody will say somethin' eventually. So let's—"

Suddenly, J.D. sat up and pointed toward the street. "Look!" he hissed.

In the moonlight we could see Satan strolling across the Railroad toward Ain't Pitty's driveway, oblivious that we were sitting in the shadows of the porch.

"I bet he's headed for the chicken coop," whispered Eric.

"Reckonin' day is here, y'all. C'mon."

Moving quickly to the corner of the house, we watched as Satan made his way past the lean-to and across the patio. Staying in the shadows, we followed at a distance. As we passed the picnic table, J.D. grabbed one of the pillowcases we had folded earlier but forgotten to take inside.

Moving past the garden, we could see Satan's shadow crouched low and stalking the chicken coop in slow motion. But as low and

137

slow as he was, the chickens sensed trouble and were getting loud and active.

Motioning for us to spread out, J.D. whispered, "We're gonna corner 'im."

The wicked look in J.D.'s eyes made me wonder exactly what he intended to do with Satan once we caught him. Regardless, I moved farther out to help block the cat's escape.

Butted up against the side of the coop was a storage bin where the chicken feed and coop supplies were kept. As Satan inched closer to the bus, I could tell J.D. was planning to corner him between the bin and the coop. As we closed in around him, the only way Satan could go was up, and the lid to the bin was wide open.

Just as predicted, by the time Satan realized we were behind him, he was trapped. Snapping his head around, he arched his back, puffed out his fur, and rolled his big tail straight up in the air. His eyes narrowed to burning slits as he began a long, gravelly hiss and pawed at the air with big, sharp claws, one of which was missing.

That damn cat's madder'n hell, and somebody's gonna get hurt.

For a split second, it looked as if Satan might claw a path right over one of us to try to escape, but instead he turned and half-jumped, half-clawed his way to the top of the bin, realizing too late there was no place to go except down. Despite his frantic clawing, Satan fell into the bin and J.D. slammed the lid down, trapping him inside.

The closed lid muted the noise, but the demonic sounds coming from inside the bin were like nothing I'd ever heard. It was as if the real Satan was in there with the four-legged one, both wreaking havoc and destroying anything they could get their claws into.

"I hope folks around here are sound asleep," I muttered, looking to make sure no lights were coming on. "We sure don't want to have to explain this."

The battle inside the bin continued for almost half an hour. Finally, when the noise stopped, J.D. found a stick and beat on the top and sides of the bin until Satan was so riled up, he went on another bin-killing rampage.

"Stop, J.D.!" I hissed. "You're gonna wake the dead!"

"That's enough," insisted Eric.

"Hush, y'all. If we let Satan out now, he'll tear us to shreds. I know what I'm doin'."

J.D. repeated the box beating until no sound came from inside the bin, regardless of what he did to the outside of it. Cautiously lifting the lid, we peeked in. Satan was lying limply across a large pile of shredded chicken feed and mangled straw—his eyes glassy, mouth open, and chest heaving. Leaning in quickly, J.D. grabbed the exhausted cat by the scruff of his neck and stuffed him into the pillowcase. In his frazzled stupor, Satan could manage little more than a faint "how dare you" hiss.

With the conquered cat and stick in hand, J.D. headed back to the patio and up the driveway to the edge of the Railroad. The rest of us were concerned Satan might get a second wind and make mincemeat of anybody who happened to be too close, so we hung back. Checking to make sure no cars were coming, J.D. ran across the Railroad, opened Miz Lettie's mailbox, pushed Satan in, and slid the pillowcase off as he slammed the little metal door shut.

Sprinting back to Ain't Pitty's driveway, he grinned. "That'll teach that damn cat to pick on helpless little lizards . . . and me."

In triumph, J.D. led the parade back to the chicken coop to clean up the aftermath of the reckoning. We sure didn't want Ain't Pitty to see her supply bin torn all to hell.

"Aren't you worried he'll suffocate?" asked Sandra, looking back toward the mailbox.

"Naw. The mailbox isn't airtight. It has little holes in the sides so he can get air. He just can't move much. I'll go over in the mornin' and let 'im out. But for now, that damn cat deserves every bit of what he's gettin'."

When the bin was cleaned up, we made our way back to the front porch and our rockers. It had been a long day, and we were tired. Across the Railroad, Miz Lettie's mailbox was deathly quiet.

Gathering eggs the next morning did not take long. The hens had laid only one all night.

"Somethin' must've spooked 'em," muttered Ain't Pitty. "Y'all see anythin' funny down there this mornin'?"

"No, ma'am, not a thing," replied Eric.

"That damn cat may have been prowlin' around and got 'em spooked, Ain't Pitty," offered J.D., winking at us.

"Well, let's see what they can do today."

After a breakfast of thin pancakes with fig preserves and thick strips of bacon, we cleared the dishes while Ain't Pitty made her shopping list. We had volunteered to go grocery shopping with her at the Piggly Wiggly in Geneva, in hopes she would let us know what was going on with Sheriff Coker.

"Eric," whispered J.D., "make sure Ain't Pitty stays inside a few more minutes. Nettie and I are gonna go let Satan outta the mailbox. It's gonna get hot in there quick, since the sun's up. We'll meet y'all at the car. Nettie, I'm gonna open the door from the side, but take a stick just in case Satan comes out fightin'."

Running up the driveway, intent on pardoning Satan from his metal prison, we reached the Railroad just in time to see the mailman pull up to Miz Lettie's mailbox and reach for the handle.

Panicked, I looked at J.D. His eyes were bulging, and his mouth was wide open in a loud but silent scream. There was nothing to do but watch as the unsuspecting mailman pulled the little door open.

From the way Satan sprang out of his tin tomb, we could tell he had recovered from the reckoning and was more than ready for round two. The crazed cat landed on the unsuspecting mailman with teeth bared, back arched, and claws out.

What have we done?

We witnessed just the beginning of the front-seat battle between good and evil, but the Satan-inspired yells and the wild flailing of arms and tails left no doubt about who was winning.

"Oh, shit! C'mon, Nettie."

We ran back down the driveway and jumped into the Oldsmobile as the others were coming down the steps.

"C'mon, Ain't Pitty. Let's go! Let's go!" yelled J.D., slapping the car door from the outside, his voice high pitched and nervous.

Eric, Sam, and Sandra looked at us as if to say, *What the hell happened?*

"Hold your horses, J.D.," answered Ain't Pitty, as she crossed the patio. "You feel all right? You look pale."

"Yes, ma'am. I'm fine, just fine. Just ready to get goin', that's all."

As Ain't Pitty backed the Oldsmobile onto the Railroad, we saw the mailman running from his abandoned car across Miz Lettie's yard toward her front door, arms up and waving. Satan was nowhere in sight.

"Hmm," said Ain't Pitty. "Lettie must be gettin' a special-delivery letter. Wonder who it's from."

J.D. closed his eyes and slid down the front seat as if his long, leggy spine had turned to jelly.

Grateful to be sitting in the back, I looked out the rear window and was relieved to see the mailman had made it inside Miz Lettie's house.

We should've helped him. I'm not sure how, but we should've helped him.

By the time we reached Geneva, so much color had drained from J.D.'s face, Ain't Pitty asked him again if he was feeling all right. Nodding, J.D. made an effort to sit up straighter but then slid right back down, his eyes closed and his face damp with sweat.

Pulling into one of the slanted parking spaces in front of the Piggly Wiggly, Ain't Pitty gave us marching orders.

"Li'l Bit, you and Sharon come with me. The rest of y'all, be back here in an hour."

It always puzzled me when Ain't Pitty gave us instructions involving time. She never wore a watch, and none of us had one, so the starting and ending time of an hour was anybody's guess. Regardless, we usually managed to be in the right place at the right time anyway.

After Ain't Pitty and the little ones disappeared into the store, I told the others about our late arrival at the mailbox and Satan's attack on the mailman.

"Oh, God," moaned Eric, "we killed 'im. I'm goin' to military school for sure!"

"Oh, be quiet!" snapped J.D., managing to get some spunk back. "Nobody can prove it was us . . . uh . . . me. At least, I don't think they can. Plus, the mailman was runnin', so we know he's not dead, and he must not be hurt too bad if he could run that fast."

J.D. sat down on the sidewalk, his dirty-blond head hanging low.

"That damn cat gets me even when it's not me he's gettin'! Sheriff Coker's definitely gonna be waitin' for us this time."

We sat down like dominoes next to J.D. and attempted to offer some curbside comfort, but we knew there was going to be trouble. Whatever Satan had done to the mailman was our fault. Pastor Flemming once said most folks knew right from wrong; it was just that wrong sounded better at the time. He was right.

We were still curb sitting when Ain't Pitty returned with a cart full of groceries.

"Load 'em up," she ordered.

When Ain't Pitty finished running all of her errands, she took us to the Tastee Freez, but not even the thought of cold, sweet ice cream got us talking very much, except of course to tell the scooper what we wanted.

"Chocolate." "Chocolate." "Strawberry." "Chocolate." "Chocolate." "Vanilla." And lastly, Li'l Bit's yell of "chocolate" as he tried to pull himself over the raised counter to see inside.

Ain't Pitty got herself a bottle of Cherry Coke as the rest of us headed to the car, slowly licking our five-cent scoops and our worries.

Ain't Pitty fancied herself an expert on ice cream. She ate only home-churned and always added a little of her secret ingredient to it. While she never said what the secret ingredient was, we knew anyway because we had watched her make it for years. She would put overripe peaches or blackberries in a mason jar, add a little sugar, cover the fruit with yeast water, and place a saucer over the top. She would then set the concoction on the shelf so it could "rest" for a few days. When the fruit had turned to a thick liquid, she would strain it into an old brandy bottle and put it back on the shelf until she or someone else churned ice cream. She had given us specific instructions to leave the special ingredient alone, which was okay by us. Years ago we had snuck a taste and ended up having to brush our teeth and gargle with salt water to get rid of the pucker. We suspected that if Ain't Pitty made her secret ingredient in a still in the swamp, instead of in her own kitchen, Sheriff Coker would be paying her a visit.

The ride back to Ain't Pitty's was an anxious one. Most likely, Sheriff Coker, Miz Lettie, and the mailman would be waiting for us and we would soon know the consequences of Satan's actions and ours. But as Ain't Pitty turned into the driveway, there was not a car or a person in sight. We all breathed a sign of relief, but J.D.'s combined sigh and moan was so loud it got Ain't Pitty's attention.

"You're gettin' a dose of tonic when we get inside, J.D. You've been acting squirrelly all morning."

J.D. moaned again and closed his eyes while the rest of us giggled. Ain't Pitty's tonic was the nastiest-tasting stuff in the world. It was guaranteed to make you gag, and if you managed to keep it down, the only thing it did was loosen your bowels.

We carried the groceries inside and put them away while Ain't Pitty made homemade pimento-cheese sandwiches and sliced fresh peaches for lunch. When the dishes were cleared, she asked us to carry the last of her eggs up to Granny.

"She wants to do some bakin', and the little ones and I wanna tell tall tales under the oscillating fan, don't we?"

"Yeah!" they yelled, running to climb up on Ain't Pitty's chest-high bed.

From experience, we knew the tall tales and the soothing noise of the fan would have them napping in short order.

Putting the remaining eggs in a basket, we headed out the door.

The afternoon was growing more hot and humid by the minute, and even with flip-flops on we had to run from one shady spot to another to escape the heat radiating from the road.

"Somethin's really wrong, y'all," said J.D., returning to his thoughts from last night. "The Crossing, the nut man, and now Satan and the mailman, and still nobody's talkin'? Nobody's bangin' on Ain't Pitty's door, lookin' for us? Somethin's wrong."

"You sound disappointed we didn't get caught . . . yet," said Eric.

"No, I'm not disappointed, smart-ass. It's just not makin' any sense, that's all. Any way I figure it, somebody should be sayin' or doin' somethin'."

"Then why aren't they?" I asked.

"I don't know. I just don't know, and it's makin' me crazy!"

Even Cilly's house was quiet as we passed by. We could usually count on her being in the porch swing, listening to her radio at full blast, and shooting us the bird. But today the swing was empty.

"Even Jessie's not out," said Eric, looking toward Miz Maddie's house.

Jessie's mower was sitting in its usual place, and his rocker and tree chair were empty.

"He probably mowed this mornin', when it was cooler. It's so blasted hot now, we could fry these eggs on the street," whined Sam.

"Huh-uh," insisted J.D. "Somethin's up. I can feel it."

Even the roly-polies were hiding from the heat as we went up Granny's steps, but inside the air felt a good ten degrees cooler.

Gotta be the trees.

Granny was in the den, watching her weekday story and busily snapping beans. I was never sure what her TV story was about, but Granny talked to and about the folks on the television as if they were close friends.

"There's Kool-Aid in the refrigerator and sugared pecans on the table. My story will be over in a few minutes, and I'll be in," Granny said as we hugged her.

Granny's sugared pecans were famous. Each fall, when the pecans were ready for picking, one of Uncle Ben's helicopter-pilot friends from Rucks would detour on his way to Field 10 and hover over Granny's backyard for a few minutes. The intense vibration and wind created by the rotors dropped more pecans from her trees than any amount of hand shaking and picking could ever do. It would take days to gather all the nuts that fell.

Once they were shelled, Granny would soak some of the pecan halves in water and crushed sugar cane and then bake them until the sugar coating was crunchy. She bagged the nuts for family, friends, and, most important, the accommodating pilot and crew from Rucks. Rumor had it that even the Rucks commander was fond of Granny's pecans, especially if she soaked his in Ain't Pitty's secret ingredient.

Granny came into the kitchen and put the beans in the sink to soak. Then, pulling a pink Fiesta pitcher full of cold water from the refrigerator, she refilled our glasses.

"It's too hot for y'all not to be drinkin' somethin' every hour or so."

"Yes, ma'am."

Refilling the pitcher at the faucet, she added, "I hear Salter Lee got hurt this mornin'. He's the mailman for Crystal Springs."

Uh-oh!

"Apparently, somebody put Miz Lettie's ol' tomcat in her mailbox last night, and when Salter opened the box this mornin', he got clawed up pretty bad." Looking straight at J.D., she added, "Y'all wouldn't know anythin' about that, now, would you?"

Granny was not asking a question, she was making an accusa-
tion, and our dead silence and bowed heads confirmed our guilt. Up
to now, she had never said much about our rumored practical jokes,
but this time someone had gotten hurt, and she was not about to let
that go.

Granny folded her arms and leaned against the refrigerator
while we fingered worn spots in her red Formica table.

"Salter Lee's a good, hardworkin' man who never hurt anyone.
It's a shame he got hurt because of some young'uns' prank, don't
you think?"

"Yes, ma'am, it sure is a shame," agreed J.D., shaking his bowed
head but not looking his granny in the eye.

"Is there anythin' we can do to help Mr. Lee?" I asked, guilt
getting the best of me.

I felt J.D.'s big foot kicking at me under the table.

"Glad you asked. I talked with Salter's wife a bit ago. They've
been at Doc Anderson's office all morning. Salter had to get over
twenty stitches, a tetanus shot, and a penicillin shot. Needless to say,
he's not feelin' very well. I told 'em I'd fix their supper this evening
and you all would bring it over. And while you're there, you will
apologize and volunteer to do any and all of the chores and errands
they need to have done, even if it takes all week. Understood?"

"Yes, ma'am."

Granny looked at us with snapping eyes, knowing we would
not dare disagree or fail to do everything she said.

"Be back here at five. I'll have a supper basket ready by then."

The look on J.D.'s face was pure misery, but he managed to
mumble, "Yes, ma'am."

Taking Ain't Pitty's eggs from the basket, Granny's tone sof-
tened some and she changed the subject.

"The family's high-summer picnic is this Sunday. I want y'all
there and on your best behavior." Then, with a wink, she added,
"I'm makin' a Lane cake, and I don't want to bring any of it back
home. It's too fattenin'."

Everybody loved Granny's Lane cake. It was six layers of made-from-scratch yellow cake, with sweet butter, gooey caramel, chopped pecans, and coconut between each layer and on top. It took at least twelve eggs, a pound of butter, and most of a day to make.

"I'm gonna need some extra butter from Tilly's, so how about y'all get it for me?"

Going to her pie safe, Granny pulled out a bag of raw pecans and an empty Butter Bell crock and set them on the table.

"Take these to Tilly when you go, please."

"Yes, ma'am."

Grabbing the bartering goods, we headed out the back door. If we climbed the fence and crossed the corner of the high school football field, we could walk straight down First Street to Tilly's side of town. This route was cooler because the Women's Guild had planted trees all along First Street as part of their Beautify Crystal Springs program. Problem was, most folks traveled the Railroad.

"Wonder how she found out," Eric said, climbing the fence.

"I don't know," grumbled J.D., helping Sandra over. "But if Granny knows, other folks have to know, so why isn't anybody else talkin' about it?"

"Maybe they think somebody else did it!" said Sandra.

"Yeah. And maybe pigs fly!" snapped J.D.

"Well, it doesn't do any good to worry about it now," I said.

"Nettie, Sheriff Coker's just waitin' to send all of us to the juvenile detention center in Dothan. So there's plenty to worry about. If we don't know what's goin' on, we can't plan, and if we can't plan, we can't stay out of his crosshairs."

"I know. But we can't do anythin' about it, can we? So all I'm sayin' is, let's worry when we have somethin' to worry about."

"By then it may be too late."

"I'm worried about Salter Lee. Two shots and twenty stitches is a lot," said Sam.

"Well, that's just somethin' else we can't do anythin' about, isn't it?" snapped J.D., regret written all over his face.

There were no cars in front of the café, but Mr. Short was sitting at the counter when we walked in. This time of day, he usually brought freshly butchered meat for Miz Tilly's supper special and stayed to have a cup of coffee.

I never understood why folks drank hot coffee on hot days until I started drinking it. Then I realized there was something comforting about holding a warm cup and sipping the milky liquid. It just made the day a little better.

"Hey, Miz Tilly. Hey, Mr. Short."

"Hey, young'uns," grinned Miz Tilly. "What brings y'all to town?"

Sam leaned over the counter and set the pecans and crock down.

"Granny would like some butter, please. If you have plenty."

"Sure. I always have 'nuff for Miz Susie. Eli brought in a fresh batch last night. Just let me get these chicken parts to cookin'."

Miz Tilly took three plump chicken legs out of the thick buttermilk they were soaking in and dipped them in a bowl of beaten eggs. Then she placed them in a brown paper bag filled with fresh flour, salt, pepper, paprika, and a little bit of garlic powder and sugar. Closing the bag, she shook it until the legs were covered. We had watched Miz Tilly fry chicken for years and knew she would arrange the pieces in the oversize iron skillet so they were not touching. She said this allowed the bubbling peanut oil to brown and crisp all the parts evenly.

Going to the sink, Miz Tilly washed her hands and dried them on a hand towel that was as white as the bleached apron she had on. For all the cooking she did day in and day out, Miz Tilly's aprons were always clean, crisply starched, and ironed.

When we asked why she bothered so, she said, "If a cook's apron isn't clean, most likely her food isn't either."

Pulling Coca-Cola glasses from the shelf, Miz Tilly filled them with iced tea.

"Y'all must be parched on a devil's day like this. Drink up!"

I had gotten in the habit of folding my arms across my half lemons whenever we came into Miz Tilly's, hoping she would not feel the need to say anything else about my woman parts. Luckily, today she was focused on frying chicken and filling butter crocks.

"Here's Miz Susie's, and this one's for Salter Lee."

Damn! She knows. I'm not sure how, but she knows.

J.D. moaned and laid his head down.

Well, at least now we know how Granny found out.

"Get your head off my clean counter, J.D. Take the lesson that's comin' your way with your head up. Y'all need to think about what you're doin' before you do it, so good folks don't get hurt."

"Yes, ma'am."

Looking out her front window, she added, "If what I heard about the Crossing this mornin' is true, y'all might wanna head out my back door right now. Sheriff Coker's car just came around the corner, and he's headed this way."

Miz Tilly gathered our glasses while Sam grabbed the butter crocks. Sailing off the swirling stools, we scurried around the counter, through Miz Tilly's storage room, and headed for the back door. As the last in the fleeing line, I peeked around the corner and saw Mr. Short get up, give a knowing nod to Miz Tilly, and reach for the door just as Sheriff Coker came in.

"Hey, Sheriff."

"Hey, Short. How are you? It's been a long time."

"It has, Sheriff—too long. I just got a nice side of beef in this mornin'. Stop by for a visit on your way home, and I'll have two thick rib eyes waitin' for you."

"That's mighty nice of you, Short. I need to talk with Digger for a few minutes anyway, so I'll swing by."

Gosh! I wonder if Mr. Digger called him about last night.

Easing the screen door closed behind me, I knew Miz Tilly and Mr. Short had just saved us from facing the Sheriff.

Hurrying down the back steps, we ran past the loading dock of the Feed and Seed, waving to Mitchell as we went by. He was sitting in the shade on a stack of old seed bags that stayed propped against the far end of the dock.

Damn! He's just so pretty.

Once we were a safe distance from the café, J.D. stopped.

"Y'all go on to the senior center and wait for me. I'm gonna sneak back to Miz Tilly's to see if I can hear what Sheriff Coker has to say."

"Are you crazy?" hissed Eric.

"I've been tellin' y'all somethin's off, and I aim to find out what it is. Now go . . . please."

Not waiting for a response, J.D. turned and headed back to the café.

"C'mon," Eric said reluctantly. "Let's go."

Pushing through the hedge surrounding the backyard of the senior center, we ran up the long flight of steps to the patio-like porch. It held several picnic tables and a couple of charcoal grills, and strings of lightbulbs crisscrossed its exposed-beam ceiling. The porch sat high enough for us to see J.D. slip through Miz Tilly's back door. Checking to make sure no one else was around, we settled down at the table with the best view of the café to watch and wait. I could also watch Mitchell as he looked back and forth between Miz Tilly's and us.

We've gotta let him know what's going on.

It was a long time before we saw J.D. leaving Miz Tilly's. He jogged over to the loading dock, talked with Mitchell for a minute, and then the two of them headed our way.

I could feel myself start to blush.

"I see that," teased Sam.

Yeah. You and everybody else.

J.D. and Mitchell bounded up the stairs two at a time, sending a wave of energy over the entire table as they slid onto the bench across from us.

"Hey, Mitchell," said Eric.

"Hey, y'all," he replied, smiling at me.

"Okay, J.D., what did you hear?" asked Sam.

"I was right: somethin' *is* off. I hid behind the storage-room door and could see the Sheriff through the crack. Miz Tilly made him somethin' to eat, and, wouldn't you know, she set his plate down and then leaned into the doorjamb right in front of me. I couldn't see or move! Hell, I could hardly breathe, 'cause I was afraid I'd scare her. She stayed there the whole blasted time."

"Dummy!" laughed Eric. "She knew you were there!"

"No, she didn't."

"Oh, yes, she did. She was protecting your scrawny butt."

"Okay, okay! Maybe she was. But it doesn't matter. I could still hear 'em talkin'. The Sheriff said he'd been in Samson for the better part of two days."

"Well, that explains a lot," I said.

"Wait. Y'all need to hear the rest of this. Miz Tilly asked him if the toilet paper bandits and catnappers were over there."

"Toilet paper bandits and catnappers!" giggled Sam. "That's what she called us?"

"That was also for your benefit, J.D." chided Eric.

"Will y'all please let me finish? This is important! The Sheriff said he didn't have time to worry about kids' pranks because a little girl from Samson disappeared night before last. She was walkin' home from a friend's house and never made it. She disappeared without a trace. He said another little girl from over near Opp disappeared the same way last fall, and they found her body dumped in a swamp a few days later. She'd been 'saulted."

"What does ''saulted' mean?" asked Sandra.

"Well . . . uh . . ."

"It means whoever took her hurt her really bad before he killed her," interrupted Eric. "What kind of sick son of a bitch does that, especially to little kids?"

"Evil ones," I replied. "Miz Tilly had to be thinkin' about Luke."

"Yep. That's why Sheriff Coker came to see her. He thinks whoever took the little girls may be responsible for Luke's disappearance, too. He wanted to know if she could remember anything else about the time Luke disappeared—if there were any drifters around or if she had seen anythin' strange goin' on around town that might link the cases."

"Could she?"

"Not really. She said Eli had seen a bunch of cars at the Feed and Seed's loading dock one night when he was late bringin' the butter in, but he just figured they had a poker game goin'."

"Poor Miz Tilly."

"Sheriff Coker asked her to call him if she remembered anythin' else."

"Mitchell, you were in Opp last winter. Did you hear anythin' about all this?" asked Eric.

"Huh-uh."

Mitchell's tone did not match the look on his face.

He does know something. Wonder what. He's just not saying. Wonder why.

"I hope the little girl from Samson makes it home safe and sound," said Sandra.

"Men who like to hurt kids are not likely to let 'em go," said Mitchell flatly.

He's not talking about the little girl; he's talking about himself.

We suspected Mitchell's frequent bruising was coming from his pa or possibly Otis Pierce, but when we questioned him about it, he always insisted that he had fallen or wrecked his bike. We even talked with Ain't Pitty and Uncle Ben about it, but they said until Mitchell was willing to tell the Sheriff who was hurting him, there wasn't much anyone could do.

Maybe we can get him to talk.

"No wonder folks keep tellin' us to stay close to home," said Sam.

"Well, J.D., did Miz Tilly know you were behind the door or not?" asked Eric, as if trying to lighten the mood.

"Yeah, she knew."

"Ha! Told you so! You were lucky she saw you, and not the Sheriff."

"Uh-huh. She said the same thing."

"So, are y'all the ones who decorated the Crossing last night?" asked Mitchell.

"Did you see it?"

"Yeah. Everybody at the store walked over to take a look. Two ladies from the Women's Guild were in the store early to buy a rake long enough to pull the toilet paper out of the trees. Y'all shoulda heard 'em! They were not happy."

"Did they say who they thought did it?"

"Yep. Y'all."

"Did they say anythin' about the cat and the mailman?" asked Sandra.

"Sandra!" yelled J.D.

"What? It's all right if Mitchell knows, isn't it?"

"It's okay, J.D.," said Mitchell. "The Crossing wasn't the only thing being talked about this mornin'. Miz Lettie was in a little while ago and told anybody who'd listen what happened. She insisted y'all were responsible and that the Sheriff hung up on her when she called to tell him about it. I don't know what she was more upset about, her cat hurtin' Salter Lee or being hung up on."

"We weren't plannin' on anyone gettin' hurt," moaned J.D., laying his forehead down on the picnic table.

Just then, a farm truck pulled up to the loading dock and honked the horn.

"Gotta go, y'all," said Mitchell. "Take it easy."

"Hey, Mitchell," called Sam, "we're goin' to a picnic Sunday after church. Wanna come?"

"Sure!"

"Great! Meet us at Ain't Pitty's about lunchtime."

Sometimes sisters can be real friends.

We made our way up the path to Salter Lee's house in slow motion. None of us was sure what was going to be said or who was going to say it, but we kept going. Just as J.D. took a deep breath and raised his hand to knock, the door opened and Salter Lee was standing there. His weathered black face had stitches over his left brow, down his cheek, and in front of his left ear. There were also scattered stitches, bandages, and assorted scratches on his neck and arms.

Oh, God! Look what we did!

I had never felt guilty about any of the pranks we'd pulled until now.

Finding his voice, J.D. stammered, "Uh . . . Mr. Lee . . . sir . . . our granny . . . Miz Campbell . . . wanted us to bring supper . . . bein' you had such a bad day 'n' all . . . and if you have any chores, we'll . . . I'll . . . be happy to do 'em for you . . . all of 'em."

J.D. held the picnic basket out, but Salter Lee stepped back and opened the door wide.

"Y'all c'mon in."

Setting the basket on the dining room table, J.D. sighed.

"Mr. Lee, I put the cat in the mailbox. I was gonna let him out this mornin', but you got there before I did. I'm really sorry. I never meant for anybody to get hurt."

Quiet echoed up the walls as Salter Lee lifted the blue-checkered towel covering the basket and took a long, slow sniff.

"Mmm-mmm. Miz Campbell sho can cook! Miz Lee can cook, but not like this." Then, winking at us, he added, "'Course, I'll not be tellin' her that."

Lifting an angel biscuit out of the basket, he took a bite.

"That biscuit's lighter'n air."

Taking another bite, he closed his eyes, as if committing the taste to memory. Finally swallowing, he sat down on a nearby ladder-back chair and crossed his legs.

"Yep, today's been a little rough. But thank the good Lord it was me openin' that mailbox this mornin'. That ol' feral cat woulda half-killed Miz Lettie."

J.D.'s face went pale and he swallowed hard, as did the rest of us. We had not thought about what would happen if Miz Lettie had opened the box. We didn't like her because Ain't Pitty didn't like her, but none of us wanted to see her hurt. We also knew Salter Lee was right. Satan would have torn Miz Lettie to pieces.

"I don't believe y'all meant to hurt anybody, but you did, and it coulda been a lot worse. Just what did that ol' cat do to deserve spendin' the night in that hot mailbox?"

Dead silence. How could we possibly explain our years of battles with Satan?

J.D. started rambling about the chicken coop, Wilbur, and Satan's attacks on him, but before he finished, Salter Lee interrupted.

"Now, let me see if I have this right: there were five of y'all against one ol' cat that was just doin' what all cats do?"

Hearing it said like that, Satan's reckoning did not seem so just anymore.

Salter Lee did not push for an answer; I think he saw it in our faces.

"I was plannin' on mowin' and trimmin' the hedge on Saturday, bein' that's my day off 'n' all. But with these stitches 'n' such, I'd best rest for a bit. How about y'all take care of those chores for me?"

"Yes, sir."

At the door, J.D. stopped

"Mr. Lee, I know we shoulda . . . coulda . . ." J.D. was seldom at a loss for words, but he was now. Giving up, he stuck his right hand out and said, "I hope you feel better soon. I really do."

Salter Lee smiled and shook J.D.'s hand.

"Apology accepted, son. Y'all listen to your better angels next time. They'll save you from having to worry about all the shoulda, coulda, wouldas."

We weren't surprised to hear the fancies tinkling that night. At the dinner table, Ain't Pitty and Uncle Ben repeated Granny's stinging words about Salter Lee's getting hurt and added a few of their own. It was one of the few times I felt as if we had disappointed them.

"Before y'all go to Salter Lee's on Saturday, pick and snap another basket of beans and shuck an armload of corn to take with you. I'll have a basket of eggs ready to go as well."

"Yes, ma'am."

Pausing, but not moving, Ain't Pitty cleared her throat.

"And no more gallivantin' around after dark. When the sun goes down, y'all can go between here and Granny's, and that's it. And no one goes anywhere alone, ever. Understood?"

"Yes, ma'am."

"Okay. Don't stay up too late."

"Yes, ma'am."

"That was strange," Eric whispered as the tinkling faded. "We just got punished and protected at the same time."

"Yeah," added J.D. "But at least we didn't get restricted to the porch. They'll never know if we go someplace other than Granny's after dark. We'll just have to be extra careful."

"That little girl disappearin' has the whole town spooked," I said.

"Well, there are too many of us for anyone to try anythin'," reasoned J.D.

"I know, but it's still scary."

"Now, don't go turnin' into a scaredy-cat—we still have another TP-in' to do."

"Look, I'm not scared, and you know it. Somethin' bad is happenin' around here, and we need to be careful. Maybe we should just forget about the last TP-in'."

"Why? TP doesn't hurt anybody, and we've been plannin' it for weeks. We need to finish what we started."

"Yeah, but the Judge's yard would be our third."

"So?"

"Didn't Ain't Pitty say bad things always happen in threes?"

"Oh, that's right," said Sam.

"Hold on, y'all," said Eric. "We don't have to decide now. Let's see how things go for a while and then decide."

"Okay, but don't y'all start turnin' chicken now," warned J.D.

Chapter 14

A tradition of the Crystal Springs Campbells was to have a high-summer picnic at Uncle Red and Ain't Ivy's farm. They had a hundred acres outside of town where they raised corn and hogs. The picnic was always a good time, especially if the ain'ts left us alone and if we didn't bother the uncles. The one exception was Uncle Red. He seemed to enjoy having us around. He was a quiet man with a lopsided grin who loved talking about his farm and ways of growing a good corn crop and breeding award-winning hogs. Uncle Red never told anyone why his pork tasted so much better than everybody else's, but we suspected it had something to do with the big patch of scuppernong grapes growing next to his hog pens. When the grapes were ripe, he treated his hogs to some every day, saving just enough to make a batch of scuppernong wine for himself and Ain't Ivy.

Uncle Red's hogs were big and dirty, and the biggest and dirtiest one of them all was his oldest brood sow, Queen Lola. This massive momma hog was legendary, not only because of her size but because she produced litters of fourteen to fifteen piglets every time she was bred, which was at least twice a year.

"Queen Lola's the reason we have a little money in the bank for a rainy day," Uncle Red would say. "She takes good care of me, and I take good care of her."

Queen Lola's favorite thing to do on hot, lazy days was to wallow in the big, shaded mud bath located at the far end of her pen.

We had watched her lie there for hours, occasionally flicking her corkscrew tail at bothersome flies. But all we had to do was rattle a candy wrapper, and that big ol' hog would jump up like a piglet and come snort at the ground under our feet.

When we rolled into the farmyard, dozens of Campbell folks of all ages were already there—some we knew and liked, and some we didn't. The ones we didn't like were mostly the ones who didn't like us or anybody else, for that matter. These sour folks seldom had anything nice to say about anybody, so we did as Ain't Pitty advised: "Leave 'em be. They're just unhappy folks who don't have anythin' better to do than wallow in their own misery. Kick their dust off your flip-flops and move on."

Some of these misery-loving folks gave us a hard stare as we got out of the Oldsmobile, probably because of Mitchell. Ain't Pitty had prepared us for this possibility last night, saying that Mitchell might be judged by things he had no control over, like his pa.

"And I'm sure my ears will burn for bringing a stranger to a Campbells-only event. Either way, we're givin' these folks manna for their misery. Just stay with Mitchell, and if anyone gives y'all a hard time, just keep smiling and keep walking—it'll drive 'em nuts."

I saw Granny take note of the hard stares around the yard. In her world, the Campbells were kind and gracious, so she moved quickly to nip any potential problems in the bud. Giving Mitchell a big hug, she said, "I'm so glad you could come picnic with us. It's good to have a fresh face here!" Her actions silently dared anybody else to do less.

Across the yard, the ain'ts were unpacking picnic baskets and distributing food across long picnic tables. Most of the uncles were standing around the steps of the summer kitchen, talking about the weather and taking turns hand-churning a half-dozen ice-cream makers, each containing a different flavor.

Up near the cornfield was Uncle Red's barn, which was filled with bales of hay and farm tools. To the left of the barn was a rusty metal tepee where Uncle Red stored his old but still-running Farmall tractor and its attached feed wagon. Beyond these buildings sat a hundred acres of tall corn that would soon be ready to harvest. The sweet corn would be used to feed people, and the rest would feed their livestock.

We saw Uncle Red coming out of the barn, a big smile on his face. He had traded in his usual sun-blocking khaki overalls and oversize safari hat for a lightweight blue plaid shirt and a pair of faded blue jeans. We could tell he was excited about something as he hugged everybody.

"Queen Lola's birthin' another litter of piglets, ten so far."

Some of the kids begged to watch, but the ain'ts said absolutely not, at least to their own. Fortunately for us, Ain't Pitty and Uncle Ben knew we would find a way to get down there, so they said nothing. But before we could sneak away, Ain't Ivy started ringing the cast-iron dinner bell that hung in the backyard.

"It's a wonder we don't hear that damn bell at Ain't Pitty's," said J.D., covering his ears.

"Uncle Red needs to hear it on the other side of the cornfield," yelled Sam.

"Yeah. Well, it's a miracle Ain't Ivy's not deaf!"

As soon as Uncle Red finished the blessing, we loaded our plates with ham biscuits, fried chicken, deviled eggs, and pepper slaw and headed under the tepee to eat. It was cool there, and, more important, it was out of the ain'ts' sight. We ate quickly, downed the last of our lemonade, and stacked our trash on a nearby bench. Slipping out the back of the tepee, we crossed behind the barn and headed down the winding path to Queen Lola's pen.

Climbing the fence, we could see the Queen lying on her side in the soft, squishy mud. When she saw us, one floppy pink ear perked up and her dark, pink-centered snout wrinkled up as she sniffed the air to see if we had treats. Squirming around next to Queen Lola's massive belly was a squiggling mound of muddy pink piglets, all rooting to reach one of her many full teats. Down by the Queen's tail was a big pile of bloody gray stuff.

"What's that?" asked Li'l Bit, pointing at the slimy mound.

"Looks like monster oysters, except for the blood," said Sandra.

"Ugh!" I moaned. "I'm never eating oyster shooters again."

There's not enough saltines or Tabasco in the world to make me for-
get this.

"That's what the piglets were in when they were inside Queen
Lola," said J.D.

"Yuck!" said Li'l Bit.

"Sure is a messa pigs," said Sharon. "How'd they get inside
Queen Lola, anyway?"

"The daddy pig put 'em in there," replied Sandra.

"How?"

"Don't know, don't care."

"Okay, y'all," said Sam. I think it's time we changed the sub—"

"Uh-oh!" said Eric. "Here comes Uncle Red."

As we watched his checked shirt coming down the path, Queen
Lola lumbered to her feet, shaking piglets off her belly and dragging
her full teats in the mud. Turning stiffly, she sniffed at the bloody,
oyster-like mess that had been at her tail and with a wide-open
mouth began chomping at it with her back teeth.

"Ohh! Uggh!" echoed up and down the fenceline. A wave of
nausea washed over me, and I felt the lunch I had just eaten coming
back up. Hearing the others, I knew I was not alone. With the exception of Mitchell, J.D., and Eric, who seemed to be trying to control their retching by sheer willpower, the rest of us proceeded to
vomit our recently eaten lunch right into the pen. Queen Lola, who
apparently preferred the look of what we were throwing up to what
she was eating, lumbered over and proceeded to gobble up the
hunks of partially digested food lying in the mud. A second wave of
nausea hit as we were trying to get off the fence, and one by one we
hit the ground like a bunch of curled-up roly-polies.

"Well, now," chuckled Uncle Red. "I reckon y'all shoulda listened when folks said not to come down here."

Pulling a blue bandanna from his back pocket, he wiped Sandra's mouth clean and moved on to the next groaning lump of flesh.

"That was the grossest thing I've ever seen in my life," whimpered Sam.

"Yeah" was all I could manage to mutter, the taste of vomit still strong in my mouth.

"I'm never gonna have a baby if I have to do that," moaned Sharon.

"Oh, c'mon, y'all!" nagged J.D., helping Sam and Sharon to their feet. "It's not that bad."

"Oh, yes, it is," I said.

"Here, Nettie," said Mitchell, helping me up and handing me his handkerchief. His hand felt smooth and strong.

"This is just what animals do," said J.D. "Isn't that right, Uncle Red?"

"But . . . but . . . why?" croaked Li'l Bit, whose skinny little frame was still spread-eagle in the grass, his skin pale green.

"Because it has hormones Queen Lola needs to make milk for the piglets," replied Uncle Red, slipping his arm under Li'l Bit's shoulders and sitting him up.

"But Ain't Pitty said horrormones are what grew hair on Cilly's mom's face."

Struggling not to laugh, Uncle Red replied, "Well, I guess they do that, too."

When we were all on our feet, we began a slow walk back to the picnic, but the closer we got, the stronger the smell of food was and the queasier we became.

"May we walk the farm road, Uncle Red?" I asked. "It will give everyone's stomach time to settle."

"Sure, just don't be long. The leaves are curlin' and the bees aren't flyin', so there's a storm on the way. And stay outta the gully—I'm not aimin' to pull y'all outta there today."

At least once a summer, we walked the dirt road surrounding Uncle Red's cornfield. Thick trees and brush bordered the road on the right and across the back. But the side leading back to the barn was bordered by a deep gully that ran half the length of the field and then took a slow right turn, ending in a deep runoff pond. The gully, which had been formed by years of heavy rain combined with the slope of the land, had fascinated us since we were old enough to climb up and down its crumbly sides.

Stepping into the road, we could see the rutted pattern of Uncle Red's tractor wheels in the soft dirt. Running down the middle of the road was a strip of grass with an occasional mound of fire ants, which we cut a wide circle around. The sting of those little red devils lasted for days, and if we happened to get more than a couple of bites at one time, we would be lame for a week. The road was narrow, so we paired up: J.D. and Eric led the way, Mitchell and I were in the back, and everybody else was in the middle.

"Well, that's all the excitement I needed for today. I don't want to eat again for a week!" groaned Sam.

"Me neither!" agreed Sandra.

"Aw . . . c'mon, y'all. It's just nature bein' nature," teased J.D.

"Well, there are just some things nature should keep to herself," I snapped, pushing Queen Lola's feast out of my mind and pressing Mitchell's handkerchief against my lips until the wave of nausea passed.

"Mitchell, let me take this to Ain't Pitty's and wash it. If you put it back in your pocket now, we'll both smell like vomit."

"That's okay—you can keep it," laughed Mitchell. "I have more."

"Are you sure? It feels really nice, and it doesn't look like a regular handkerchief."

"It's not. My momma made it. She told me I should always keep a good handkerchief with me."

"Are you sure? It's special. Don't you want it back?"

"It *is* special—that's why I want you to have it."

"Oh. Okay. Thanks."

"You're welcome."

"You must miss your mother a lot."

"Every day."

According to Wiregrass lore, a good corn crop should be knee-high by the Fourth of July. If it was true, Uncle Red's corn was ahead of schedule. It had lots of young cobs with silky tassels that tickled our skin as we brushed by. The number of cobs depended on the height of the stalk, and the height depended on the rain, which there had been plenty of.

"Gosh, look!" said Eric, pointing to the back of the field. The whole corner of Uncle Red's cornfield was gone.

"Holy cow!" said J.D., picking up what was left of a mangled stalk. "This was hand cut, and not well. Uncle Red would never have done this. Somebody's stealing his corn."

"Look," said Eric, pointing at the tree line. "That's where they came in."

A truck-size hole had been pushed through the brush, and there were tire tracks leading in and out.

"We've gotta let Uncle Red know."

"Maybe we oughta double back and tell 'im," suggested Sam. "Plus, he was right—there's a storm comin'."

We could see a black, mountain-shaped thunderhead forming in the distance.

"But we wanna see the gully!" yelled Li'l Bit and Sharon.

"I'd like to see how deep it's gotten since last summer," added Eric.

"Gully," voted the rest of us.

"Okay, y'all. But we need to move fast," warned J.D.

We picked up our pace, but it wasn't long before we saw jagged bolts of lightning on the horizon and heard thunder rumbling our way. As usual, we started counting the seconds between the lightning flash and the thunder. "One Mississippi, two Mississippi, three . . ."

"Damn!" yelled J.D., as thunder clapped right over us. Lightning was now stretching higher and wider, and the air was tinted green, signaling the likelihood of skin-cutting hail.

"We're gonna get wet, y'all," yelled J.D. Kneeling down, he called to Li'l Bit. "Climb on! Your legs can't move you as fast as we need to go. Eric, you get Sharon!"

Giant plops of rain had begun to fall by the time we made the left turn leading back to the barn, and there was no time to say "Mississippi" between the earth-shaking thunder and the wicked lightning. We stopped at the turn just long enough to look in the steep, jagged, V-shaped gully. It was as wide at the top as Uncle Red's barn, deeper than the tepee was tall, and deeply rutted. Rainwater and downstream runoff leading the storm were already flowing fast at the bottom.

"Any bigger, and it's gonna take out his corn," yelled Eric. "Dirt's too soft to hold it!"

Thunder cracked again, and we started moving as fast as J.D. and Eric could manage with the little ones on their backs. The rain was falling so hard, the road changed to mud and the rows of corn blurred to gray. Suddenly, J.D. stopped. I could see that part of the road in front of him was washed out by the widening gully. Forming a line, we moved closer to the corn, which was whipping around so hard the leaves slapped and stung our skin.

"We gotta tell Uncle Red about this, too!" yelled Eric. "That washout's big enough to swallow the whole front end of his tractor!"

Just then, a bolt of lightning struck so close we heard the ear-splitting crack as it hit the ground. The tingle under our feet and the smell of singed corn made us move even faster.

Whitewater was surging through the gully now, and I could feel my feet slipping and sliding in my flip-flops, which were slipping and sliding in the mud. Reaching another washout, we were forced to move close to the stinging corn again.

"Be careful!" shouted J.D., as he scrambled deeper into the corn. "The road's goin'!"

Turning to follow, I felt the ground under my feet give way and I started a muddy slide toward the fast-moving current.

Oh, God!

As I opened my mouth to scream, I felt two strong hands grab my arm and heard Mitchell yell, "Hold on. I've got you!" Then someone grabbed my t-shirt and back over the edge of the gully I came, three of us landing in a muddy pile.

"Holy cow, Nettie!" yelled Sam. "Are you okay?"

"I think so."

My hands were trembling as Mitchell and Sam helped me to my feet, minus my flip-flops, which were now floating somewhere downstream.

"C'mon, y'all!" yelled J.D. "We gotta move before we all end up in the water."

That's when we heard it—a chugging sound approaching from somewhere deep in the corn. With the help of the lightning, we could see Uncle Red's tractor rumbling toward us, mowing over the corn as it approached.

Pulling the wagon up next to us, he yelled, "Climb in! Get in the middle and pull that tarp over your heads."

Underneath his safari hat, Uncle Red looked worried as he counted heads. Scrambling into the wagon, we put Li'l Bit and Sharon in the middle and covered ourselves with a plastic tarp. Uncle Red turned the tractor back into the corn and began working his way back to the tepee.

Most of the time we were grateful for the cool breezes that came with summer storms, but this time the wind was bone-chilling cold. We were muddy, wet, and scared, and the only part of me not trembling was where Mitchell's arm was draped around my shoulders.

It seemed like forever before we got back to the farm, and the storm was still raging as we pulled under the tepee and escaped the stinging rain and hail. Uncle Red turned the tractor off and twisted around in his seat.

"Y'all okay?"

We managed to nod as he jumped from the tractor and helped us down. Sitting down on a nearby crate, he pulled Li'l Bit and Sharon onto his lap, cradling them to keep the wind off.

"Thank you, Uncle Red," said J.D. "If you hadn't come when you did, we all might have gone for a muddy swim."

We gave Uncle Red a group hug, thankful he'd been paying enough attention to know we weren't back and might be in trouble.

Everybody should have an Uncle Red.

When the downpour slowed, we ran across the hail-covered backyard to the summer kitchen, where Ain't Ivy and Ain't Pitty were waiting with towels and mugs of hot lemonade. As we dried off, we told Uncle Red about the missing corn.

"Yep. I know. Best I can figure is somebody snuck in a few nights ago and took it."

"But why? To eat?" asked Sam.

"Not likely. I figure they stole it to make liquor. Farmers around here have lost part of their crops to moonshiners for years. Last summer, I got a dog to help guard the field, but they just cut his throat and left him in the middle of the road for me to find. I've called Sheriff Coker, but he says he has to catch 'em in the act, or at least catch 'em with the corn, to be able to lock them up," lamented Uncle Red. "He said it was like chasing shadows. Those thieves turn off their lights and run the back roads and fields all over the county."

Bad, poor men. They don't have anything to lose.

When it was time to leave, Uncle Red walked us to the car.

"I'd appreciate y'all comin' to help pick up the corn I had to run over to get to ya. If we get it picked up quick, I can save it for feed," he said with a wink.

It took us three days to get all of the cornstalks picked up, loaded up, and ready to be processed for silage. The only good part of those three hot, sweaty days was we got to eat a lot of leftover ice cream. We also got to see the gully up close again, including the washout that almost swallowed me. I shivered, both at the memory and at the fact that Mitchell and Sam had saved me.

Surveying the damage, Uncle Red said he was going to have to figure out a way to either fill in the washouts or shorten the rows of corn, both of which would cost him money.

"Why don't you plant wiregrass on the sides of the gully, Uncle Red? You get enough of those roots into the dirt, and they'll hold anythin'. Wiregrass never washes away."

"That's a great idea, Nettie. Wonder why I didn't think of it before? Woulda saved myself a lotta dirt and a lotta corn! Now all I need to do is figure out how to stop those thievin' moonshiners before somebody gets hurt."

Chapter 15

At least once or twice a summer, Ain't Pitty would let us take a float trip, which was an all-day inner-tube ride down Sandy Bottom Creek. After the long, hard days we put in at Salter Lee's and Uncle Red's, we were ready for a float and decided to go on a Sunday so Mitchell could go with us. It was the first time he had been on an all-day float, and he was as excited as Li'l Bit and Sharon, who were also going for the first time.

After breakfast, Sam, Sandra, and I packed a picnic lunch as J.D. and Eric tied the inner tubes to Jigger's roof. Once we were ready to go Sharon sat on J. D.'s lap, Sandra moved to the front, and Mitchell squeezed into the back next to me. His Zesty smell was a welcome change from crickets and eucalyptus oil, and I was very aware that our arms and legs were touching.

Ain't Pitty drove north to the halfway point between Samson and Opp and turned onto the dirt road leading to the High Water Bridge boat landing. This drop-off point was about ten miles upstream from Sandy Bottom Bridge, where we would exit the creek late in the afternoon.

Ain't Pitty brought Jigger to a stop near the water and repeated her usual instructions: "Be careful and watch out for the little ones! Be out of the water and on your way home by the time the sun's at your shoulders, or you're gonna be late for supper."

Handing Sam and me our lunch, which she had divided into

two waterproof bags for insurance, she waved and turned Jigger for home.

Sandy Bottom Creek was big by most creek standards. In some places, it was deep and as narrow as thirty feet, with whitewater rapids. In other places, it was shallow and as wide as eighty feet, which allowed the current to just mosey along. As with the Crystal Springs pool, most of the clear water came from natural springs scattered at different points along the creek bed, but once or twice a summer, the area got a storm bad enough to muddy the water and change the number and shape of the small beaches dotting the shoreline.

At the edge of the water, we tethered our inner tubes to our ankles using pieces of clothesline Uncle Ben had cut for us. For extra safety, we tethered Li'l Bit's waist to J.D. and Sharon's to Eric. Both of them could swim, but the creek could be unpredictable at times and it would not take much for them to get into trouble. J.D. waded into the water to show them different positions to take in the tube, based on what the water was doing.

"If the water's deep, you can put your feet down in the hole of the tube. If the water's shallow, lie on your stomach or back; otherwise, your feet will pay the price. If we're goin' through whitewater and you want to go fast, be on top of the tube, and if you want to slow down, just move to the middle. Most important, remember to keep your feet pointing downstream no matter what."

A light fog was lingering just above the water as we waded in, which made for an eerie, mysterious start to the float. I knew the fog would stay until the sun was high enough to burn it off, and then the day would get hot fast.

We started out floating together, but the current spread us out across the creek. I could not help but notice that Mitchell would paddle to catch up with me or hold on to a branch of some kind until I caught up with him. Sam also noticed and floated by with a grin on her face.

Smart-ass.

By midmorning we heard the roar of the Rucks choppers approaching. Their thumping rotors caused our tubes to shake and the water to ripple all the way to the banks. Mitchell never took his eyes off the choppers from the time the first one appeared until the last one disappeared.

"You like watchin' them?" I asked, amazed at the stupidness of my question.

Of course he likes them, dummy. He was watching them, wasn't he?

"Yeah. When my mother was alive, we'd watch 'em every night. I can't wait to be old enough to join the army and learn how to fly 'em."

"That's great. Maybe you'll be stationed at Rucks and we'll be watchin' you fly over in a big Huey one day."

"I hope so."

"I have no idea what I'm gonna do when I get out of school. I haven't even thought about it yet."

"I think about it all the time."

I could not help but wonder if Mitchell's hurry was more about getting away from his pa than it was about flying choppers.

Rounding a bend, we floated up to a tree that had fallen like a bridge across a narrow section of the creek. Its root system formed uneven but usable steps up to the trunk, which made a nice platform for us to jump from. We floated under the trunk and tethered our tubes to the downstream side of the roots.

While the rest of us climbed up, J.D. and Eric went into the water to see if it was deep enough to jump and to make sure there were no hidden stumps or branches that could cause problems. Surfacing and giving us the okay, they treaded water while Li'l Bit and Sharon took their first jumps and dog-paddled back to the steps.

"Okay, no diving, but we can do ten jumps each, and then we have to go," said J.D. "We need to stay on schedule if we're gonna reach Sandy Bottom Bridge on time."

We lined up to take turns jumping, cannonballing, and flipping our way into the water, hooting with laughter when someone landed an occasional belly flop.

As Mitchell and I sat on the tree trunk, waiting for our turn, he bumped my shoulder and whispered, "Thanks for inviting me. This is fun."

"You're welcome. I wasn't sure your pa would let you come."

"I didn't ask him. He's hardly ever home, and if he is, he doesn't care if I'm there or not, unless . . ."

Mitchell fell quiet.

"C'mon, Nettie. Your turn," called J.D.

I got up and flipped into the creek. Touching the sandy bottom, I looked up through the clear water and could see a wavy Mitchell sitting on the trunk above me. For a brief moment, I tried to imagine what his life must be like when he was not with us, and it hurt my heart.

Finishing our last jumps, we tethered up and pushed off into the current. For the next hour, we floated under trees dripping with Spanish moss and by fields of ripening corn and peanuts. We passed an old house and barn that had proven to be no match for the creek's floodplain and waved to the sweaty farmer tending the adjacent field. Floating under an old railroad trestle, we slowed down long enough to bounce echoes off its underside.

"We'll be at the cypress tree soon," called J.D., as we floated out of the shadows of the trestle. "Time for lunch."

Sam and I had managed to keep the bags mostly dry, so, if we were lucky, the food would be, too.

"Remember to pee before you get out, y'all. We want that water well downstream before we get a drink," J.D. said.

We had an honor system when we were in water. We did not pee where we swam, and if we saw somebody peeing upstream from us, of either the two-legged or fur-legged variety, we sounded a pee alert, which meant we did not drink the water for a thousand Mississippis.

The sun was directly overhead when we floated up to the tiny island marking the halfway point of our trip. In the middle was an old cypress tree whose drip line shaded most of the island and whose root knees were well above the sand. The tree looked worn and weary after years of buffering whatever happened to float over the island during high water, but it was still standing and its leaves were still green.

Pulling our tubes onto the beach, we found a good spot among the roots to sit and divvy up the food. We had no plates or napkins, so our laps and wet t-shirts had to do.

When the food was gone, we leaned back against the smooth roots and closed our eyes, thinking about whatever happened to cross our minds.

"J.D., do you have a girlfriend yet?" asked Eric.

Opening one eye, J.D. asked, "And you want to know this *why*?"

"Just 'cause."

"He does," volunteered Sandra, moving just fast enough to escape J.D.'s hand as he sat up and made a grab for her.

"That's enough."

"Her name's Claudia, and she's sweet on him, too," yelled Sandra, dodging left and right to escape capture. "He walked her home from school every day and called her to say good-bye the day we left for Crystal Springs."

"That's enough, I said," warned J.D. again, as he rubbed sand down her back.

"Well," drawled Eric, "it's gonna happen to all of us eventually."

"Havin' a boyfriend isn't so bad," giggled Sam. "As long as he doesn't have BO and knows how to kiss."

"I don't have a boyfriend, and I don't want one, neither!" declared Sharon. "They're just trouble."

"And just how would you know that, prissy?" asked Sandra.

"Because I see you mopin' around when some boy you like doesn't pay you any attention, that's why!"

"Huh, you don't know anythin'."

"Danny sure seems to be meeting you at the pool a lot these days, Sam," grinned J.D.

Danny was the young deputy we had met when Elmer Fudd accused us of stealing his nuts.

"He's a lot nicer and better smelling than John Thomas, that's for sure."

"Has he kissed you yet?" asked Sandra.

"Not yet." Sam grinned. "But summer's not over."

She's not the least bit shy talkin' about all this stuff.

"What about you, Nettie?" asked J.D. "You sweet on anybody?"

Uh-oh.

"Nope," I replied, nervously trying to bury my feet in the hard sand.

"Well, I don't know about that," teased Sam. "If she'd give him half a chance, Andy Stockton would be there in a minute."

"Hush up, Sam."

How'd she know that? And why the hell is she blabbing it now?

Fourteen-year-old Andrew Stephen Stockton had been a play-mate since our sandbox days. We had climbed trees, waded creeks, played softball, and sat together in church since we'd decided to be best friends, in the first grade. He was the best outfielder on our neighborhood softball team, and I was the best shortstop, so we worked well together. I had even gone to the Virginia State Fair in Richmond with him and his parents last fall. We rode all the rides, mooed at all the award-winning cows, and shared cotton candy until we were sticky from head to toe. But as we were riding the Ferris wheel one last time, Andy changed everything. He put his arm across the back of the seat behind me. I asked him if he had a cramp or something, but he said no, he was just resting his arm. I told him to get it back where it belonged or he'd be sorry, and then I scooted to the far corner of the seat.

By the time we got home, the Ferris wheel was forgotten. But things changed again just before we left for Crystal Springs. Andy and I were packing up softball gear at the end of a neighborhood game, when he asked me to go steady with him. All I remember after that was running for home, leaving Andy to carry all the equipment by himself.

Andy was my best friend, but he'd changed things I did not want changed. Now, Sam had told everybody about it, including Mitchell. I wasn't sure why her telling him upset me more than her telling the others, but it did.

I had not thought about Andy since we'd gotten to Crystal Springs, and it was strange to think about him now. For a moment, I wondered what he was doing and what I would say to him when I got home.

Coming out of my daydream, I realized Mitchell was watching me with a funny look on his face.

"Okay, Mitchell, your turn. You got a girl?" asked Eric.

"Nope. Not yet."

Tossing a pebble at me, J.D. piped in, "Well, I think I know someone who might be interested in the job."

Damn you, J.D.

All I could do was stare at the lump of sand covering my feet.

"Okay, Eric, how about you? You're the one who brought up all this boyfriend-girlfriend stuff. Do you have a girl?"

"Kinda. Her name is Jane, and we've been to the movies a couple of times."

"Ever kiss 'er?" asked Sandra.

"Not yet. Momma said I'd be in trouble if I did anythin' more than hold her hand."

"Yuck!" yelled Li'l Bit, getting up and brushing the sand off his low-riding campers. "Whadda y'all wanna hold an ol' girl's hand for, anyway? You'll get cooties!"

"Silly thing—you hold my hand all the time, and I'm a girl," teased Sam.

"Well, that don't count! Momma *makes* me hold your hand!"

Embarrassed by the laughter, Li'l Bit headed to the water.

"Can we get goin'? It's gettin' hot just sittin' here."

"Yep, it's gettin' hot in more ways than one!" laughed Sam, gathering up our lunch bags.

The afternoon was lazy, hot, and humid, and the next stretch of creek was a great place to catnap because of the slow-moving current and long tunnels of tree shade. Lying back, we could see specks of sunlight reflecting off the water onto the quivering leaves in the canopy

"It looks like a thousand lightning bugs up there," I said.

"Yeah, it's beautiful," said Mitchell. "I could stay here all day."

"Me too."

Around the next bend, Mitchell and I floated up to a small cove of rocks that had rolled down the bank into the creek. A small, lazy whirlpool had formed in the middle and captured a perfectly shaped green leaf. It was swirling slowly around and around, caught in a current strong enough to keep it prisoner but not strong enough to pull it under. Hopping off his tube, Mitchell picked up the leaf and set it down in the free-flowing current.

"Why'd you do that?"

"I guess I didn't like seeing it trapped."

Like you.

For the better part of two hours we floated along, listening to the whine of the locusts echo above us and watching the fish feeding ripples disappear as they went deep to avoid the midday heat.

"Hey, y'all, we're gonna pass the beach where we found that old ice house. Wanna stop?" asked Eric.

"Yeah," replied J.D., shading his eyes to look at the position of the sun. "We're doin' okay on time. We can see if anybody else has been around there."

"Are y'all talkin' about the old ice house off Choctaw Road?" asked Mitchell, turning pale.

"Yeah. You know it?"

"Yeah. And y'all don't wanna be anywhere near there."

"Why?" asked Eric. "What do you know about it?"

"Nothin' . . . I . . . I just heard a lot of mean drunks hang around there, that's all."

"Well, that explains the old moonshine jug we found," said J.D. "Let's just pull up to the beach and take a quick look. If anybody's around, we'll leave."

Mitchell opened his mouth to say something else but stopped.

He really doesn't want us to go.

"Wait, J.D. If Mitchell thinks—"

"It'll be okay. We'll take a quick look and be gone."

I could feel tension rising in Mitchell, but he didn't say anything.

"Let's talk with J.D. again," I whispered. "Maybe we can change his mind."

"No. If he's set on going back to the ice house, it's better if I'm with 'im."

"Why?"

"Because . . . well, just because."

I didn't like the answer, but Mitchell paddled ahead to catch up with J.D. and Eric before I could say anything more.

After pulling our tubes onto the beach. Li'l Bit and Sharon headed to the honeysuckle patch they had found the last time, and the rest of us searched the beach for boot prints.

"Nothing here," said J.D. "Let's check the building."

Walking single file, we headed across the field, disrupting resting bugs and butterflies and sending them flitting across the tall grass.

"Watch your step," warned J.D., as a big black snake and a couple of her babies slithered down the path ahead of us, disappearing into the grassy shadows.

As we neared the ice house, we heard the sound of a motor. Ducking down and peeking through the grass, we saw an old car pull up and stop.

"I wanna get a closer look at who's in that car," whispered J.D. "Y'all stay here."

"Wait!" urged Mitchell, grabbing J.D.'s arm. "That looked like Otis Pierce's car, the one he parks near our trailer. You don't wanna mess with him, J.D. He's mean, real mean. He'll hurt ya."

"Not if he doesn't know we're here," whispered J.D. "I wanna see what he's up to. He didn't come all the way out here just to drink from a jug. Remember the little t-shirt we found in there?"

"Oh, shit, J.D.," hissed Eric. "You don't think he had somethin' to do with that little girl disappearin', do you?"

By now, Mitchell was as pale as the sand.

"I don't know, but whoever it is, they're up to somethin'. Mitchell, you and Eric come with me if you want, but the rest of y'all stay here, stay down, and stay quiet."

Mitchell hesitated a split second, before following J.D. and Eric.

From behind the grass, we could hear two car doors slam and the faint creaking of the ice house door opening. We could also hear men talking but not what was being said. Suddenly, J.D., Eric, and Mitchell came scrambling back down the path, motioning for us to stay low and head back to the beach.

"Okay, who were they and what were they doin'?" I asked when we hit sand.

"It was Otis Pierce and the biggest man I've ever seen, with a machete the size of my arm," replied J.D. "Mitchell was right. We need to get outta here."

We got Li'l Bit and Sharon, tethered up, and pushed off into the current, staying quiet until we were well downstream. J.D. motioned for us to huddle, so we maneuvered our tubes together, keeping the little ones floating well ahead of us. Mitchell held on to my hand, instead of my inner tube, and his fingers were ice cold.

"Could y'all see what they were doin'?" whispered Sam.

"Nope," replied J.D. "All I could see was Pierce goin' into the ice house, carryin' a jug. The monster-man with the machete stayed outside. His face alone was enough to scare the pants off me. He was the strangest color I've ever seen—not red, not brown, but both, almost cinnamon colored."

"Mitchell, do you know who he was? Have you seen him before?"

"Yeah," replied Mitchell, his voice flat. "His name's Gris. He's a swamp Cajun from over in Louisiana. He used to cut cane, and he's mean as a snake. He runs with Otis Pierce and Pa."

The look on Mitchell's face made me shiver.

"What are we gonna do?" I asked.

"Whaddaya mean?" replied J.D., glancing nervously over his shoulder. "We didn't see the little girl, and they weren't doin' anythin' wrong. They're just scary, that's all."

"Should we at least tell Ain't Pitty? She'll know if anythin' needs to be done."

"If we tell Ain't Pitty—or anybody else, for that matter—they'll get even more spooked and we'll spend the rest of the summer on the porch, or, even worse, they'll send us home. You want that?"

"Maybe she'll just tell us to stay away from the ice house."

"Yeah, or the creek that runs near it, or the road that runs by it, or even this side of town," snapped J.D.

"What do you think, Mitchell?" I asked.

"I don't want y'all gettin' into trouble or havin' to go home, but you need to stay away from that ice house and those men. They're dangerous."

He's protecting us, but who's protecting him?

"That, we can do," agreed J.D.

"C'mon!" called Li'l Bit, tugging at his line. "Y'all catch up."

Pushing out of the huddle and into midstream, we continued the float. As we rounded the last bend before we were to exit, we drifted past an old man casting his line into the water near some tree fall. Tall and thin, he had a black-and-white beard, round spectacles perched on the tip of his nose, and a floppy old hat on his head. Waving as we floated by, we were careful not to disturb him or any nearby fish.

Once we were past the quiet zone, J.D. asked, "Anybody know that ol' fella? He looked familiar."

"No. And it's a little early to be fishin'," said Eric.

"Maybe he just got off work," suggested Sam.

"I wonder if he can see the ice house from where he is," J.D. said. "He's close enough to the intersection with Choctaw Road, he could've seen somethin'."

"Why would he be lookin'?" I asked.

"Hmm, good question. I don't know."

When we reached Sandy Bottom Bridge, we pulled our tubes out of the water, wrapped the tether lines in and out of the holes, and tucked the ends under the wrapped line to hold them snug for the roll home. Hoisting the tubes to our shoulders, we headed up the hill toward the road, J.D. and Eric carrying their tubes, as well as Li'l Bit's and Sharon's. Once on hard pavement, they would be able to roll their own.

The sun had dropped behind the trees, so the pavement had cooled enough that our now-summer-tough feet could handle the heat. Our flip-flops would never have lasted the whole float, and I wasn't taking any chances with my second pair of the summer, so we had left them lined up on the patio.

We had not walked far when we heard a car coming up behind us. Looking nervously over his shoulder, J.D. watched as it rolled by. I could tell he was really on edge when he did the same thing with the next car.

"Y'all, I think we need to get off this road for a little while. If Otis Pierce and the big Cajun come this way, they may put two and two together and figure out we were at Sandy Bottom Creek, since there's no other place to swim or float on this side of town. Let's cut up to Hardshell Hill and wait to see if they come by."

"Good thinkin'," said Eric. "If we sit at the very top, we can see Choctaw Road and the turnoff to the Railroad."

Scurrying past the old church, we made our way up to a big oak tree at the top of the hill.

"Funny y'all should come all the way up here," said Mitchell. Pointing to a plain white headstone at the far edge of the oak's drip line, he added, "My momma's buried right over there."

"She's in the shade. That's good." *What a dumb thing to say.*

"Glad you noticed. She loved sittin' in the shade. Pa said he didn't care where she was buried, so I picked that spot."

Mitchell pulled up a nearby clump of daisies by their roots and walked down to his mother's grave. Getting on his knees, he dug a hole near her headstone, tucked the roots of the daisies in, and covered them with dirt. He stood and dusted off his hands, then climbed back to where we were sitting.

"I hope they grow."

"That was a sweet thing to do, Mitchell."

"She loved daisies, and I really loved her. I miss her so much."

Now's your chance—ask him.

"How'd she die?"

"Pa said she fell and hit her head. But I don't know for sure."

"What do you mean? Do you think he hurt her?"

"No . . . maybe . . . I don't know."

"Look!" yelled Eric. "There they go!"

Scanning Choctaw Road, we saw the car from the ice house moving through the intersection.

"Good call, J.D.! They would've passed right by us."

Chapter 16

The next day was blistering hot and especially muggy, even for the Wiregrass, so we did our chores early and headed for the pool. We figured it was going to be crowded but were still surprised to see a dozen folks in the water and around the wall when we arrived.

Going down the steps, we could hear two ladies talking about a deputy catching a man and woman goin' into the little storage house at the Crossing last night.

"The deputy was parked in the woods with his headlights off and saw them go in," said one lady. "Apparently, they tried to run but didn't get very far."

"Ha!" whispered Eric. "I wonder if it was the same man and woman we saw. Talk about shameful things!"

"Yeah, but the more important question is, why was the deputy sittin' in the woods in the middle of the night in the first place?" asked J.D.

"Hmm, do you suppose he was watchin' for us?"

"Could be, I guess. But why now and why there? It's not like we've ever TP'ed the same place twice, except for Miz Lettie's."

"Maybe they weren't watchin' the Crossing at all," I suggested. "Maybe they were watching the loadin' dock."

"That's what I was thinkin'. Ain't Pitty has said for years Willie Ray sends the legal stuff out the front of the store during the day and the illegal stuff out the back at night. We've just never been able to see 'im do it. But now, Willie Ray knows the Sheriff is watchin' and he'll be more careful."

"It's a shame that silly couple sneakin' into the little house messed things up."

"No, it's not a shame; it's luck. That coulda been us sneakin' in."

Cilly and John Thomas showed up about lunchtime. According to the whispers around the pool, they were likely to be named homecoming king and queen this fall, because no one had the nerve to run against them. We also heard John Thomas was secretly dating a girl in Geneva.

I didn't like Cilly, but if what folks around the pool were saying was true, I felt sorry for her.

"Thank heaven for 'Dear Jane' letters, huh, Sam?"

"Yeah. Really."

After lunch, I was surprised to see Mitchell arrive.

Well, this afternoon just got a lot better.

Coming down the steps, he waved and dove in. I watched as he swam to the springs, grabbed sand, and rode the bubbles back up, pulling himself out of the pool next to me.

"Hey, you."

"Hey, you back."

"Glad you're here, Mitchell," said J.D. "How'd you manage to get off?"

"Just lucky. It's so hot the customers weren't coming in, so the dock manager let me go early."

"Wait here a minute," I said. *He's gotta be hungry.*

I knew Miz Tilly usually took Mitchell something to eat after her lunch rush was over, but I figured there would be no bag of food today, since he'd left work early. I was also pretty sure Miz Tilly's bag usually had something for his supper as well. In return,

Mitchell dumped Miz Tilly's trash and washed out the cans to keep the critters away before he biked home.

"Here you go," I said, handing him the extra peanut-butter sandwich Ain't Pitty had packed.

"Thanks. How'd you know I didn't have lunch?"

"Lucky guess."

I wasn't sure what or when Mitchell ate when Miz Tilly and Ain't Pitty weren't feeding him, but at least now he was getting good food on a regular basis.

By the time we climbed out of the pool, the sun was setting, most of the crowd had left, and our hands and feet looked like prunes.

"That's the way to spend a hot-as-hell day," said J.D. as we flip-flopped home.

"Mitchell, do you think your pa will be mad because you didn't work this afternoon?" I asked.

"He probably won't even know."

I hope so.

Supper was ready by the time we reached the patio, and Ain't Pitty was coming out the door with a large pitcher of tea.

"Y'all rinse off and set the table."

"Guess what we heard at the pool today, Ain't Pitty," said J.D., sliding under the shower.

"Probably nothin' I wanna hear, but tell me anyway."

J.D. explained about the man and woman being caught at the Crossing.

"Well, I'll be. That'll keep the tongues of the Women's Guild waggin' for a while."

When we explained that the deputy might have been watching the loading dock of the Feed and Seed, Ain't Pitty looked grim.

"Well, it's about damn time."

After dinner, I helped Mitchell load his bike into the trunk of the Oldsmobile while Uncle Ben went to get the car keys.

"See you tomorrow when I get off?" he asked.

"Sure. We'll meet you here. Ain't Pitty said something about goin' night fishin' tomorrow."

"Sounds like fun. I'll bring my fishin' pole."

"In the car, Mitchell," prompted Uncle Ben when he came back, winking at me and walking between us.

Sliding into the front seat, Mitchell grinned and waved.

Lord, please don't let his pa be home.

The sun had been down for hours, but the night was not cooling off.

"If a breeze doesn't start stirring soon, we may have to sleep on the porch," whined Sam.

We had done it before—pulled mattresses off the beds and onto the front porch in hopes of catching any breeze too weak to make it through the bedroom windows. Ain't Pitty was not crazy about having her good bedding on the concrete, but we knew she wouldn't say anything—hot was hot.

Even the Railroad was still, except for Satan, whom we could see slinking across Miz Lettie's porch.

"Well," muttered J.D., "that damn cat is staying pretty close to home these days. Maybe his reckoning did some good after all."

"Maybe for little lizards and Ain't Pitty's chickens, anyway," I added.

I was still trying to figure out the good and bad parts of the reckoning. I missed Wilbur and was glad we had punished Satan for killing him, but I also felt bad about what Satan had done to Salter Lee, which had happened only because we'd scared the damn cat half to death and stuck him in Miz Lettie's mailbox. Even after he'd gotten hurt, Salter Lee did not blame Satan. He said Satan was only doing what all cats do, which implied we were wrong to have punished him. But what about justice for Wilbur and the chicken and even J.D.? Satan had clawed him up twice. That damn cat hurt people and things I cared about and needed to be punished, or so I thought. If Salter Lee was right and we were wrong, then what were we wrong about? The way we punished Satan or the fact that we had punished him at all? Good and bad, right and wrong were getting all twisted up in my head when it hit me.

It's not about that damn cat at all. It's about us. We left the bus door open when he killed the chicken, we were TP-in' Miz Lettie's yard when he attacked J.D., and we were feeding Wilbur on the porch and made him an easy target. Satan was able to wreak all this havoc because of us.

I was debating whether to share my revelation with the others, when J. D. cleared his throat and spoke.

"I think we should do the last TP-in' job tonight."

All of the rockers stopped.

"I dunno, J.D.," said Sam. "This summer's been tough. Maybe we shouldn't."

"Yeah," agreed Eric. "We've really been pushin' our luck."

"Wanna stop?" snapped J.D. "Are y'all really ready to stop?"

I could not tell if J.D. was in favor of what he had just asked or not, but there was something different in his voice.

He's not asking if we want to stop tonight's TP-in'; he's asking if we want to stop TP-in' forever—stop our secret nighttime activities forever.

It was quiet on the porch until Sandra whispered, "Not yet."

"Not yet," said Sam.

Part of me was ready to stop—the part that was feeling guilty for the trouble we had caused. But another part knew once we stopped, summers as we had always known them would be over.

I'm not ready for it to end—not yet.

"I . . . I . . . guess not."

Eric was the last one to speak, and I could hear the reluctance in his voice.

"Okay. One and done?"

"One and done," replied J.D.

Going into the stifling bedroom, we changed into our dark clothes, strung our lines with the last of the TP, and slipped quietly out the door. Staying in the shadows, we made our way up the Railroad until we were across from the Judge's house. In the moonlight, it looked big and scary, just like haunted houses I'd seen in the movies.

This has trouble written all over it.

According to our plan, J.D. and Eric would TP the front porch, Sam and Sandra would do the bushes around the front, and I would do the rose garden on the side of the house. Our starting and ending point would be a narrow opening in the hedge across the Railroad from the Judge's yard. The hedge was thick and dark and would be a good place to hide if we needed to.

There was just enough moonlight to see where we were going, and the lightning bugs helped give shape to the trees and bushes in the Judge's yard. J.D. and Eric went first, dashing across the street and up into the shadows of the house. After a few minutes, when lights did not come on, the rest of us ran across and split up. Sam and Sandra started on the shrub line, and I headed around the house.

The Judge's rose garden had at least two dozen shoulder-high bushes in full, sweet-smelling bloom. I knew the roses were different colors, but in the dark they were just different shades of black, white, and gray. Moving quickly, I zigged and zagged among the flowers, snagging the soft paper on hundreds of thorny stems.

The Judge is gonna have his hands full getting this stuff off.

When I had finished the last square on my last roll, I stuck the empty cardboard tube in the closest bush and turned go.

At that moment, a deathly cold, bony hand grabbed my arm, jerking it so hard I thought it was going to come out of its socket. Whirling around, my mouth wide open and sucking air, I found myself looking into the very angry face of a bearded old man. Suddenly, I was whirling and falling into an endless black pit . . . then nothing.

I did not know what it was supposed to feel like to faint, but as I began the long swim back through murky darkness to being awake, I knew I did not like the feeling. I was lying on an uncomfortably stiff and scratchy sofa in a place I did not recognize. Turning my head, I saw the others standing stair-step in the center of the room, looking pale and frightened. In front of them was the old man we had seen smoking a pipe at the Fourth of July picnic, the same one we had seen fishing on the bank near the ice house, and the same one I'd seen right before I fainted. It had to be the Judge. Dressed in a baggy plaid robe with matching pajama pants and black slippers, he was pacing slowly back and forth, staring at my cussins and rubbing his thin beard.

When he saw me move, the Judge shifted his attention my way.

"Nice to see you back among the land of the living, young lady."

Walking over, he picked up my hand and pulled me to a sitting position.

"Care to join your fellow trespassers and vandals?"

I knew what trespassing meant from our backyard-grave and nut-stealing experience, but I did not know what a vandal was.

Doesn't matter. The way the Judge said the word made it clear it didn't mean anything good.

Placing me in the lineup between Sam and Sandra, the Judge resumed his slow, beard-rubbing pacing.

After a minute, he turned a chair to face us and sat down, crossing his arms and legs.

"Now, the question is, what am I going to do with you?"

Pausing, he looked at the phone on a nearby table.

"I could call Sheriff Coker. He's been saying you five are behind all the mischief that's been happening around town this summer, and other summers, for that matter. I'm sure he'd be glad to haul you over to the juvenile detention center in Dothan for the night. But then he'd have to turn around and haul you right back here tomorrow morning to be in my courtroom by nine o'clock, which doesn't seem fair to him, now, does it?"

The Judge got up and started pacing again.

"I could also call Mrs. Campbell and your aunt and uncle, wake them up out of a sound sleep, and have them come over here to see the mess you made of my property. I'm sure they'd call your parents and let them know about your illegal nocturnal activities, which would probably lead to some form of punishment and an early departure from Crystal Springs."

Sitting down again, the Judge added, "Or I suppose we could just save everybody but us a lot of time, trouble, and sleep and go ahead with a court session right here and now, since you all will end up in my courtroom tomorrow morning anyway."

Gesturing with open hands, he added, "We can just get on with what the law says is appropriate punishment for your misdeeds. What would you all think about that?"

My throat was so dry and my fear so deep, I could hardly breathe, much less speak. There was no sound coming from the others, either.

"Hearing no objections, let's get started." Sitting up straight, the Judge pulled the phone table in front of his chair and used his curved pipe to rap loudly on the top. Then, in a voice loud enough to wake the dead on Hardshell Hill, he boomed, "Hear ye! Hear ye! The lawful court of Geneva County, Alabama, is now in session, the Honorable Amos R. Thorton presiding. The good people of Crystal Springs and Geneva County, Alabama, have cause to bring charges of trespassing and vandalism of private property against the five minors currently before me. Since I am witness to the specifics of these crimes and actually caught the perpetrators in the act, I find they have no adequate defense and, therefore, are at the mercy of this court."

The Judge walked over and stood in front of J.D.

"How do you plead, son? Guilty or not guilty?"

J.D.'s voice was barely recognizable as he whispered, "Guilty, sir."

"And you?" he asked, stepping in front of Eric.

"Guilty, sir."

The Judge kept moving down the line until all of our confessions were on record; then he sat back down at his makeshift desk.

"Well, at least you're not trying to make excuses. There's something good to be said for that." Sighing, he banged his pipe on the table again. "I hereby find all of you guilty of trespassing with the intent of malevolent mischief. I also find each of you guilty of willfully vandalizing my porch, my shrubs, and, most importantly, my award-winning rosebushes. Do any of you have anything else to say before I sentence you for your crimes?"

I took a chance and glanced at J.D. out of the corner of my eye, hoping he would come up with something to save us.

J.D. looked at me and raised his hand.

"Sir . . . uh . . . we're really sorry. Not just about gettin' caught—"

"Yeah, really," interrupted Sam, slapping her hands over her mouth in an "I don't believe I actually said that out loud" motion.

J.D. shot her a dirty look and continued.

"We're really sorry for TP-in' your yard, sir, especially your roses. You worked hard on them, and we were wrong to mess them up. I talked the others into it, sir, and if anyone should be punished, it's me."

Leaning forward on his elbows, a skeptical look on his face, the Judge asked, "And I should believe this sudden declaration of remorse and acceptance of responsibility because . . . ?"

Dead silence.

"In the thirty years I've been on the bench, I've never met a criminal who wasn't sorry—not because he committed a crime, but because he got caught. Being sorry doesn't mean a thing, young man, unless it is motivated by sincere regret and concern for the victim, and right now I do not believe your concern, or the concern of your accomplices, is for me or any of the other victims of your long-running shenanigans. Nor do I believe your accomplices were unwilling participants. Sincere apologies are usually accompanied by a change in the behavior that caused the apology to be needed in the first place. Considering your history, I am not convinced your behavior, nor the behavior of your accomplices, will change just because you happened to get caught tonight."

You're wrong, Judge. We have *changed. We just didn't realize it until now.*

In desperation, J.D. tried one more time. "It was a stupid thing to do, sir, and I promise—we promise—we won't do it again. Not to you or anybody else . . . ever."

The Judge cocked his head to the side and raised his eyebrow.

"I understand you were also really sorry after the Salter Lee episode, but it seems being sorry then has not changed your tendency to cause trouble for innocent folks, now, has it?"

My heart hit the floor with a thud.

Good grief! How'd he know about Salter Lee? Think, Nettie. Think! If we're gonna get out of this mess, we've gotta come up with something quick! Something like . . . the truth. Oh, Lord, help me.

"Judge . . . sir?" I asked. "Have you ever made a choice you knew better than to make?"

The Judge's face went dark, and he squinted his eyes, but I pressed on.

"I don't mean any disrespect, sir. It's just, the way I figure it, folks don't change fast. And sometimes they make the same mistakes while they're workin' on trying to figure things out. We almost didn't come tonight, but you were the last one on the list, so we felt like we had to finish what we started, but we almost didn't come— really . . . almost."

Curiosity instantly replaced the look on the Judge's face.

"I see. And just where did this 'list' come from?"

Oh, God! I just gave up Ain't Pitty!

"Uh, we made the list, sir. We made it when we got here this summer." *So much for telling the truth.*

Coming to stand in front of me, the Judge asked, "And just how did you decide who was going to be placed on this list?"

"Well . . . we'd get ideas by walkin' around town, lookin' at different places."

"Hmm," muttered the Judge, rubbing his beard again. "No one ever put you up to doing this . . . TP-in', as you call it?"

"No, sir," said J.D., answering before I could. "No one ever told us to do any of it. I decided who we TP'ed and when."

Something in J.D.'s voice caught my attention. I admired the way he had jumped in to protect Ain't Pitty, but his voice did not make it sound like he was protecting someone who was guilty. He sounded like he was protecting someone who was innocent.

I had always assumed the annual TP-in' list came from Ain't Pitty, but thinking back now I realized I had never heard her mention it and had never actually heard any of the cussins say who created the list. If Ain't Pitty didn't do it, whoever did had to know why people were on the list and how to stock supplies in the front bedroom without being seen.

J.D.'s not protecting Ain't Pitty; he's confessing.

"And how did you decide who went on the list, young man?"

"Just like Nettie said, sir: I just walked around town and picked places that looked like good targets."

I knew J.D. wasn't telling the truth, and I understood why. People went on the list if they caused problems for Ain't Pitty. He loved her very much—we all did.

"Then what was the continued attraction to the house across the street from your aunt's? I understand vandalizing her home has become a summer tradition of yours."

J.D. swallowed hard. "Well, I guess 'cause she was close . . . sir."

"Right," said the Judge, going back to his seat. "You all should be ashamed of yourselves."

I am now. I just don't know why I wasn't before.

"You must have gone through a lot of toilet paper during the course of the summer. Where did you get it? Did you buy it?"

"No, sir. We borrowed—uh, snuck—it from our aunt's house, sir."

Looking skeptical, the Judge pressed harder. "No one ever noticed all that toilet paper was missing?"

"Well, sir, our uncle brings cases of it in from Rucks—Fort Rucker, sir—and I guess when there's nine people livin' in a house with one bathroom, no one questions the amount of toilet paper bein' used."

"I see your point." The Judge chuckled. "I believe I understand now. And while I do not know why and how it all began, I do know where and when it will end. It ends here and now." Looking at us over the rim of his glasses, he added, "Do you understand your days of conducting similar activities in or around Crystal Springs and Geneva County are over?"

"Yes, sir."

Leaning back in his chair, the Judge began to look concerned.

"It's dangerous for children to be wandering the streets at night unsupervised. Bad things can happen when those who care about you are not watching. Can you imagine what your families would go through if something bad happened to you?" The Judge got up and walked over to the window. "You all should consider yourselves lucky you were caught by somebody who was not intent on causing you harm."

I wasn't sure how he'd gotten to the part about considering ourselves lucky, but I was not there yet. In fact, I considered us pretty unlucky to have gotten caught on our last, probably forever, TP-in'.

"Some children are not as lucky," continued the Judge, looking through his reflection.

"Judge, are you talkin' about the little girl from Samson? Did they find her?" asked J.D.

The Judge turned around quickly. "No, they haven't. Do you know something about her?"

"No, sir. Well, at least I don't think I do, sir. But there've been some 'spicious things goin' on over the past few weeks. Stuff you and Sheriff Coker might want to know about."

"Explain yourself, son."

Taking a deep breath and leaving very little out, J.D. told the Judge what had happened the night we TP'ed the Crossing and saw the truck pull up in front of Wilkes's.

"Could you all tell who the third person in the front seat was? Who was sitting in the middle?" the Judge asked intently.

"No, sir. We were hidin' in the hedge next to the post office and couldn't see over the hood, but the hair color was light."

"Could you tell if it was a girl or a boy?"

"No, sir."

"Hmm. And you're sure it was Ames and Pierce in the truck?"

"Yes, sir, I'm sure. We've seen them around a lot this summer. There was also someone in the back of the truck. We couldn't tell who it was, but he was really big."

"Digger Wilkes said the same thing. He called the Sheriff that night and said he saw the truck pull up and that there might have been a little girl inside. The deputies could not find the men or the truck that night, but the Sheriff increased the number of patrols around Crystal Springs and out Choctaw Road where the men live."

Good ol' Mr. Digger. He called the Sheriff about those men but not about us.

"Those men are scary, sir."

"Yes, son, they are."

I could see J.D. relax a little as he went on to explain how we found the boot prints on the beach at Sandy Bottom Creek and followed the path to the old ice house.

"We could tell somebody'd been in there," he added, describing the cot, the brown jug, the child's t-shirt, and the lantern.

"We floated Sandy Bottom Creek today and went by there again."

"Yes. I saw you."

"That was you? I thought so," said Sam, surprised again that she had spoken out loud.

"Yes. The Sheriff and I have been keeping an eye on that ice house for a while now. Did you all see who was there this afternoon?"

"Yes, sir. We saw Otis Pierce and a man named Gris. He's a big, cinnamon-colored fellow, Judge. And he carries a really big knife, a machete. I think he might've been the one in the back of the truck at Wilkes's that night, but I can't be sure."

The Judge's face looked even more troubled.

"I see. I trust you all will never go anywhere near that ice house again?"

"Yes, sir."

Mitchell shouldn't be around the ice house or those men, either.

"Judge?" I asked. "Are you gonna put those men in jail?"

"Well, young lady, before I can put people in jail, I have to have proof they've broken the law, and sometimes that kind of proof is hard to come by."

"It would be really good if you could."

"And why is that?"

"Well, sir, Ames's boy, Mitchell, is a friend of ours. He's a good guy, and I know he's not involved in anythin' bad, even if his pa is. His pa hurts him, Judge, a lot."

"I know about Mitchell. I knew his mother. She was a good woman, and I'm glad you all have befriended the boy." Pausing, the Judge cleared his throat. "Have you actually seen his father or any of the other men hurting Mitchell in any way?"

"No, sir."

"Has Mitchell ever told you his father or any of the other men hurt him?"

"No, sir."

"Therein lies the proof I need to act. If Mitchell will come to Sheriff Coker or me—or any adult, for that matter—and tell us what's going on, we can help him, but until then, it's hearsay."

We have to get Mitchell to talk.

"Is there anything else you all can tell me, or do I have it all?"

"No, sir. I think that's 'bout it," replied J.D.

"Well, then let's see if we can bring this . . . uh, trial to a close."

The Judge sentenced us to be back at his house at eight o'clock the next morning, and we were not to leave until we had picked up every piece of toilet paper in his yard and his rosebushes looked as good or better than they had before we'd taken liberties with them. Then he escorted us out his front door and watched from the porch until we reached Ain't Pitty's.

Once we were out of earshot, we all started talking at once.

"Holy cow, Nettie!" said Sam. "I thought he'd killed you! He came around the house carryin' you like a dead rag doll. You were so pale and limp. I was so scared, I couldn't even run."

"Yeah," added J.D., "we were all scared. He carried you up the front steps and said if we didn't follow him into the house right then, there would be hell to pay."

"I'm so sorry! I never saw him comin' until he grabbed my arm. I've never been so scared in my life, and I don't remember a thing until I woke up in his house."

"Don't feel bad, Nettie," said Eric. "I have a feelin' we would've gotten caught anyway. I think you just happened to be the first one he got to."

J.D. looked back at the Judge's house.

"You know, we forgot the carport on the first TP-in', the floodlight on the second one, and now this. What did we forget?"

No one answered, but the looks on our faces made it clear that we were all thinking the same thing.

We didn't forget anything. We made the wrong choice. We should've listened to our better angels. They tried to tell us not to do it, but we didn't listen. Now, here in the dark, our lesser angels are having a good laugh.

As we reached Ain't Pitty's porch, a hot wind started blowing and jagged lightning shot across the sky. We could see a stacked-up, black-on-black thunderhead rimmed with pink-tinged heat lightning and jagged, up, down, and sideways lightning flashing inside the cloud all at the same time.

"Wow!" said Eric. "That's either the most amazing thing I've ever seen or the scariest. And it's heading our way."

"Well, that's just great!" snapped J.D. "Now we get to pick wet, windblown toilet paper off those damn sticky rosebushes tomorrow."

"Looks like we're getting a dose of our own medicine," I said.

"And we'll consider ourselves lucky to have the chance, huh?" prompted Eric, reminding us to be grateful we were not on our way to the detention center.

"Lucky? Are you kiddin'?" snapped J.D.

"No, I'm not kiddin'. We're damn lucky."

"Well, if we are, luck sure has a strange sense of humor."

"It's gonna be a long day tomorrow. Maybe this storm will cool things off enough so we can get some sleep," said Sam.

Strong gusts of wind started whipping tree limbs in different directions at the same time, and the almost-constant lightning was turning night to day.

"C'mon, y'all," I said. "We need to get inside. This one's gonna be bad."

Going in last, I hooked the screen door and shivered all the way to my toes, not because of the storm, but because I sensed something even worse was coming.

The next morning, we ate breakfast in silence, hoping to avoid a conversation with Ain't Pitty about the Judge for as long as possible, but as we finished eating, the phone rang.

Uh-oh! Nobody calls this early.

When Ain't Pitty came back from answering it, she looked upset.

"Something important has come up that I need to go see about. I'm gonna drop Li'l Bit and Sharon off at Granny's. The rest of y'all stay together and stay in town until I get back."

"Yes, ma'am."

Look at her face! That call had to be from the Judge!

We watched from the kitchen window as Ain't Pitty and the little ones climbed into Jigger.

"We're in such trouble," said Sam.

"Well, now's a hell of a time to figure that out," snapped J.D.

"Let's just hope she doesn't tell Granny. She'd tell Momma for sure," added Eric.

Gathering garden baskets, we headed to the Judge's house. As expected, the storm had shredded the multiple layers of toilet paper into soggy slivers that tore into even smaller slivers when touched. The rose garden was especially bad because the thorns caught the slivers and held on to them like prisoners. In the interest of self-preservation, we decided to work on the roses together, especially since the Judge was standing in the window, watching us and drinking his morning coffee.

We worked quickly and quietly until his car pulled out of the driveway and headed for what we assumed was the courthouse. Most likely he would be there until evening, so as soon as he was out of sight, we slowed our pace.

The sun was high and hot as hell before we had the rose garden back to normal.

"C'mon, y'all," said J.D. "Let's go get some water and something to eat. I'm parched."

Making a quick run back down the Railroad, we drank a full pitcher of tea and gobbled up last night's leftovers. Thankfully, Ain't Pitty was not back, so there was no explaining to do . . . yet.

The afternoon was sweltering hot and our backs were aching by the time we pulled the last bits of shredded toilet paper from the shrubs. As if on cue, the Judge pulled into the driveway just as we stood to stretch.

Without saying a word, he made his way to the front of the house and motioned for us to sit on the steps. He then began a slow examination of each tree, bush, and piece of furniture from the front, back, and sides. Saving the rose garden for last, he disappeared around the corner of the house. When he finally returned, he looked at our scratched and bloodied hands and arms.

"Well, was it worth it?"

"No, sir," we replied in unison.

"Good. Then go and sin no more."

I was not sure why he chose to use the same line Pastor Flemming used on Sunday mornings, but I was positive I would never hear those words again and not think about my thorn-cut fingers and stinging arms.

As we got up, the Judge added, "By the way, I need to talk with your aunt and uncle this evening. I'll be there about eight o'clock, and it would be better if you all were not there."

Uh-oh!

"Yes, sir."

As soon as the Judge closed his front door, we headed for the Railroad.

"Damnation!" snapped J.D. "You'd think after we gave him all that information and spent the day from hell cleanin' his yard it would be enough! Why's he gotta tell Ain't Pitty and Uncle Ben?"

"We should've expected it," said Eric. "He *is* the Judge, after all. He has to tell somebody."

"If I didn't have to, I'd never touch another piece of toilet paper again," whined Sandra.

"Nothing like a constant reminder that we screwed up," agreed Sam.

Reaching the patio, I was disappointed to see it empty.

"Mitchell's usually here by now. He must have had to work late."

I tried not to let the disappointment show through, but seeing him would have been the only good part of a really bad day.

"Well, it's just as well," said Eric. "He doesn't need to be caught up in all this mess. He has enough to deal with."

We could see Ain't Pitty in the kitchen, fixing dinner, and the little ones were in the garden. Bracing for the worst, we rinsed off the blood and dirt and went inside.

"Y'all set the table, please," said Ain't Pitty, looking distracted.

Giving us a quizzical look, J.D. shrugged his shoulders. If she knew, she was not letting on, so there was little for us to do but wait.

Dinner was quiet, too. Both Ain't Pitty and Uncle Ben looked as if something was on their minds, but neither was talking. On the counter I noticed a tray with a pitcher of fresh lemonade and four of Ain't Pitty's good glasses.

She's expecting company; gotta be the Judge. Wonder who the fourth glass is for.

When the dishes were done, Ain't Pitty sent Li'l Bit and Sharon to the chicken coop and us to Granny's with a basket of vegetables.

"Don't go wanderin' around, y'all," she called through the kitchen window. "Stay at Granny's until I call for you."

"Yes, ma'am."

The evening air was hot and sticky as we made our way up the Railroad, but at least the sun was not beating down on us anymore. There was no sign of the Judge as we passed his house and now-spotless yard.

"Maybe he changed his mind," said Eric.

"Naw," said J.D. "He'll be there. The big question is what's gonna happen to us once he tells Ain't Pitty and Uncle Ben. They're not gonna be able to let this slide."

Eric's going to military school, and we're going home—that's what's gonna happen.

Granny was at the kitchen sink, washing her supper dishes, when we walked in.

"I was wonderin' when y'all were gonna show up."

Something in her tone of voice made us stop.

"Uh, just thought we'd stop by," said J.D.

"And bring you some vegetables," added Sam.

"And here I was, thinkin' y'all'd come to tell me about spendin' the day cleanin' up your mess in the Judge's yard."

Oh, hell!

Any remaining hope of getting out of this mess without Granny's knowing left us like air escaping a pinpricked balloon. Now, there was nothing left to do but fry in the heat of her stare.

"How did you find out, Granny?" croaked Eric.

"It's none of your business how I found out. Sit down."

Why in the world had we been dumb enough to think she and others would not find out? The whole damn town went up and down the Railroad, so by now what we had done and the fact we had gotten caught were probably welcome gossip fodder.

"Did you call Momma?"

"No. I've not called her . . . yet."

"Are you gonna send us home?"

"I could, and, if the truth be known, I should. For smart young'uns, this was a really stupid thing to do! Especially after all the other stupid stuff y'all've pulled. Did you really think we wouldn't find out? What in the world possessed you to do such a fool thing?"

Because we're dumber than a box of rocks, that's why. We knew better! And did it anyway.

Granny was really worked up now and was not bothering to wait for answers. "The Judge, for heaven's sake! With Sheriff Coker just waitin' to catch y'all pullin' another dumb stunt. Messing with the Judge's yard makes it look like y'all were tauntin' him, the Sheriff, and everybody else in town!"

It was rare to see Granny angry, and she was angrier now than I had even seen.

"I'm surprised the Judge didn't call the Sheriff and have him—"

Stopping mid-sentence, she looked at our badly scratched-up hands and arms.

"Do those hurt?"

"Yes, ma'am."

"Good. I'm glad! Pain is a wicked but effective teacher."

Any sliver of hope for sympathy went out the window with those stinging words.

"The only reason the Judge didn't have you all hauled to Dothan is he saw a speck of good in you. Heaven knows how, but he did. Otherwise Pitty, Ben, and I would've been sittin' at the courthouse all mornin'."

Looking desperate, J.D. started, "Granny, we—"

"Hush up! I'm not done."

Lord! She's not taking prisoners.

"I really thought y'all would've stopped all this nonsense after you got Salter Lee hurt. You got lucky then, not because you deserved it, but because we thought you'd learned a lesson. Well, you didn't, and now your lucky streak is over." Looking right at J.D., she warned, "Pull another stupid stunt like this, and you're goin' home and your summer vacations in Crystal Springs will end. Understood?"

"Yes, ma'am."

"Now, what do you have to say for yourselves?"

"Granny, we shoulda . . . uh . . . coulda . . . ," stammered J.D.

Granny put her hand up. "Stop. All the 'shoulda, coulda, wouldas' serve no purpose now."

"What?"

"You did what you did, and all the 'shoulda, coulda, wouldas' in the world can't undo it. They're just words of regret at getting caught."

Salter Lee said the same thing.

"Regret doesn't make a wrong right; it just says you knew better than to do what you did. If you all had thought about the 'shoulda, coulda, wouldas' before you acted so stupidly, regret would have no place to land now."

There was nothing to say. Granny was right, but only partially. We had thought about the "shoulda, coulda, wouldas" for everything we had done. But it had been through our eyes and not those of the folks we were targeting.

"Granny," asked Eric, "why'd you decide not to call Momma?"

Granny's shoulders slumped as she answered.

"Because Crystal Springs is a good place to learn the 'shoulda, coulda, woulda' lessons, and you don't have many summers left to learn them. It's a much better place than the military . . . school."

Military! She doesn't want Eric going to military school. She lost one son to war and doesn't want to lose a grandson the same way.

Looking into her eyes, I realized how painful it must be for her to hear the choppers go over day and night, knowing there were sons in them who would never see their mothers again.

Granny got up and reached for a plate sitting on the counter. Removing the waxed paper, she sat fresh divinity on the table.

"Now, y'all have three weeks before your folks get here to take you home. I suggest you mend as many fences in that time as you can, and I'll be watchin'."

Home.

Granny had just given us the first reminder that Labor Day, which marked the end of our summer in Crystal Springs, would soon be here. It was the crowning blow to a pitiful day.

Getting up from the table, we headed for the comfort of Granny's front porch to wait for Ain't Pitty to call. Leaving the kitchen, I saw a long-stemmed red rose sitting in a vase in the window.

Chapter 17

Daylight was fading as we settled in on the porch after Granny's tongue-lashing. The bugs were getting active, and we could smell fresh-cut grass, which meant Jessie was nearby.

"Did y'all see the rose in Granny's kitchen window?" I asked. "It's one of the Judge's."

"Granny never has roses in her window," shot back J.D., looking startled.

"Well, she does now."

"Okay, so she does. How do you know it's one of his?"

"Really? Are you kiddin'? Who knows those damn roses better'n me?"

"Oh, gross!" groaned Eric, covering his eyes.

I assumed he didn't like the mental image he was getting.

"I think it's sweet!" giggled Sam.

We all looked at her as if she had grown three heads.

"What? Maybe he's sweet on Granny, and maybe that's why we're not sittin' in Dothan right now."

"Hmm. Good point," I replied.

"Well," cautioned J.D., "we've got a bigger issue to deal with than the Judge givin' Granny a rose. If he is the one who told Granny what we did, then why does he still need to talk with Ain't Pitty and Uncle Ben?"

Staring at the giant mophead hydrangea next to me, I got a sinking feeling.

"Oh, gosh! What if he still thinks Ain't Pitty was involved with the TP-in'? Remember? He asked if anybody put us up to it. That would explain why he wants to talk to her and why she and Uncle Ben were so quiet at supper. I think we got Ain't Pitty in big trouble."

"Good grief! Can this thing get any more screwed up?" complained J.D.

"Well, we've gotta do somethin'," said Eric. "We can't just let it happen."

"Eric's right," added Sandra. "There's gotta be a way we can get Ain't Pitty off the hook without gettin' ourselves in more trouble."

"Maybe," said Sam. "But the bottom line is, we are, and maybe she is, too, and there may not be anythin' we can do about it."

Eric slid to the edge of his seat and rubbed his face with both hands.

"Look, we chose to do it. And it really doesn't matter if Ain't Pitty knew or not. But Sam's right—the Judge knows it was us, and, based on what he said last night, he may think Ain't Pitty's involved. Maybe we should just go down there and tell him again that she wasn't."

J.D. got up and started pacing.

"You're right, at least partly. I think we need to go down there and at least listen to what the Judge has to say. If he blames Ain't Pitty, we'll have to step up."

"We can't," cautioned Sam. "The Judge told us not to be there."

"Well, what the Judge doesn't know won't hurt 'im."

"What?"

"Stay calm, everybody! We can sneak down there and listen to what they're sayin'. If Ain't Pitty isn't in trouble, we'll leave and the Judge will never know we were there. But if she is in trouble, we'll have to take our chances and talk with 'im."

"How are we gonna know where they're meetin'?" asked Sandra.

"We'll have to sneak down there and take a look. If they're on the front porch or the patio, we can hear them without a problem. If they're in the kitchen, we're gonna have to stand under the rollouts and hope we can hear enough to know what's goin' on. If they're in the livin' room, I can sneak into the front bedroom and listen from the passageway."

Hearing no argument, J.D. was off the porch in two strides and we were on his heels. Reaching Miz Sadie's backyard, we slipped past her clothesline and stopped at the back of the storage shed. We did not have to wait long to know where Ain't Pitty and the Judge were meeting—we could hear voices on the patio.

Motioning for us to be quiet, J.D. and Eric gave us a leg up onto the low end of the shed's slanted roof and then pulled themselves up. Once on our knees, we inched our way to the top. As our eyes popped over the edge, we looked through the branches of the oak tree and could see Ain't Pitty, Uncle Ben, the Judge, and Sheriff Coker sitting at the picnic table.

"Oh, gosh!" whispered Sandra. "They're gonna put her in jail!"

"Be quiet or get down!" J.D. hissed under his breath.

Straining to hear, I could make out only a few words—such as "night," "trouble," and "danger"—and I could have sworn I heard one of them say "Mitchell."

As it got dark, Ain't Pitty got up and turned on the outside light, flooding the patio, the shed's roofline, and our eyes with light. If the folks at the picnic table happened to look up, they might be able to see us through the leaves. J.D. motioned for us to back up, so we began a slow crawl away from the edge.

The work of the day had been long and hard, and after being in one position for so long, our muscles were not going backward easily. Suddenly, a loud, rough whooshing sound came from where Sandra had been. We looked just in time to see her pigtails fly over the lower edge of the roof. Then there was a thud and a long, low moan.

"Quick!" hissed J.D. "Run!"

We scrambled off the roof, gathered up Sandra, and started a frantic run through the dark shadows of Miz Sadie's backyard.

What happened next, we could only watch in slow motion. J.D., his long legs putting him a full stride ahead of the rest of us, ran blindly into Miz Sadie's clothesline. The thin rope caught him right across the neck and stretched three feet in the direction he was running. Then, like a slingshot, the line snapped back, lifting J.D. off his feet and sending him flying backward into a dark blob on the ground. We could hear him groan as air was forced unwillingly out of his lungs.

"C'mon, Nettie! Help me!" snapped Eric.

We flew back to the blob and each grabbed a limp arm, pulling J.D. to his feet and into a dead run at the same time. We just made it to the far corner of Miz Sadie's house as the four from the patio came around the lean-to. Not waiting to see if they were still coming, we kept going at an all-out run, even though the noises coming from J.D. as he tried to breathe and run at the same time were like nothing I'd ever heard.

Finally reaching Granny's porch, we helped J.D. to the glider. His skin was pale, his eyes teary, and his chest heaving out as much as his stomach was heaving in.

"Well, so much for that bright idea!" Sam gasped.

We could hear the phone start ringing inside.

"It's gotta be Ain't Pitty," I said. "Quick, sit down."

We scurried to find seats as the front porch light came on and Granny came out.

"Good, you're here." Turning to go back inside, she added, "If J.D.'s not breathin' right in a few minutes, come get me. And just so you know, y'all are spending the night with me."

As the door closed and the light went off, we let out a collective sigh across the porch.

"Is nothin' gonna go right?" Eric whined. "How could she tell? She can't even see that well!"

"I have no idea," I replied, getting up to check on J.D., who was lying back against the cushions, his skin clammy but warm.

"Are you okay?"

"Am I bleedin'?" he asked in a pitiful, frog-like voice.

"I don't think so, but I can't see very well. It's too dark."

"Wait a minute," said Eric. "I saw a pack of matches on the table."

As the match head flared to life, Eric lit a nearby citronella candle.

"I don't see any blood, but you've got a big red welt goin' from ear to ear."

"That's gotta hurt," said Sam, wincing. "You want an aspirin or somethin'? We're out of Bactine, but we can get some goo from Ain't Pitty's aloe vera plant to put on it. There's not much that stuff can't fix."

"Huh-uh. I don't want anybody else knowin' about this." Fingering the welt, he added, "I think I left my head back at Miz Sadie's."

"No, it's still attached, and you'll be happy to know you're three inches taller now than you were just a little while ago," Eric quipped.

J.D. managed a little laugh and sat up. "This thing feels like a rope! If anybody sees it, they'll know I was on that fool roof!"

"With the way our luck's been runnin', what makes you think they don't already know?"

"True. But they don't know I almost hung myself! How the hell am I gonna hide this?"

"I've got a blue bandanna you can tie around your neck like a sweatband," offered Sam. "I'll sneak down to Ain't Pitty's and get—"

"I'll be damned! I'm not wearin' some sissy scarf!"

"Suit yourself."

"After all this, we still don't know exactly what they were talkin' 'bout," Eric said. "But whatever it was, it didn't sound like Ain't Pitty was in trouble—or us, either, for that matter."

"It didn't, did it?" agreed J.D.

"Maybe Granny was wrong. Maybe there's still a little bit of luck runnin' our way."

As J.D. recovered, we resigned ourselves to spending the rest of the evening on Granny's porch.

"Look, Jessie's in his tree chair," said Sandra.

We couldn't see his face, but we could see his shadow leaning back in the cup of the old tree.

"Looks like we're not the only ones spending the evening watching the cars go up and down the road," J.D. grumbled.

"I still think he's watchin' us."

"So? He's not hurtin' anythin'."

It wasn't long before we heard a souped-up car coming around the bend with the radio blaring. John Thomas was driving, and Cilly was all but sitting in his lap. As they passed by, we saw their middle fingers sticking through the open window.

"Jackasses," snapped Eric.

"Yeah," agreed Sam. "But you gotta feel sorry for 'em. I'm just not sure which one to feel sorrier for."

"Like deserves like, and those two are definitely alike," I said, as another set of headlights flashed across the porch.

"That's Ol' Man Ames's truck," said J.D., sitting up higher.

We could see Mitchell's pa in the driver's seat and Otis Pierce beside him. Stopping the truck in front of Granny's, they stared at the porch.

"Uh-oh," I said.

"Wonder what the hell they want," Eric added.

"I don't know," said J.D., jumping up, "but I'm gonna find out! I'm sick 'n' tired of those bastards causing problems, and tonight is not the night to mess with me!"

Damn! He's going after them!

"J.D., stop!"

"Don't do it!" yelled Eric, as he made a grab for J.D.'s arm and missed.

With no choice but to follow, we headed across the yard.

Mitchell's pa saw us running toward them and started laughing. Then he hit the gas and the old truck lurched down the street.

"Come back here, you son of a bitch!" J.D. yelled after the truck.

"Just what the hell would you do if they did?" snapped Eric.

"I don't know . . . somethin'."

"Yeah, somethin' stupid. That hangin' musta made you crazy. Those men can hurt us, J.D., and I mean *really* hurt us. We're already on their radar, and now you go and pull somethin' stupid like this."

Turning back toward Granny's, we saw Jessie standing by the road.

"He must think we're crazy," muttered Sam.

"He knows who the crazy ones are, and it's not us," said J.D.

"We've gotta tell somebody about this, y'all," I said.

"What're we gonna tell 'em, Nettie?" countered Eric. "That we saw creepy men drivin' up the street? That's not against the law. And we were the ones runnin' after them, not the other way around."

"I know, but I bet Ain't Pitty or the Judge would wanna know they're comin' around here."

"Not yet," said J.D. "The last thing we want to do is make things worse for Mitchell, and if we call the law on his pa, Mitchell will pay the price."

"Gosh, you're right. I hadn't thought about it like that."

He's got trouble if we do and if we don't!

It wasn't long before the Field 10 choppers crossed over and Granny called us inside. The rule at her house was that when she went to bed, so did we, or at least we pretended to.

When we were sure Granny was asleep, we closed the bedroom door and Sam and J.D. slipped out the back window. They were going to sneak down to Ain't Pitty's to get a piece of her aloe vera plant for J.D.'s neck and find Sam's blue bandanna, which J.D. finally admitted he was going to need if his hanging was to remain a secret.

It was a long time before they climbed back in the window, and their faces said something was wrong.

"What is it?" asked Eric.

"Ames and Pierce were sittin' across the street from Ain't Pitty's with their headlights off, that's what. Sam and I stayed in the shadows, so they didn't see us, but we sure as hell saw them."

"What do you think they wanted?" I asked.

"Hell if I know, but I'm sure it wasn't a social call. They took off when one of the Sheriff's deputies drove up the street."

"Thank goodness he was pat—. Wait a minute. They never patrol the Railroad this time of night. Wonder wh—"

"Sam thought it was Danny."

"Ah, that explains it."

"Well, whatever the reason, I'm glad he was there," said Sam.

"Me too," said J.D. "Anyway, when the coast was clear, we snuck into Ain't Pitty's and made sure all the doors were locked and got our stuff."

"You didn't tell Ain't Pitty and Uncle Ben what happened?"

"Not yet. They would've wanted to know what we were doing down there in the middle of the night. Besides, those ol' men aren't stupid enough to come back. The deputy saw them and is patrolling the area."

"Still, Ain't Pitty and Uncle Ben need to know."

"I know they do. We've just gotta figure out what to say and who to say it to so nobody gets hurt."

J.D. went to the bathroom to put the magic goo on his neck while the rest of us climbed into bed, dirty clothes, dirty faces, and all. It had been an exhausting day.

We were sleeping so soundly the next morning, Granny had to call us to breakfast. But when she saw our smudged faces and dirty, slept-in clothes, she made us go clean up before we could sit at her table.

When we returned to the kitchen, Granny eyed the bandanna around J.D.'s neck. It looked funny, but it covered the welt. Pulling her medicine basket out of the cabinet, she poured two aspirin and laid them down by J.D.'s plate.

We were on our second helping of biscuits and sausage when Ain't Pitty arrived. The look on her face said last night's meeting with Sheriff Coker and the Judge had not gone well. I braced for bad news as she poured herself a cup of coffee and sat down.

"The phone call I got yesterday morning was from Sheriff Coker. He said Mitchell was at Doc Anderson's and that he'd been beaten . . . badly."

A gasp went up from the table.

"Mitchell told the Sheriff that it was too dark for him to see who did it, but he managed to get away from whoever it was and run. Danny, Sheriff Coker's deputy, found him on Choctaw Road, tryin' to make it to town in the middle of a bad storm. He's the one who took Mitchell to Doc Anderson's."

Thank God they were patrolling that road!

"Is he okay?" I asked.

"He's hurt, but Doc says he'll be all right."

"Thank God!"

"Even though Mitchell says he doesn't know who did it, Sheriff Coker thinks his pa and Otis Pierce were involved, so he's not letting Mitchell go home . . . yet."

"Good!" said J.D.

"Sheriff Coker brought Ames and Pierce in for questioning, but they denied knowing anythin' about the beatin' and insisted

Mitchell be released, but Sheriff Coker refused. They left angry, and the Sheriff thinks they're likely to cause trouble."

That's what they were doing here last night.

"Mitchell also wouldn't settle down until the Sheriff called me to make sure y'all were okay. Seems like he thought the same folks who hurt him might try to hurt y'all as well, but he wouldn't say who and he wouldn't say why." Scanning our faces, she added, "If Mitchell's pa and Otis Pierce are the ones who did this, why would they want to hurt y'all?"

Hurt us? Why? What did we do? Dummy! What did Mitchell ever do to deserve all the hurt he's been through? Those crazy men don't need a reason to hurt.

"I don't know why they'd want to hurt us, Ain't Pitty," replied J.D. "I really don't. But we saw 'em last night . . . Ames and Pierce . . . we saw 'em."

J.D. explained that we had seen Ames's truck stop in front of Granny's and that he and Sam had seen the same truck sitting across the street from her house a little while later.

"Danny Grimes came by on patrol and scared 'em off."

"They must have been lookin' for Mitchell," said Ain't Pitty. "The Sheriff needs to know about this." Then she asked the question I figured she already knew the answer to: "If y'all were supposed to be here, how did you know those men were sitting in front of my house?"

J.D. slowly untied the bandanna around his neck to reveal the welt and proceeded to tell Ain't Pitty and Granny about our eavesdropping on the shed roof, his near hangin', and the trip back to Ain't Pitty's to get some aloe vera goo and the bandanna.

"We figured it was y'all on the roof."

"We just wanted to know what the Judge was gonna say, Ain't Pitty."

"I see. And it didn't matter that the Judge said for y'all not to be there and that I told you to stay at Granny's until I called you?"

"Yes, ma'am, it mattered. We were just worried about . . ."

"About what?"

"About you."

"Me? Why me?"

"Uh . . ."

"Because we were afraid that you were gonna be in trouble for what we did," I explained. "If you were, we were gonna tell the Judge it was all our fault, which it was. If you weren't, we were gonna just sneak back to Granny's."

"I see."

"Well, at least you're not trying to make excuses," said Granny. "There's something good to be said for that."

That's what the Judge said.

"Do you realize how dangerous it was for you to be out there in the middle of the night with those no-good men prowling around?" asked Ain't Pitty.

"Yes, ma'am."

"Don't do it or anythin' like it again. You could have been hurt, or worse. The Sheriff and his men are keepin' a close eye on things around here now, but no more runnin' around at night, and y'all stick close to home during the day. If you want to go someplace out of town, even the lake, I go with you."

"Yes, ma'am."

"Ain't Pitty, where's Mitchell?"

"He's stayin' at Pastor Flemming's for now and wants y'all to come over." As we scrambled to get up, she added, "Don't wear the boy out—he's been through a lot. Stay together, stay in town, and be home by suppertime. Li'l Bit and Sharon are stayin' with me today."

The meeting at Ain't Pitty's last night wasn't about us at all. It was about Mitchell's getting the hell beat out of him.

We ran all the way to Pastor Flemming's house and sprinted up the sidewalk. Mitchell and the Pastor were sitting on the front porch, drinking coffee.

"And a good morning to you all!" boomed the Pastor.

All we could do was stare at Mitchell, who was looking back at us through one black eye and one that was almost swollen shut. There were also cuts and bruises on his face, neck, arms, and legs. I had never seen anyone who had been beaten before.

There's gotta be cuts and bruises we can't even see.

"I don't understand, Pastor. What part of this is good?" I asked.

"This part."

"How? How is it good?"

"Because Mitchell is safe now. And he's with folks who care about him."

But look at the price he paid!

"You all have a seat," said Pastor Flemming as he stood up. "I think Mitchell is more than ready to spend some time with folks his own age. Mitchell, I'm going to walk over to the church office for a while. You take it easy and you all stay together, either here or at Mrs. Miller's or Mrs. Campbell's. Just let me know where you are and if you need anything. You know where I am."

"Damn, Mitchell, you look awful," said Eric, as the Pastor headed down the sidewalk.

"Gee, thanks."

"Are you hurtin'?" I asked, sitting down beside him.

"Some, but I just got a lot better. Nothin's broken, just bruised and sore."

Then, in front of God and everybody, Mitchell picked up my hand and held it.

"Mitchell, who did this?" asked J.D.

"I'm not sure. It was dark. I couldn't see."

"How many were there?" asked Eric.

"Two or three."

"Did they say anythin'?"

"Yeah," said Mitchell, shuddering. "They said for me to make sure my friends stayed away from the ice house, or they'd get hurt, too."

They saw us! That's why he was beaten up. That's why those men were in town last night. They weren't looking for Mitchell; they were looking for us!

J.D.'s knees buckled as he grabbed the arm of the rocker to sit down.

"I told them I didn't know what they were talkin' about, but they didn't believe me. They said they'd found footprints around the buildin' and driveway a while back and that they saw us in the field near the creek the day of the float. They said they were gonna teach me a lesson about mindin' my own business and send y'all a message at the same time; then they just started swingin' and kickin'. It's a good thing they were drunk, because they had a hard time stayin' on their feet. I managed to run away while they were stumblin' around and hid in the woods along Choctaw Road. They drove back and forth a long time lookin' for me, but when that bad storm hit, they gave up and left. I was almost to the Railroad when Danny found me. He took me to Doc Anderson's."

"Mitchell, did your pa and Otis Pierce do this?" I asked.

"It was dark. I don't know who it was."

"That's bullshit and you know it, Mitchell. Who else could it have been?" Eric snapped. "Otis Pierce and the Cajun were the only ones who could have seen us in the field that day. You have to tell the Sheriff it was them."

Mitchell shook his head, conflict written all over his face.

"Then we'll tell him."

"No! You can't say anythin'! I told you! I don't know who it was. Y'all need to stay out of it and stay away from the ice house. Whoever it was, they'll hurt you and those you care about if you don't!"

"But, Mitchell, we—"

"No. You don't understand. Just stay out of it! Please!"

I shivered. There was real fear in Mitchell's eyes. Not for himself, but for us.

"Okay, okay. Stay calm. It's not good for you to be upset now."

"Look," I said, "we may not need to say anythin', at least right now. From what Ain't Pitty said, the Sheriff already thinks your pa and Otis Pierce were involved, so he may keep you from havin' to go back to your pa anyway."

"Please," Mitchell begged. "Just don't say anythin'. You don't know what they can do. Promise me. Please promise me."

Looking around at the rest of us for agreement, Eric said, "We promise, at least for now."

"Good."

J.D., who had been surprisingly quiet, leaned forward. "Mitchell, I'm sorry, so sorry. You told us not to go to the ice house, and I pushed you into it. I caused this."

I knew what the word "devastated" meant, but I hadn't known what it looked like until now. The look on J.D.'s face tore at my heart.

"No! No, you didn't," insisted Mitchell. "Nobody made me go anywhere. I made the decision, nobody else. This wasn't the first beatin' I've had, and it won't be the last. Men who do this don't need a reason to hurt people. That's what they do. That's all they know how to do. But at least this time I had someplace to go and someone to go to, and you have no idea what that meant to me."

"But I should've listened. This happened because I didn't, and I'm sorry. Sorrier than you'll ever know. I'm not sure I even knew the meaning of the word until now."

"Well, that's one apology you can just keep, because this beating has given me a way out."

Over the next few days, we did not hear much, except that Sheriff Coker brought Mitchell's pa and Otis Pierce in for more questioning. The two men continued to deny knowing anything about the beating, and without positive identification, the Sheriff had to release them. Danny had even come to see Mitchell twice, asking if he could remember anything at all about who had hurt him, and each time Mitchell had said no.

We did not understand his decision but were glad he was finally away from his pa and the others and tried to keep his mind occupied with happier things. During the day, we took him to some of our favorite swimming places, including a spot near Geneva where the Choctawhatchee and Pea rivers merged. At the fork was a big tree with a knotted rope hanging from one of its limbs that we used to swing out over the river. After dropping into the water, we'd let the current carry us down to a nearby boat ramp where it was easy to climb out.

Walking back to the fork with Mitchell, I touched one of his fading bruises.

"They're almost gone."

"Yeah. They don't hurt anymore. I've been rubbin' vinegar on 'em. Momma always said it helped bruises fade faster."

"Ain't Pitty says you're a lot like your momma."

"She did? Good—I'm glad. Pa always said Momma was no good and that I should forget about her. But he's wrong. I try to do something she taught me to do every day. That way, I'll always remember her."

"Ahh, like keeping a handkerchief with you all the time and using vinegar on bruises?"

"Yep."

"What else did she teach you?"

"Well, she taught me to choose happy."

"What?"

"She said life was about choices, and that you can choose to be angry and unhappy all the time or you can choose to be happy. She told me to always choose happy. No matter what."

"Choose happy. I like that. But how can you do that when the bad stuff's happenin'?"

"I try to think about happy things, like stuff Momma and I used to do and what it will be like when I get old enough to fly helicopters.

Momma always said to put the happy thoughts and good memories on a big, open shelf in my mind so I could pull them down whenever I needed them."

"What do you do with the bad memories?"

"I wash them off, tie them up in a box, and put them in a closet in the back of my mind. That way, each day is a fresh start."

Oh my gosh! That's why he smells like Zest all the time!

"It must be hard keeping the bad memories away."

"Yeah. Sometimes it's really hard. But Momma said you have to let go of the bad stuff; otherwise, you just spend your life relivin' the same pain and you never get to happy."

I'll bet there are a lot of tied-up boxes in that closet.

The next evening, Ain't Pitty decided it was time to introduce Mitchell to her version of swamp fishing.

"We're gonna wade into that?" he asked, staring at the black, murky water. "You're kiddin', right? You can't see where you're goin'."

"That's life," said Ain't Pitty, stepping in.

"I can't."

"Sure you can."

"But . . ."

"Takes courage, Mitchell, and faith that what's on the other side is worth it."

"You can always stay on the bank and fish with the little ones if you want," teased J.D. as he and Eric waded in.

"Ignore 'im, Mitchell," I said. "I don't like it either, but once you're in, it's not too bad if you concentrate on the fish and not the other things you think are swimmin' around you."

Mitchell slid his flip-flops off and took his first steps into the mushy water. I could tell he didn't like it, but he set his jaw and stayed with us every mucky step of the way.

Once we could get our lines close to where the dead trees were, the fish started biting and it didn't take long to get Mitchell's mind off of where the lower half of his body was.

"This is the biggest bass I've ever caught," he said, attaching the foot-long fish to his stringer.

Ain't Pitty just looked at him and winked.

Coming out of the water, we introduced Mitchell to the second part of swamp fishing that took courage: pulling the leeches off.

"Nothing like leeches to make you forget about your other aches and pains," he chuckled. Grimacing, he started pulling off the slippery little bloodsuckers. "We ought to take these things over to Doc Anderson. He said in the old days they used them to heal people."

Looking at Ain't Pitty, I knew some healers still did, just not in the same way.

Church on Sundays was another part of Mitchell's new life. Pastor Flemming had taken him shopping in Geneva and bought new shorts, t-shirts, tennis shoes, and a white shirt for Sunday mornings. The Pastor also went to see Willie Ray to let him know Mitchell would not be coming back to work. Willie Ray told Pastor Flemming that he was meddling too much in other folks' business. But, according to Mitchell, the Pastor told him folks *were* his business.

This Sunday, I was sitting in my usual spot next to the window, watching two flies try unsuccessfully to find an escape hole in the screen, when I noticed Pastor Flemming was more intense with his sermon than usual. He was preaching about neighbor loving.

"When thinking of our neighbors, the ones we like, the ones we don't, and even the most despicable among us, remember, the good Lord loves every one of them just as much as he loves you and me. And he stands ready to forgive them for their sins and transgressions just as quickly as he stands ready to forgive us." Shaking his head, he added, "Sometimes it's beyond us to understand why this is, especially when we see the bad things some folks do. But it is what it is, and we should be on our knees in gratitude and praise for it. Why? Because each of us is the recipient of this forgiving grace, and without it where would we be? I doubt many of us, myself included, would fare very well if God's judgment mirror were placed in front of us right now and we did not have the Lord's promise of forgiving grace in our souls."

At first, I figured Pastor Flemming was talking about the men who had hurt Mitchell and was wondering how you went about forgiving that kind of bad, but then he included everybody and it hit me.

We're going straight to hell!

I had never considered our secret nighttime activities as forgiveness-needing bad. But listening to Pastor Flemming now, I wasn't so sure. It was like he was talking to us, like he knew everything we had done to cause folks problems.

When the last hymn ended, Pastor Flemming came down the steps to the center aisle, raised his right hand and said, "Go in peace. Have courage. Hold tight to what is good. Return no one evil for evil. Strengthen the weak, help the suffering, and honor all people. Love and serve the Lord and take joy in the power of the Holy Spirit. Amen."

Walking down the aisle, the Pastor positioned himself to greet his flock as they headed out.

For once, I was glad Granny made us sit in the front pew and that I was on the end. It meant I would be the last one out and could talk with the Pastor without everyone hearing.

Granny thanked Pastor Flemming for a "real nice" sermon and made her way down the front steps of the church, followed by the rest of the cussins and Mitchell.

At last, the Pastor shook my hand.

"And just how are you today, Miss Nettie?"

"Fine, thank you."

"Good! It's a beautiful day to be fine!"

I didn't let go of his hand as he straightened up and turned to go back into the church.

"Pastor, may I ask you a question?"

Squatting down, he replied, "Of course, Nettie. Ask away."

I was more than a little uncomfortable having his big, dark eyes and full attention on me and stumbled trying to get the words out.

"I . . . well . . . uh . . . I was wonderin' . . . if you don't think what you're doin' is bad, does it still count? Does it still need forgivin'?"

Lights started dancing in Pastor Flemming's eyes as he answered.

"Well, Miss Nettie, that's a very good question, and being bad is an interesting thing. There are lots of ways to be bad, and all of us are bad at one time or another. It's just the nature of folks. The difference is, folks who choose to listen to the Lord will usually hear from him about whether what they are doing is good or bad and whether they need to be forgiven."

"I've never heard the Lord tellin' me any of that, Pastor. I've never heard him tellin' me anythin' at all."

"Oh, I think you have," said Pastor Flemming. "You just may not have realized it. You listen to the Lord with your heart, Nettie, not your ears. It was the Lord speaking to your heart today that made you want to ask the question in the first place, and it will be the Lord speaking to your heart that will lead you to the answer."

"Oh," I replied, not sure I believed him. "But how will I know it's him doin' the talkin'?"

Looking out across the front lawn of his church, Pastor Flemming replied, "Because you'll feel as if you've just stepped out of the hot sun into the cool shade."

Still holding on to my hand, he stood up.

"Think about it for a while, Nettie, and if you still have a hard time hearing what your heart's trying to say, just let me know and we'll figure it out together."

Chapter 18

Our annual trip to Wayside Beach in Panama City had everything we needed for a perfect day: miles of sugar-white sand; emerald-green water; a shady picnic pavilion with an outdoor shower; and the Miracle Strip Amusement Park, with its bumper cars, octopus ride, putt-putt golf, Starliner roller coaster, and the tallest Ferris wheel in the South. By the end of the day, we had done everything except the Ferris wheel and were headed for it, when Ain't Pitty called out.

"Last ride of the night, y'all. We need to be headin' home."

Lining up, Mitchell and I loaded last, and as we sat down he put his arm across the back of the seat behind me, just like Andy had done last fall, but this time I did not slide to the corner. I liked having Mitchell close, and his arm felt warm where it touched my shoulders.

"I see that," called Sam from the gondola in front of us.

This time Mitchell and I just smiled and waved. Her teasing didn't bother me nearly as much as it once had, and Mitchell actually seemed to enjoy it.

For a split second, I thought about Andy and wondered what he would say if he knew where I was and what I was doing. He would not be happy, but, as strange as it seemed, I wanted to talk with him. He was my best friend, and before he'd asked me to go steady we talked about everything.

Our gondola finally made it to the top and stopped. A gentle breeze was blowing, and moonlight was sparkling like diamonds on the water in the gulf.

"It's like we're on top of the world. Don't you wish you could just fly around out there?"

"One of these days, I will," replied Mitchell. "But right now, I'm happy where I am."

Mitchell was spending most nights at Ain't Pitty's now. She and Pastor Flemming agreed it was easier than getting him back to Church Street every night. We had offered to let him squeeze into the bedroom with us, but Ain't Pitty just shook her head and made up the living room sofa for him. Now, by the time we got up in the mornings, Mitchell was already in the kitchen, helping Ain't Pitty cook breakfast.

As a surprise, Uncle Ben invited Mitchell to spend a day at with him at Fort Rucker. Uncle Ben had met a pilot named Lieutenant Duke Morrison, who had come to Rucks to train on a new chopper called the Kiowa. The lieutenant volunteered to show Mitchell around and, as a final surprise, took him for a ride in the new chopper, letting him handle the joystick as they flew over the massive base.

When he and Uncle Ben finally got home, Mitchell was not as excited and talkative as I'd thought he would be. In fact, at supper he was almost too quiet.

Don't be nosy, Nettie. He'll talk when he's ready.

As Ain't Pitty got the little ones ready for bed, the rest of us headed to the front porch. The night was clear and sweet smelling, and the crickets were full throated.

"Mitchell, have you heard whether you can stay with Pastor Flemming this fall?" asked J.D.

"Not yet. But I've decided I'm never going back to Pa."

None of us was surprised by this. The topic had come up many times in our late-night "what if" discussions.

"Well, if it comes to that, you can't stay around here," said J.D. "He'd come lookin' for you for sure. You'll have to head to me in Mobile or Eric in Dothan, and we'll help you from there."

"I have your addresses and phone numbers memorized."

And you have mine.

"Mitchell, did you ever try to run away before?" I asked.

"Momma and I tried . . . twice, the last year she was alive. Pa was drinkin' most of the time and hurtin' us whether he was drunk or not. The first time we tried to run, we didn't have enough money to get far enough, fast enough. Pa found us and threatened to kill us if we ever tried to leave again. But we knew we had to try. He was gonna kill us either way."

"What did you do?"

"Momma started savin' all the money she could find, and the night we were gonna leave, she showed me where it was hidden. She'd cut a hole in the back pages of her Bible and tucked the money in so you couldn't tell it was there. She told me if our plan didn't work I was to take the Bible and run."

"What was your plan?" asked J.D.

Mitchell didn't answer for a while, but then it seemed as if a wall in his mind came down and he started talking.

"When Momma was alive, we'd sneak over to Field 10 at night so I could watch the choppers. We had a hiding place in the woods near the fence, about a mile from our trailer. Usually the soldiers guarding the fenceline couldn't see us, but one night the guard had a dog with him. The dog must have scented us, because he stood at the fence and barked and carried on until we came out from behind the brush."

"A German shepherd?" asked J.D.

"Yeah. A big one."

"I bet it was the same one that spotted us at Field 10 a couple of summers ago."

"Yeah," agreed Eric. "If that soldier hadn't been so nice, we would've been dogmeat."

"Could be," said Mitchell. "The soldier's name was Lance, and his dog's name was Max. They were both nice, especially after Max calmed down. Momma explained that I loved helicopters and liked to watch the nighttime liftoff, so Lance let us stay. He talked with us a long time that night, and afterward he and Max started meeting us there. He'd tie a white shoelace to the fence close to our hiding spot on the nights he was patrolling, and when we saw it, we'd tie one of my handkerchiefs to the fence to let him know we were there. We talked about everything. He told us about being in the army and about his family's farm in Oklahoma, and we told him about Pa. Sometimes we'd stay so late we were afraid Pa would get home before we did. He always came in late and woke up mean."

They must have lived in fear all the time.

"Lance would get upset whenever he saw new cuts and bruises on us, because he knew how we got them. He wanted to go after Pa, but Momma wouldn't let him. She was afraid of what would happen to all of us. One night, Lance told us he had received orders to ship out. He was being sent to Vietnam and wanted us away from Pa before he left. He gave us money and helped put a plan together for us to get away. The night before he was to leave, Lance hid his car in the woods near our path to the fence. We were to take it and drive to his family in Oklahoma."

Mitchell took a deep breath and stared at the moon. I could tell he was in a bad memory box.

"That night, Pa left after supper like he always did. And as soon as it was dark, we headed for Lance's car. We were almost there when we saw Pa and Otis Pierce following us down the path. We tried to run, but they caught us. Pa said we were fools to think he didn't know where we were sneaking off to at night."

Mitchell closed his eyes and leaned back as if his head hurt.

"They forced us back to the trailer, and when we were inside Pa started hittin' Momma in the face. She was bleedin' really bad. I tried to help, but Otis Pierce shoved me into my room and locked the door. I could hear her screamin', and I was bangin' on the door, yellin' for them to let her go, but it didn't do any good. Then the screamin' stopped."

Oh, God. He heard his mother die.

"I could hear them movin' around in the trailer; then they drove off. About an hour later, they came back and Pa jerked me out of my room. He said I had to go to the hospital, because my worthless momma was either dead or dyin'.'"

There was nothing but stunned silence as Mitchell got up and walked to the edge of the porch.

"I started hittin' Pa, yellin' that he'd killed her, but he put his hands around my neck and slammed me so hard against the wall, I got dizzy and couldn't breathe. He said he didn't kill her—that she had fallen and hit her head, and if I told anyone any different, I'd be next. On the way to the hospital, he and Otis Pierce were talkin' fast and actin' real nervous. From what I could tell, they had planned to take Momma over the state line into Florida and throw her in the Blackwater Swamp, but one of the Sheriff's deputies stopped 'em for speedin' before they could do it. They lied and told the deputy Momma had fallen and they were tryin' to get her to the hospital. The deputy turned his red lights on and led them to the emergency room. When they got there, the doctor told 'em Momma was dyin' and if any family wanted to say good-bye, they'd better get to the hospital quick. The deputy knew Momma and volunteered to come get me, but Pa wouldn't let him. He was afraid I'd tell the deputy what happened, so he and Otis Pierce came to get me instead. On the way back to the hospital, Otis Pierce grabbed my throat and said, 'If anybody asks, you tell 'em she fell—nothin' more. Say anythin' else, and I'll tie you up and throw your ass in the swamp, just like we were gonna do your momma, but you'll be awake when you hit the water.' "

How could anyone be that evil?

"By the time I got to the emergency room, Momma was gone."

"Oh, God," whispered Sam.

"Didn't the Sheriff do anythin'?" asked J.D.

"He tried. But Otis Pierce told everybody that he saw the whole thing and that Momma fell, just the way Pa said."

"Did the Sheriff talk with you?" asked Eric.

"Yeah. But Pa kept interruptin' and sayin' that I didn't see what happened. Sheriff Coker finally put me in his police car so he could talk to me without Pa bein' around. He asked over and over again if Pa and Otis Pierce were the ones who hurt Momma . . . but . . . they'd just beaten her to death and threatened to do the same thing to me." Mitchell's voice cracked. "I was scared out of my mind . . . so I told the Sheriff I didn't see anythin'."

Forcing my shocked arms and legs to move, I got up and put my arms around Mitchell, and Sam got up and hugged us both.

"I've never told anybody what happened until tonight," said Mitchell.

"Well, I'm not gonna hug ya," said J.D., clearing his throat. "But I'd like to tie those bastards' hands and feet together with barbed wire and throw their asses in the swamp."

"Yeah. And let them be wide awake to see the gators comin'," added Eric.

"I'd be happy just to have 'em locked up," said Mitchell.

"Did your pa find the money in the Bible?"

"No. When we got back to the trailer that night, he tore Momma's suitcase and pocketbook apart. He kept hittin' me, tryin' to get me to say where she hid the money—yellin' that she wouldn't have tried to run again if she didn't have money—but I just kept sayin' I didn't know. When he and Otis Pierce finally left, I picked up Momma's things and found the Bible lyin' underneath the hand-kerchiefs she'd packed for me. If Pa saw it, he never realized the money was in it."

It was right under his nose, and he was too blind to see it.

"The next day, some lady from the county came to the trailer to make sure I was all right, but Pa wouldn't let her in. As soon as she left, he hooked the truck to the trailer and moved us north, to the other side of Opp. We stayed there until this past spring, when Willie Ray talked Pa into coming back to Crystal Springs to drive the truck for the Feed and Seed. He told Pa that everybody had forgotten about Momma and didn't give a damn about me."

"Guess he knows different now," said J.D.

"I put the Bible by my bed in plain sight, but Pa never touched it. Pastor Flemming took me to the trailer to get my things when the Sheriff had Pa in for questionin', and the Bible was still there."

"Mitchell, if you had the money, why didn't you run away again?" asked Eric.

"I didn't have anyplace to go, and I knew if Pa and the others caught me, they'd kill me for sure. I figured I could take the beatin's until I turned eighteen; then I'd join the army . . . Once I'm inside that fence, they can't touch me."

Field 10. That's why he went there. He wanted in.

"Well, you have a place to go now," said J.D.

"Do you know if Lance ever found out what happened?" I asked.

"I didn't know anythin' until today when I went to Rucks. Lieutenant Morrison served with Lance in Vietnam. They were friends, and he promised Lance if he ever got back to Rucks, he'd try to find out if we were okay. Lance's parents had written him that we never made it to Oklahoma. When the lieutenant got sent back to Rucks this summer for more trainin', he found out Uncle Ben was from Crystal Springs and came to see him. That's when they arranged for me to spend the day at the base. The lieutenant took me to a buildin' where all the names of the Rucks soldiers who've died are written on the walls. Lance's name was there." Pulling something out of his pocket, he added, "The lieutenant said Lance asked him to give this to Momma and me."

It was a tattered handkerchief.

"It's the one Momma used to tie on the fence."

Chapter 19

For the working folks of the Wiregrass, Labor Day was a celebration of slowing down. Crops were harvested, the fields were being turned to rest, and most of the garden vegetables had been eaten, canned, or frozen. It was a time for folks to relax and enjoy summer's end.

Like the Fourth of July, the Labor Day celebration took place at Geneva County Lake and was another daylong, community-wide event. For us, it was bittersweet. On the one hand, it was a fun day, but on the other, it announced we would soon be going home.

"I can't believe summer's almost over," I grumbled, loading a picnic basket into the Oldsmobile.

"Me either," said J.D., putting the fishing poles on top of Jigger.

"I can't believe I have to serve after-school detention when I get back," whined Eric.

"But . . . ," said Sandra.

"I know, I know. It's a hell of a sight better than military school."

"Yes. Be grateful."

"I am, kinda."

"I'm not ready to leave, either," complained Sam.

"Yeah, and I know why," teased J.D. "D-a-n-n-y."

"Save your teasin' for somebody who's bothered by it, J.D.," quipped Sam.

"Ha! You are and you know it."

Danny had been patrolling the Railroad a lot, but we weren't sure if it was to protect Mitchell or to see Sam. He had finally gotten up the nerve to ask her out, but Ain't Pitty had said no.

"He's older than you, Sam. And I don't care how nice he is—you're not goin' anywhere with him by yourself. You can invite him
over here if you want, but nothin' more."

Sam was not happy, but she agreed and invited Danny to join
us on the front porch in the evenings. He and Sam would sit in the
swing, whispering and holding hands. They'd already exchanged
mailing addresses and telephone numbers, so I figured Danny was
going to be around for a while.

*Hope she doesn't get a "Dear Jane" letter from him. Uh-oh! What if
I get a "Dear Jane" letter from Mitchell?*

We had never talked about being girlfriend and boyfriend, but I
was crushed at the thought that whatever we had might end.

*Slow down, Nettie. You don't even know where Mitchell will be next
summer.*

Pastor Flemming had picked Mitchell up earlier this morning
for a meeting with the Judge. He was going to find out if he had to
go back to his pa today.

Please, Judge! Don't send him back.

For the farmers, the Labor Day celebration was the closest thing to a
fair Geneva County had. They planned all year for this day because
it gave them an opportunity to show off what they did best, see
what other farmers were doing, buy what they needed, and sell
what they didn't.

Livestock the farmers did not want to feed over the winter or
animals the high school's Future Farmers Club had raised for the
past year would be shown and sold at a makeshift stockyard near the
lake. Just like on the Fourth of July, there would be all kinds of
booths and activities again, as well as a bluegrass concert in the dell,
beginning at dusk.

Pulling into the parking area, we could see the booths were getting busy and many of the animals had already arrived. Ain't Pitty stopped Jigger to let us out.

"Y'all stay together."

"Hey, there's Uncle Red," said Sandra, pointing toward an open hay-bale pen. Uncle Red was unloading Queen Lola, who had been bathed and brushed shiny.

"It musta taken Uncle Red hours to get the mud off that momma hog," I said.

Queen Lola was popular with all ages, and curious folks were already gathering to ooh and aah her. She, on the other hand, was not nearly as impressed with them. Lumbering to the middle of the pen, she lay down and closed her eyes, despite the Future Farmers Club members circling around and measuring everything from her floppy ears to her corkscrew tail. They wanted to know how Uncle Red had raised such a massive hog and what feed he used to make her offspring taste so good. He talked with them for a long time, but I never heard him mention the scuppernongs.

There was also lots of food around. If it grew in the summer and was good to eat, one of the booths was selling it. Miz Tilly had a variety of berry pies she was selling to raise money for the fire department, and the ladies of the Women's Guild were selling everything from ham biscuits to peach ice cream. These same foods just happened to be featured in their annual *Women's Guild Cookbook*, which was also for sale. Miz Lettie was working the counter, dressed in her usual pumps and pearls.

"Do you suppose she's ever worn flip-flops and a t-shirt in her entire life?" asked Eric.

"Naw, she's wound too tight for that, but I bet she makes a good cookie," said J.D.

The kissing booth was also open for business again. As usual, the cheerleaders and football players were part of the kissing teams, but there was no sign of Cilly or John Thomas. Passing the lineup of cheerleaders, we overheard someone say they had broken up.

"Jeez!" whispered Sam.

"Doesn't surprise me," said J.D. "Guess John Thomas dumped her for his Geneva girlfriend."

"I don't believe I'm gonna say this, but I feel sorry for Cilly. At least now she can move on to someone better."

"Yeah. Just not me."

"Wow! Would you look at that," said Eric, pointing to the pink side of the kissing booth.

Standing at the counter was Noni. Dressed up, dolled up, and puckered up, she planted a big kiss on the first fellow in line and then called for the next one to step up. It was still early, but the scoreboard indicated she had raised the most money so far, by far.

"Ha! Look what we started," laughed J.D.

"You know, you're right," said Eric. "Y'all wait here a minute."

Sprinting to the booth, he got in Noni's line, and when it was his turn, he laid a dollar down and gave her a good ten-second, on-the-mouth kiss. When it was over they talked for a minute, and Eric left smiling. As he rejoined us, we stared in disbelief.

"What?"

"What? Hell! What was that all about?" demanded J.D.

"Just finishing what you started. I never got to meet her on the Fourth of July—like you promised her. So this was the next-best thing, and it wasn't bad. In fact, it was good."

J.D. looked as if he were going to give it a try, but Eric grabbed his arm.

"Don't you even think about it."

Rucks was also part of the Labor Day celebration. Pilots would fly in four or five different types of choppers and land in the grassy field just east of the lake. Once they powered down, they would then let folks climb in and explore every inch of the machines. In return, the pilots and crews received some of the best home-cooked

food in the Wiregrass and would take baskets more home to Mother
Rucker when they joined the nightly migration returning from
Field 10. We were especially excited about seeing the choppers this
time because Lieutenant Morrison was going to fly in the new
Kiowa.

We had arranged to meet Mitchell and Pastor Flemming at the
choppers after their meeting with the Judge, but they were already
there when we reached the field.

Hmm, I'm not sure if this is a good sign or a bad one.

I wasn't sure how long it took to decide someone's future, but I
was hoping the meeting had lasted long enough to make Mitchell's
new life permanent. However, neither he nor Pastor Flemming said
a word about it when we arrived.

We spent the next few hours climbing into and out of choppers.
Saving the Kiowa for last, we talked with Lieutenant Morrison a
long time. He was very glad to see Mitchell and gave him an enve-
lope with his contact information in it. They were going to write
each other, and when Mitchell was old enough, Lieutenant Morrison

was going to help him join the army and take the right steps to
learn to fly.

Thank you, Lord, for bringing the lieutenant into Mitchell's life!

Finally, when even Mitchell had had enough of the choppers,
Pastor Flemming left to help set up the church's picnic and we
headed down Lake Road. We were hungry, thirsty, and ready for a
rest, and Ain't Pitty's table would provide all three.

After supper, Ain't Pitty and Uncle Ben decided to go visiting and
we decided to take a swim. Sliding out of my flip-flops, I pulled off
my shorts and reached for a towel but stopped. I had worn a t-shirt
over my swimsuit all summer, but now I knew it had to go.

Enough already, Nettie!

Grabbing the hem with both hands, I pulled the soft fabric over
my head and tossed it on the ground. The afternoon air felt smooth
and tingly against my skin, and the fact that I had half lemons and a
waist did not seem like a problem anymore.

"Finally!" said Sam. "I thought you'd never take that thing off."

"Well, it's off now."

By the time we dove in, everybody else had reached the far side
of the dock.

Swimming underwater, I popped to the surface near Mitchell.

"Boo!"

Laughing, I leaned back to smooth the hair out of my eyes. As I
came up, Mitchell grabbed my hand and pulled me toward him.

"Nettie, you're the prettiest girl I've ever laid eyes on, and I like
you, a lot."

At the beginning of the summer, I would have gotten red-faced
and tongue-tied, but not now.

"No one's ever said that to me before, but I like it, and I like
you, too, a lot."

"Boy! That's a relief! I was nervous 'bout tellin' you."

"Do you wanna know what I called you the day I first saw you in Slater's?"

Mitchell hesitated, as if he was not sure the memory was a good one.

"Yeah, I guess."

Smiling, I dipped down to let the cool water flow over my shoulders.

"I called you Pretty Boy 'cause you were the prettiest boy I'd ever seen."

"Ha! Really?"

"Really."

Taking off swimming after the others, I called back, "I still do!"

When Mitchell caught up, the grin was still on his face.

By late afternoon, Ain't Pitty and Uncle Ben were playing Frisbee with the little ones, and the rest of us were drip-drying on the bank.

"Hey, y'all," said J.D. "Sun's behind the trees and the fish are comin' up."

Digging around in Jigger, we found some crickets, pulled our fishing poles off her roof, and flip-flopped down to the dock.

Mitchell and I climbed onto the railing and tossed our lines in the water. He still had not said anything about the meeting with the Judge, but I couldn't wait any longer.

"So, did you find out if you get to stay with Pastor Flemming this fall?"

"Yeah. I'm not stayin' with 'im."

My heart sank like a rock.

"Are they sendin' you back to your pa?"

"No. They're not doin' that."

"Thank God! But where are you goin'? Can you come back next summer?"

"I don't need to come back, because I'm not goin' anywhere."

"Okay, enough! Where are you stayin'?"

"Hey, don't get upset. I'm just teasin' ya. Your Ain't Pitty and Uncle Ben have offered to let me live with them and go to school in Crystal Springs. The Judge made it official today."

"Oh my gosh! That's so great!"

I threw my arms around him in a hug that sent both of our fishing poles into the water.

"Shushes" started coming our way from all around the dock.

Ignoring them, I yelled, "Hey, y'all, come 'ere! Mitchell has great news!"

Propping their poles, the others made their way to our side of the T.

"Okay, let's hear it," said Eric, hoisting himself backward onto the railing.

"Guess!"

"Oh, c'mon, Nettie!" moaned J.D. "What is it?"

"Okay, Grumpy! Tell 'em, Mitchell."

"Your aunt and uncle have invited me to live with them and go to school here this fall."

"He doesn't have to go back to live with his pa! Isn't that great?"

Mitchell was scanning the faces of the others, as if worried they would not approve.

"Yeah! Congratulations," said J.D., slapping Mitchell on the back.

"That's terrific, Mitchell," added Eric. "They'll take good care of ya."

"Yeah, and you can help them," added Sandra.

"Did your pa agree to this?" asked Sam. "Doesn't seem like somethin' he'd be in favor of."

"No, he didn't like it one bit. Sheriff Coker, the Judge, and Pastor Flemming went to talk with him this mornin'. They let me go, but I had to listen from the car. The Sheriff said he couldn't prove Pa was involved in the beatin', but the beatin' proved I was bein' neglected and that was enough for him to remove me from the home. The Judge told Pa I'd be stayin' with a family in Crystal Springs and goin' to school, but Pa started cussin' and arguin' with 'em. Pastor Flemming tried to explain that I'd have a better chance of gettin' a good job and buildin' a good life if I could stay in one place and finish school. He even asked Pa if he didn't want a better life for me, but Pa just spit at 'em and said what he did with his own son was none of their damn business and that they had no right to take me away. Then he started yellin' at me to get outta the car."

"That had to be tough to hear, Mitchell," said J.D.

"It was. But the Judge told Pa he'd squandered any chance to be a good parent and that they did have the right to protect me. He also told Pa that he and his cronies were to stay away from me, or they'd be spendin' the rest of their days lookin' through bars."

"Good. Now they can't bother you."

"You'll love livin' with Ain't Pitty and Uncle Ben," said Sandra.

"I already do."

Mitchell eased himself into the water, intent on retrieving our fishing poles and not scaring the fish.

"J.D.," I whispered, "do you think his pa and the others will really leave 'im alone?"

"They'd be crazy if they don't."

Yeah, but they are crazy.

Chapter 20

We could hear the bluegrass band warming up in the dell as we loaded the last of the picnic supplies. Ain't Pitty and Uncle Ben were going to take the cars to the parking area, and we were going to walk Lake Road one last time. Most of the other picnickers had already gone, but as we approached the bend in the road, we saw Mitchell's pa and Otis Pierce sitting at their usual table in the woods, drinking from a jug and smoking cigarettes. They stared at Mitchell as if they wanted to bore a hole right through him, but he just kept on walking.

Uncle Ben and Ain't Pitty had stopped farther up the road and were standing outside the cars, waiting for us to catch up. Apparently, they had seen the men, too.

"Ignore them, Mitchell. They're not part of your life anymore," said Ain't Pitty. "Y'all don't dally. The music's gonna start soon."

With Ain't Pitty and Uncle Ben keeping us in sight, we resumed our walk. Mitchell and I brought up the rear.

"Are you excited about seein' your parents soon?" asked Mitchell.

"Yeah, I guess. I'm just not ready to leave."

"Next summer will be here before you know it."

"I know. But nine months is a long time. What if I don't come back, or what if you don't stay in Crystal Springs?"

Mitchell stopped and turned my face toward his.

"Yes, you will come back." Leaning forward, he kissed my cheek and whispered, "And I'll be right here waitin' for you."

Spotting a small daisy growing near the edge of the road, Mitchell picked it. Closing his eyes, he smelled it for a long time and then handed the flower to me.

"My mother said you never forget the smell of a daisy."

Putting it to my nose, I twirled it and took a deep breath.

"It smells like summer."

"Yep, this summer. Time to choose happy, Nettie."

When we reached the parking area, Li'l Bit and Sharon scampered off with other kids to catch what was left of the lightning bugs and we stopped to help Uncle Red load Queen Lola into his farm truck for the ride home. She was still lying down and showed no signs of wanting to leave.

Using a stick heated in the hot coals of a nearby grill, Uncle Red persuaded Queen Lola to get up and go up the ramp while we blocked other potential exits.

"I've never seen anythin' that big move that fast," laughed Eric, as we headed to the dell to join Ain't Pitty and Uncle Ben.

The evening had cooled, and the moon was high enough for us to see its reflection in the smooth water of the lake. Lights were strung across the top and down the sides of the temporary stage and in the surrounding trees so folks could see. With Mr. Short and his banjo leading the way, the band started playing one toe-tapping, hand-clapping song after another. They played for the better part of an hour before they stopped to take a break.

Standing to stretch, Ain't Pitty turned around and looked at us, her smile fading.

"Where's Li'l Bit and Sharon?"

Jumping up, we scanned the crowd, but the little ones were nowhere to be seen.

"They were lookin' for lightning bugs with the other kids a little while ago," said Sam.

"Y'all split up and go look for them. It's too dark for them to be wanderin' around by themselves. Girls, y'all go check around the booths, where there's light. Boys, y'all check around the water. Ben, let's you and I search the dell. They may be sittin' with other kids."

As everyone else took off, Mitchell stood still, staring toward Lake Road, a worried look on his face. As he stepped into the crowd, I started to follow, but he stopped me.

"No, Nettie. Do exactly what Ain't Pitty told you to do. I'm gonna check Lake Road."

"I'm goin' with you."

"No. You need to help Sam and Sandra."

"Don't do it, Mitchell. Don't go down there by yourself."

"I'm just gonna do a quick check of woods near the road, Nettie. If there are any lightning bugs left to catch, that's where they'll be. I'll meet you back here in a few minutes."

Squeezing my hand, he took off into crowd. As he reached the entrance to Lake Road, he turned and waved, then headed into the darkness.

My heart was pounding in my throat as I ran to catch up with Sam and Sandra. Time seemed to move in slow motion as we circled booth after booth, but there was no sign of the little ones. Intermission was over and the music had started playing again when we caught up with J.D. and Eric.

"Any sign of them?"

"No. Nothin'."

"J.D., Mitchell went down Lake Road to look for 'em by himself!"

Panic crossed J.D.'s face.

"God Almighty! Does he think his pa and Otis Pierce have Li'l Bit and Sharon?"

"I don't know. But he wouldn't let me go with him."

"C'mon!"

"Shouldn't we tell Ain't Pitty and Uncle Ben?" yelled Sam, as we dodged around parked cars.

"No time!"

The moon was bright as we turned onto Lake Road, but dark, fog-like clouds were moving like a wave in front of it, giving the woods an eerie, smoky look that sent cold shivers all the way to my toes. Familiar night sounds were all around us, but now they were loud and sharp and offered no comfort, just a level of fear I had never known.

Running as fast as we could, we rounded a long bend and ran into one another's backs when J.D. and Eric came to a sudden stop.

Stumbling toward us was Jessie, and he was carrying Sharon, his usual blank expression replaced with wrinkles of concern. Hurrying to J.D., Jessie put Sharon in his arms. She was scraped up and crying and had leaves and pine needles all over her.

"Li'l Bit . . . Mitchell . . . need help," Jessie said haltingly.

"Where are they, Jessie? Where's Li'l Bit? Where's Mitchell?" snapped J.D. so fast that Jessie had no time to answer, even if he wanted to.

"Jessie, please, where are they?" I pushed.

Jessie didn't answer, but he pointed in the direction we had come from.

"They . . . they . . . took 'em," said Sharon, sobbing.

J.D. sat Sharon on the ground and grabbed her shoulders.

"Where? Where'd they take 'em?"

"I . . . don't know . . . We . . . were playin' . . . along the road . . . and . . . Otis Pierce . . . jumped outta the bushes . . . He stuck a rag in my mouth . . . I couldn't breathe, and—"

"C'mon, Sharon! Hurry up," begged J.D.

"Please, Sharon!" I added. "Li'l Bit and Mitchell are in trouble!"

Taking a deep breath, she started again. "I heard Li'l Bit yellin' . . . Mitchell's pa was chasin' him, and Li'l Bit was runnin' . . . He almost got away but fell down . . . Mitchell's pa grabbed him . . . but Li'l Bit started hittin' him in the face and kickin' him so hard, one of his flip-flops flew off."

"Stay focused, Sharon!" I said. "What did they do then?"

"Mitchell's pa stuffed a rag in Li'l Bit's mouth and shoved him into the front of the truck. They were tryin' to put me in there, too! But I started fightin' 'em, just like Li'l Bit. Then I saw Mitchell. He ran up to the truck and was yellin' at the men to let us go or he was gonna tell the Sheriff everythin'. Otis Pierce tried to grab him, but Mitchell kicked him . . . really hard. It musta hurt, because he dropped me and fell down. Mitchell pulled the rag outta my mouth and yelled for me to *run . . . fast*! So I did."

"Then what happened?" J.D. pushed, his voice tense.

"I ran for the road. But I could hear somebody chasin' me. I was really scared, but I kept runnin' . . . Just when I reached the road, a hand grabbed my arm and pulled me into the root cave. Remember . . . the one we found on the Fourth of July?"

"Yeah, we remember. Keep goin', Sharon," said Eric.

"It was Jessie. He shushed me 'cause Otis Pierce was comin' right toward the tree. But he didn't see us. I had to hold my hand over my mouth 'cause I was afraid he'd hear me breathin', but he didn't. He just turned around and left."

"Then what?" pressed J.D.

"Jessie made me stay still, and after a while, the truck came by. We waited some more to make sure all the bad men were gone and then climbed outta the cave. I was shakin' so bad I could hardly walk, so Jessie carried me. That's when we saw y'all."

J.D. turned to talk with Jessie, but he was gone. In all the excitement, he had slipped back into the shadows.

"Sharon, we need to know where they took Li'l Bit and Mitchell. Did you hear the men say where they were goin'?"

"No. I just heard 'em yellin'."

"Think! We gotta think!" said J.D., putting his hands on his head and pacing. "Those fool men aren't crazy enough to go back to the trailer, but where else . . ."

J.D. looked at us, and we all spoke in unison.

"Ice house."

Grabbing Sharon, J.D. yelled, "Let's go!"

We ran hard and fast until we reached the parking area, where J.D. turned to Sandra.

"Take Sharon to Ain't Pitty and Uncle Ben right now! Tell 'em what happened. Tell 'em to get the Sheriff and meet us at the old ice house as soon as they can. Tell 'em Li'l Bit and Mitchell are in big trouble. *Run!*"

"How are we gonna get there?" asked Eric, frantically looking around for help.

"Jigger!" yelled J.D.

"What?" hissed Sam. "You don't know how to drive! We need to get Unc—"

"There's no time! Remember what happened to Luke and those little girls? They were just gone! Let's go!"

As we piled into Jigger, J.D. stomped her floorboard ignition button, put her in reverse, and, looking over his shoulder, backed the old car out of the pines as if he had been driving all his life. When he had enough room to turn, he put the gearshift into drive and hit the gas pedal so hard Jigger's back end slid and her tires spit out a long rooster tail of pine needles. Finally getting traction, Jigger jumped forward and up the road we went, barely slowing down as J.D. made a sharp turn onto Choctaw Road.

"Lights," yelled Eric. "J.D., turn the lights on!"

"I don't know how! The moon's gonna have to do!"

J.D. was leaning forward in the seat, his hands white-knuckle tight on the steering wheel and his foot pushed to the floorboard, trying to get Jigger to go faster. She had not hit sixty miles an hour in decades, but she did now. The intensity of the speed caused the old car to rattle in ways I'd never heard or felt before, but she stayed together and kept going all the way to the turnoff to the ice house.

Standing on the brakes, J.D. managed to slow down enough to turn into the overgrown dirt lane and then slowly inched forward, as if he was trying to figure out our next move.

"Eric, if these men have Li'l Bit, you and Sam grab him and run for the beach. You'll have a better chance if you hide in the woods next to the water. When you're sure nobody's followin' you, make your way to the boat landin' and up to the road. Maybe folks will be comin' from the lake by then and you can get help. Nettie and I'll get Mitchell and follow you. If they fight you, kick 'em in the balls. If you can't kick 'em there, put your fingers in their eyes and kick 'em in the knees. If they can't see and can't run, they can't chase us."

I heard a police siren in the distance, and relief flooded through me. Help was on the way.

J.D. eased Jigger around the bend in the driveway. We could see the ice house looming in the moonlight, but there was no truck and no one in sight, only a flickering orange glow coming from around the partially opened door.

J.D. brought Jigger to a stop and turned off the engine. Being careful not to make noise, we got out of the car and tiptoed toward the ice house. Despite the hot, humid night, I was freezing. Something was wrong, terribly wrong. I could feel it, and, judging by what I was sensing from the others, they felt it, too.

Putting his hand up to stop us, J.D. bent down and picked something up. It was Li'l Bit's other flip-flop.

Sam reached for my hand. Hers was ice cold and sweaty. I felt sick to my stomach.

Reaching the ice house door, J.D. took a deep breath and pulled it open, his fists up and ready to fight. Eric was right next to him, ready to do the same.

The heavy door groaned as it swung open. In the flickering shadows of the dingy, dark room, I could see the dirty cot turned on its side and Mitchell, his eyes closed and head tilted to the side, hanging at the end of that dirty rope.

This time as the darkness closed in, I knew where I was going and was grateful. The pain was more than I could bear.

I could feel the razor-sharp blades of wiregrass cutting into my arms and legs as I came around, my thumping head lying in Sam's lap. Her eyes were red and swollen, and she was wiping her nose on her bare arm. Even upside down, tears looked the same. As my eyes focused, I saw Danny kneeling next to Sam, and the expression on his face said what I had seen was real.

"Noo!" I screamed, sitting up, my head throbbing harder.

"Stay still, Nettie," said Sam, as she and Danny grabbed my arms.

The ice house was cast in a mixture of dark shadows and narrow beams of bright light from nearby cars. I could see Pastor Flemming's tall frame coming through the door, tears rolling down his face, Mitchell lying limp in his arms. The Judge, who I realized was standing next to me, stepped in front of us to block what we were seeing, but it was too late. I touched his leg and looked up at him with a silent plea to move. There was overwhelming sadness in his eyes as he stepped back.

As Pastor Flemming went by, I could see that Mitchell's eyes were closed and there was black soot on his neck, but there was no sign of fear or pain, just the look of sleep.

Oh, Mitchell, no!

I closed my eyes, hoping it would push the pain back enough that I could breathe, but I opened them again in a panic.

"Where's Li'l Bit?"

Struggling to get to my feet, I looked around frantically.

"Oh, God! Where is he?"

Pulling me back to my knees, Sam said, "Wait! J.D. and Eric went down to the creek with the Sheriff to look for him."

An even colder chill went through me.

If they'd hang Mitchell, what would they do to Li'l Bit?

"Nettie," said Danny, "J.D. figured if Li'l Bit managed to get away, he might have run to the beach, since he knew where the path was."

"We need to help look for him!"

"No," insisted Sam. "You passed out and hit your head. Stay put. The last thing we need is for you to faint again."

The harsh words stung, but she was right.

The Judge, who was still standing near us, added, "Be still, Nettie. There's nothing you can do right now but pray."

Sam took my hand, and we prayed over and over again that Li'l Bit was safe.

Please, God, make this not real.

Suddenly, a wave of homesickness washed over me. I wanted my momma and daddy, and I wanted to see Andy. I wanted to be anyplace but here, doing anything else but this and feeling anything else but the horrible pain.

"Look!" said Sam.

A bobbing light was coming across the field from the direction of Sandy Bottom Creek. We watched as three dark forms made their way closer. Finally, we could see J.D., Eric, and Sheriff Coker. J.D. was carrying Li'l Bit upright in his arms. Scrambling to our feet, Sam and I ran to meet them, hugging every arm, head, and back we could find.

"Li'l Bit, are you okay?" asked Sam.

Like Sharon, he was dirty and scratched up, but everything seemed to be working.

"Yeah. I wanna go home."

"He was hiding under a patch of honeysuckle near the water," said the Sheriff. "Smart kid."

The Judge took Li'l Bit from J.D. and sat him on the hood of his car, while the Sheriff headed to the ice house. Li'l Bit was shivering from head to toe.

"Here," said the Judge, putting his jacket around Li'l Bit's shoulders. "Is that better?"

Li'l Bit nodded and cuddled down into the warm jacket.

"Son, I need to know exactly what happened tonight. Can you tell me?"

"Yes, sir."

Slowly, Li'l Bit began retelling Sharon's story.

"Mitchell's pa was yellin' and cussin'. He stuck a rag in my mouth and threw me in the truck. Otis Pierce tried to do the same to Sharon, but Mitchell ran up and start yellin' and fightin' 'im. He kicked Otis Pierce so hard that he dropped Sharon and she was able to run away."

"What happened then?"

"Mitchell's pa grabbed him by the neck and hit him so hard, Mitchell fell down and didn't move. They picked him up and put him in the back of the truck; then Otis Pierce went runnin' after Sharon. But he couldn't find her. Mitchell's pa was real mad and called Otis Pierce a fool for lettin' her get loose in the first place. He said they had to leave quick 'cause Sharon was gonna tell everybody what they'd done."

Li'l Bit sighed and looked toward the ice house, as if he wanted to know what had happened.

"You're doing well, son. What happened next?"

"The men got in the truck beside me and started drivin', but they smelled so bad I started gaggin'. Otis Pierce pushed the rag deeper in my mouth to make me stop, but it made me gag more. I gagged so hard the rag came out and I threw up all over the seat."

"I doubt they were very happy about that," the Judge said under his breath.

"Noo, sir. They started fussin' and cussin' about the smell, but my throw-up didn't smell as bad as they did! They smelled like Queen Lola's pen and that old moonshine jug we found in the ice house."

The Judge suddenly stood up straight and looked at Danny.

"Deputy, did you hear that?"

"Yes, sir!"

"Tell the Sheriff to check the site of the still you all found. Those drunkards may be running, but they're not likely to leave their liquor behind. Hurry!"

"Yes, sir!"

Turning back to Li'l Bit, the Judge asked, "What happened next, son?"

"When we got here, Otis Pierce went in the ice house to light the lamp and Mitchell's pa yanked me outta the truck and tried to get the throw-up off the seat with one hand. He didn't know Mitchell had woke up and was climbin' out of the back of the truck, but I did. I saw him! Mitchell jerked me away from his pa and pushed him down on the floorboard. He yelled, 'Run, Li'l Bit, *run!*' and then jumped on his pa's back. I started runnin' as fast as I could for the creek. I heard Otis Pierce come out of the ice house and start yellin', but I kept runnin', 'cause that's what Mitchell told me to do!"

"Why did you run for the creek and not the road?"

"'Cause we found lots of good hidin' places down by the creek. We're always lookin' for good hidin' places. Right, J.D.?"

"Right, little buddy."

Pulling the coat tighter around Li'l Bit, the Judge asked, "Did those men say why they came here, to the ice house?"

"Yes, sir. Mitchell's pa said they had to get their money before they left town."

"Money?"

"Uh-huh. He said there were five jugs of it up in the rafters. He told Otis Pierce to get 'em down while he cleaned off the seat."

I remembered having seen the outline of a jug in the rafters the day we found the ice house.

"Hmm. Did he happen to say where the money came from?"

"Not exactly, but he said Willie Ray'd never miss it."

The Judge was mumbling something about there being no honor among thieves, when we heard a commotion behind us. Ain't Pitty and Uncle Ben, looking wild-eyed and frantic, were coming down the driveway. When Ain't Pitty saw us, she stopped and dropped to her knees, her hands together and her head bent. After a minute, Uncle Ben helped her up and they hurried over to us. As we all received rib-bruising hugs, Ain't Pitty started talking nervously.

"Thank God y'all are safe! We couldn't get out. Everybody was tryin' to leave the lake at the same time. We had to cut across the field to get to Choctaw Road. And when we got here, the deputy made us park and walk in—something about too many cars bein' back here."

Taking a minute to catch her breath, Ain't Pitty hugged Li'l Bit again and sighed.

"Sandra and Sharon are waitin' in the car with the deputy. He told us it would be better if they didn't come with us, but I'm not sure wh—"

Realizing something was wrong, Ain't Pitty started looking around in a panic.

"Where's Mitchell?"

The silence and tears said what she did not want to hear.

"Oh, God! No . . ."

There was only silence on the ride home. Uncle Ben had pulled Sandra aside and told her what had happened before we left, but no one was ready to tell Li'l Bit and Sharon, and, thankfully, they were not asking, at least not yet.

We were getting out of the cars as the last of the 10:00 p.m. choppers flew over. Those from the lake were in a separate group bringing up the rear. I pictured Mitchell at the helm of the Kiowa and knew I would think of him every time I heard and felt the thumping rotors of a chopper.

Once inside, Ain't Pitty insisted everyone drink a cup of chamomile tea and take a warm shower. "Maybe it will help you sleep."

When it was our turn to shower, there was none of the usual girl chatter, just numbness as we went through the motions. Emptying my pockets, I found the daisy Mitchell had given me earlier, its white petals still attached. As I stepped into the shower, the scent of the daisy mixed with the smell of Zest, and from that point on I could not tell where the tears ended and the shower water began. I sank to my knees, my chest so tight I could hardly breathe.

Just like the first time I saw Mitchell.

When we finally made it to bed, all I could hear was crying. My pillow was soaked with tears and wet hair, and I assumed everyone else's was as well. This was one night when chamomile tea and warm showers would not work their magic. Despite our exhaustion, sleep did not come until the wee hours of the morning; then, one by one, the cussins stopped crying.

When it was just Sam and me awake, she reached over and squeezed my hand.

"One breath at a time, Nettie. Just one breath at a time."

It wasn't long before Sam's breathing changed and I knew she was asleep. The silence in the room roared like thunder in my ears, and the blackness surrounding me was full of images of Mitchell—his dark hair curling against his neck, his deepwater-blue eyes, and that warm smile that just reeled me in. He was so pretty, so heart-stopping pretty. His smell filled the air around me, and I felt his lips brush my cheek—the wispy tickle of mimosa blossoms.

Slipping into a restless sleep, I heard Mitchell's voice.

Choose happy, Nettie. No matter what, choose happy.

Chapter 21

I woke the next morning to the deepest sadness I had ever known.

It's not real. It can't be.

Staring at the ceiling, I prayed to go back to sleep.

If I'm asleep, I can't feel this pain.

But sleep had gone and last night's horror took its place in my mind. I could hear the others waking up around me, but no one spoke. The smell of coffee was coming through the passageway, and we could hear movement and low voices, so we dressed and made our way to the kitchen.

Uncle Ben and Ain't Pitty, looking tired and worn, had Li'l Bit and Sharon on their laps as we came in. They were telling the little ones that Mitchell had been hurt very badly last night and had died.

"He's with his momma in heaven now, and she'll take good care of him," said Ain't Pitty.

"Mitchell loved his momma," said Li'l Bit. "I heard him tell Nettie that he missed her every day. Now he won't have to miss her anymore."

"Yeah," agreed Sharon. "And now his pa and Otis Pierce can't hurt him anymore, either!"

I found myself wishing I were six again. Wishing I did not know what had happened to Mitchell and what had almost happened to Li'l Bit and Sharon.

Sam poured coffee as we found places to sit. Setting a cup in front of me, she whispered, "Remember, all you have to do today is breathe. Just breathe."

A plate of sausage biscuits sat untouched in the middle of the table. No one was hungry. Even the thought of food was nauseating, but the warm coffee cup was somehow comforting.

We were on our second pot when someone knocked at the front door. Uncle Ben went to answer it, and through the echo of tinkling glass he came back to the kitchen with Pastor Flemming in tow. His hair was wet, and he was dressed in fresh khakis and a white button-down shirt, but his face looked bone weary. His eyes were red-rimmed, with dark circles underneath, and his wide shoulders were drooping.

"Miz Pitty, may I bother you for a cup of black coffee, please?"

Pouring him the last of the pot, she started another. He took a big sip, despite its being percolator hot, and set the steaming cup down.

"Last night was awful for all of us, wasn't it?"

Fresh tears welled up around the table. Even Pastor Flemming's eyes were glistening.

"I wanted to see how you all were doing. Were you able to sleep?"

"A little," answered Sandra.

"I don't feel like I slept at all," replied Eric.

"I watched the sun come up," said J.D.

"Have you slept, Pastor?" Sam asked.

"Not yet. Maybe later. I hope you all can take a nap today. It's important to rest, even if it's just for a little while." Looking at the plate of food, he added, "And try to eat something, even if you don't feel like it. Feeding your body can comfort your mind and your spirit."

"Pastor, did the Sheriff catch those men?" I asked.

"Yes, Nettie, he did. They are in jail right now."

"Thank God!" said Ain't Pitty.

"Amen," replied Pastor Flemming. "Last night, the Sheriff asked if I would stay at the jail for a while. Some of the deputies were struggling and in need of support. So I was able to hear what happened."

I was glad those evil men had been caught but was surprised at how little it influenced the sadness I felt. Mitchell was gone, and the fact that those men were in jail did not change that.

"How'd they catch 'em?" asked J.D.

"Actually, you all helped," replied the Pastor. "After talking with Li'l Bit, the Judge realized Ames and Pierce were not likely to leave their liquor behind, and he was right. They made the mistake of going back to their still. What they didn't know was the Sheriff's deputies knew where the still was. They'd found it a few days ago and were keeping an eye on it, hoping to catch the bootleggers in the act, and that's exactly what happened. Sheriff Coker said when they reached the still last night, Ames and Pierce were there loading jugs of moonshine into their truck and Willie Ray Booker and Teivel Slater were loading jugs into their cars. The big Cajun, Gris, was dismantling the still so they could take it with them."

"Well, I'll be da—. Oh, sorry, Pastor," muttered Ain't Pitty.

"They caught four of the five men without a problem, but the big Cajun was swinging a long machete and knew how to move around in the swamp. One of the deputies had to put a bullet through his shoulder to stop him."

Pastor Flemming's lips flattened into a wry smile. "Sheriff Coker got Doc Anderson to come make sure Gris didn't die before they could get information out of him. Doc said the bullet went clear through his shoulder, so he covered the bullet holes with Band-Aids and said any additional medical attention, including any pain medicine and the removal of the dozen or so leeches crawling all over Gris, could wait until every one of the Sheriff's questions had been answered. Gris's hands were cuffed behind his back, so all he could do was suffer with the pain and watch the little bloodsuckers crawl around and bite. Apparently, pain and leeches are great motivators to talk."

"Did the men confess?" asked Uncle Ben.

"It took a while, but they did. When the Sheriff got all five men back to the jail and in different rooms, they started fast-talking—each one trying to blame the others for every bad thing that happened. Sheriff Coker and his deputies stayed at it all night, and by this morning they'd found out that these men not only ran one of the largest moonshine businesses in South Alabama but were also part of a ring of child molesters that has been operating in the Wiregrass for a long time. The Sheriff was able to get the names of others who were involved, and the Alabama State Police are picking them up now."

"What's a mole—" started Li'l Bit, but Ain't Pitty interrupted him.

"Pastor, don't you think the little ones have heard enough? Shouldn't they go outside?"

"No, Miz Pitty, not yet. Last night these children were victims of and witnesses to some horrible things. If they are going to heal and if we are going to help them, it's better they hear the truth from us than to get bits and pieces of half-truths from strangers. Then we need to trust the good Lord to help us with the rest."

"All right," replied Ain't Pitty, sounding reluctant.

"Kids, child molesters are people—bad men and women—who like to hurt children. Mitchell knew his father, Otis Pierce, and some of the other men liked to hurt children, because they had hurt him many times. Last night, Mitchell knew if he didn't help Li'l Bit and Sharon, those men were going to hurt them, too. Mitchell was very brave."

Pastor Flemming's voice faltered, so he stopped to take a sip of coffee.

"Now, as frightening and sad as last night was, all of you are safe now. Those bad men will never be able to hurt you or anybody else again. Sheriff Coker and the Alabama State Police have arrested them for the bad things they've done, and Judge Thorton is already working to see that they spend the rest of their lives in jail."

"Pastor Flemming," asked Sharon, "what about Jessie? Is he okay?"

"Jessie's fine. I talked with Mrs. Maddie last night, and he was home safe and sound."

"I'm glad he was there to help."

"Me too, Sharon."

"Ain't Pitty," asked Li'l Bit, "can we see if Wilbur ate the crickets we put out yesterday?"

"Pastor?"

"Sure, now's a good time."

Ain't Pitty knew what had happened to Wilbur, but Li'l Bit and Sharon did not. They knew the little lizard was not coming around when we were on the porch, but they kept putting dead crickets in his corner to make sure he had something to eat. The next morning when the food was gone—quietly swept into the flowerbed by Ain't Pitty or us—they assumed Wilbur was still out there, running among the azaleas. Next summer would be soon enough for them to know the truth, especially now.

"Stay in the yard," said Ain't Pitty.

It was unlikely they understood everything Pastor Flemming had just explained, but maybe slipping back into everyday life would help with the parts they did understand. I knew there would be more questions as time went on, but for now, maybe feeding Wilbur's ghost was a good thing for them to do.

When the screen door slapped shut, Pastor Flemming continued, his voice harder.

"The Sheriff was able to confirm that Teivel Slater and Otis Pierce were responsible for abusing and killing the two missing girls and Miz Tilly's grandson, Luke."

Another shock wave circled the table.

"Dear God in heaven," whispered Ain't Pitty.

Uncle Ben looked angry and sad at the same time.

"Sheriff Coker was pretty sure these men had something to do with the disappearance of the children all along, but until the men started trying to hang each other last night, he had no proof."

I didn't think it was possible for my sadness to go any deeper, but it did. Now there were also tears for Miz Tilly and Mr. Eli. I knew deep down they had hoped one day Luke would walk back into the café. Now that hope was gone.

"Do Miz Tilly and Mr. Eli know?" I asked.

"Yes, Nettie. They do. I went with Sheriff Coker earlier this morning to tell them. They are very grateful that you all are okay."

Pastor Flemming sipped his coffee, as if giving us time to settle our thoughts.

"What about Willie Ray, Pastor? Was he involved with the children?" asked Ain't Pitty.

"Probably not. Sheriff Coker thinks Willie Ray's primary interest was the moonshine. He bragged to the deputies that he made ten times more money on liquor than he did on the Feed and Seed, and that the only reason he kept the store open during the day was to support the moonshining at night. He used the Feed and Seed's delivery truck to run supplies to Gris, who ran the still, and to haul the liquor back to the store, where they'd hide the jugs in a crawl space underneath the loading dock. When the crawl space was full, Willie Ray would call his midnight runners to come in, load the jugs, and take them across the state lines to waiting buyers. Mitchell's pa and Otis Pierce were two of his runners."

Mitchell worked on that loading dock all the time.

"Last spring, Willie Ray caught his delivery-truck driver stealing liquor and selling it on the side, so he had Gris kill him and dump his body in the Blackwater Swamp. Then Willie Ray brought Mitchell's pa back to Crystal Springs to drive the delivery truck."

"What about Mitchell?" asked Ain't Pitty. "Why'd Willie Ray hire him?"

"To help keep tabs on what his father was doing."

"Did Mitchell know what Willie Ray and his pa were up to?" asked Eric.

"Most likely. But the men said they didn't tell Mitchell much because they were afraid he'd let something slip. Apparently, he liked to talk with Miz Tilly."

"She took food to him just about every day," I said.

"Willie Ray kept a close eye on Miz Tilly, too, especially since the back of her café overlooked the loading dock. On nights he was planning to run moonshine, he'd eat a late supper at Miz Tilly's to make sure she was closing on time and going home. When he came in for breakfast the next morning, he'd make sure she was acting like her usual self."

I shivered, remembering the nights we had staked out the loading dock, trying to see if they were up to anything.

They would've killed us.

"Why'd they kill Mitchell?" I asked, my head spinning at even saying the words.

Pastor Flemming took a deep breath and his words slowed as he told us what happened after the men reached the ice house with Mitchell and Li'l Bit.

"When Pierce realized that Mitchell was holding his pa down in the floorboard of the truck so Li'l Bit could run, he grabbed Mitchell from behind and slammed his head into the door, hard. Mitchell went completely limp and stopped breathing."

My heart was in a vise.

That's the moment Mitchell died.

"When the two men realized Mitchell was dead, his pa decided to send a message to Sheriff Coker and the Judge about who had control over his son. He and Otis Pierce took Mitchell into the ice house and tied the rope around his neck."

I had never seen such sadness in anyone's eyes. Pastor Flemming's heart was broken, just like ours.

At least Mitchell didn't feel what they were doing.

"Afterward, Ames and Pierce searched for Li'l Bit, but they couldn't find him. They finally gave up and decided to get their liquor and get out of town. According to Pierce, they were headed for Mexico. Apparently, there are areas south of the border where child molesters have safe haven."

"Oh, God," said Ain't Pitty. "They were gonna take Li'l Bit and Sharon there, weren't they?"

"That was their plan."

"What about Mitchell?" asked J.D. "Did they plan to leave him alone, like the Judge told 'em to, or were they gonna try and take him?"

"Neither. Pierce said Mitchell knew too much for them to leave him behind and that he was . . . getting too old." Pastor Flemming's voice broke, and it took a minute for him to get it back. "Gris was supposed to stay long enough to kill Mitchell and then meet Ames and Pierce in Mexico."

I shivered from head to toe, and the look on Uncle Ben's face said he could kill those men with his bare hands.

How can such evil exist?

"Why didn't Mitchell tell somebody?" asked J.D., wiping tears from his chin. "Somebody who could have helped him!"

"Because those men threatened to hurt or kill him or the people he cared most about, which is what child molesters do to control their victims. But last night, Mitchell decided to fight back. He was extraordinarily brave, as were all of you. If you all had not done what you did, when you did, those evil men would have gotten away and continued to hurt other children. Now they'll never hurt anyone again."

"Why weren't they caught sooner? If everybody knew they were doin' these awful things, why weren't they locked up?"

"J.D., that's a question a lot of folks are going to be asking for a long time, and I'm not sure there will ever be a good answer." Leaning forward in his chair, the Pastor added, "But what I do know is this: There have been bad people since the dawn of time, and not all of them are locked up or ever will be locked up, which is why good folks have to be watchful. Most of the time, in a free society like ours, there is an assumption of innocence until guilt is proven. Bad people have to be caught in the act of being bad, or there has to be proof they've done something wrong, before anything can be done legally. Last night, Mitchell and you all made it possible for the Sheriff and the Judge to get the proof they needed to put these men and their accomplices away for good."

"They killed Mitchell's momma and abused him for years. How

much more proof did they need? Why did Mitchell and those other kids have to die for it to be enough?"

"I don't know, J.D. I wish I did. But a lot of folks are asking the same questions, trying to figure out what should have or could have been done to prevent all of this."

"All the 'shoulda, coulda, wouldas' in the world can't undo what happened. They're just words of regret at getting caught."

"Regret can be a powerful motivator, J.D.," replied Pastor Flemming.

J.D. was angry and looking for someone to blame, and maybe he was right. Perhaps others did have some responsibility for what happened, but I was still feeling such overwhelming grief that my mind could concentrate on little else.

"How do you make the sad go away, Pastor?"

"You can't make it go away, Nettie. But after a while the sadness will begin to ease, and when you're not looking, it will slip away a little at a time. Eventually, it will be the good things you remember most and sadness will become an occasional visitor. I believe Mitchell would want you to remember the good. He was not one to wallow in self-pity. For all the pain he had in his young life, he did not let it hold him back. He had dreams and wanted to be around good and happy people. He told me not long ago that he'd been happier this summer than he'd been in a very long time and it was because of you all. I do not think he would be happy now if he knew his friends were not. We owe it to Mitchell to let happiness back in."

Choose happy, Nettie. No matter what, choose happy.

Standing to go, Pastor Flemming asked us to pray with him.

"Almighty God, thank you for the blessing of these children and the families and friends who love them. Help all of us learn to understand Mitchell's sacrifice, and, as only you can, bring comfort and healing to our sad hearts and minds. This I ask in the name of your blessed Son, Jesus. Amen."

Pastor Flemming picked up his hat. "We're having Mitchell's funeral the day after tomorrow. Sometimes funerals are sad, and sometimes they are a celebration of a life we loved. Sometimes they're both. But, sad or not, they are a way we can say good-bye. If you all need me, I'll be near."

It had been three days since Mitchell died. Three days of mind-numbing grief that refused to leave. We were sitting on Ain't Pitty's porch, waiting to go to his funeral, and it was raining—not the usual thunderstorm type of rain, but a soft, gentle rain that dripped slowly off the hanging ferns in small, dancing splashes.

The only funeral I had ever attended was Pa Campbell's, and the only thing I could remember about it was that my momma had stood on Hardshell Hill and cried. So I was not sure what to expect except tears, and those had already been flowing nonstop for three days.

Ain't Pitty had called our mommas and daddies and told them what had happened.

"We can help the children some, and they can help each other in ways we can't. But their parents can comfort them like no one else can," she told Pastor Flemming.

She was right. We talked with Momma and Daddy on the phone for a long time after it happened, and it made us feel better to hear their voices and know they were coming to get us. Afterward, for the second time since Mitchell died, I was homesick, ready to be back in my own house and ready to see Andy. He was my best friend, and he always made me feel better.

Now, even with all of us on the porch, it was quiet. We had not talked much since it happened. We just sat together and rocked for hours on end, lost somewhere inside ourselves. Earlier, while getting dressed, I had found the white handkerchief Mitchell had given me the day of the picnic at Uncle Red's farm. Burying my nose in it now and taking a deep breath, I had to smile. It didn't smell like throw-up anymore. It smelled clean and a little like Zest. I was grateful Mitchell had given it to me, especially now.

Since the night Mitchell died, there had been a steady stream of folks coming in and out of Ain't Pitty's. Miz Tilly came with food from the café. Her eyes were red and swollen like ours, and she hugged all of us for a long time when she left. The Wilkes brothers came by with a basket full of penny candy but would not stay. They asked Ain't Pitty to let us know they were thinking of us. Salter Lee stopped by to see how we were doing, and even Miz Lettie brought over a box of cookies on behalf of the good women of the Women's Guild. We were on the porch and saw her coming but were too numb to get excited.

"I'm so very sorry to hear about the loss of your friend," she told us. Handing Ain't Pitty the cookies, she added, "Sometimes we forget what's important in this life, don't we, Pitty? I'm close. Please call me if you or the children need anything, anything at all."

Ain't Pitty didn't say a word, but there were tears in her eyes.

As Miz Lettie turned to leave, J.D. got up. "Miz Lettie, it was us . . . all these years . . . It was us, and I'm sorry—really sorry."

This time, it was Miz Lettie's eyes that filled with tears. She patted J.D.'s arm and headed back across the Railroad.

Some folks who stopped by just wanted to talk about what had happened, but Ain't Pitty cut their questions off quickly and walked them back to their cars. Finally, she put a sign on the mailbox that said NO VISITORS. The one exception was Pastor Flemming. He came twice a day. Most of the time he just rocked with us, not talking and not expecting us to talk, just being with us as we rocked for miles.

Last night J.D. told Pastor Flemming what Mitchell had said about the night his mother died—about sneaking over to Field 10, Lance's help, the Bible with the hidden money, their plan to run, and what had happened when they tried.

"The Bible's at your house, Pastor. I don't know how much money's in there, but I—we—think Mitchell would want you to have it, maybe to help somebody else."

It was several minutes before Pastor Flemming could speak.

Ain't Pitty came through the screen door in a dress and a hat. I had never seen her in a dress before, and the only hat I had ever seen her wear was a straw fishing hat.

"Yes, I own a dress, and it's respectful to wear a hat."

Uncle Ben followed her out of the door, wearing his one and only suit.

"C'mon, folks. It's time to go."

The pews of the church were packed and folks were standing three deep when we arrived. Even Lieutenant Morrison and his crew were there. The ushers said Pastor Flemming wanted us to sit in the front, where Mitchell's family was supposed to be. This time when we walked down the aisle, the pews were quiet. In front of us was Mitchell's closed oak coffin, and on the altar was a mission rocker that Mitchell and Pastor Flemming had made. Moving to the end of the pew next to the window, I took a deep breath. It was impossible for me to imagine Mitchell lying in that wooden box.

Several rows back, Jessie was sitting quietly beside Miz Maddie. Yesterday some of the ain'ts and uncles had chipped in money to buy him a new lawn mower in appreciation for his saving Sharon. This was a surprise to us, because several of them had said they didn't believe Jessie really talked to us. They said that we either made it up or were hearing things in all the excitement.

"Ignore them," Ain't Pitty had said. "Y'all know the truth, and Jessie knows y'all know. That's all that matters."

When the ain'ts and uncles had given Jessie the new mower, he'd showed no sign that he understood what they were saying. Eventually, they said good-bye to Miz Maddie and left, mumbling about wasting their money. Afterward, Jessie walked over and sat down on top of the new mower. Pulling a rag from his back pocket, he began cleaning his old mower.

J.D. had knelt down, put his hand on Jessie's shoulder and said, "Jessie, you're a good guy. Thank you for saving Sharon."

Maybe it was because no one else was around, or maybe it was just because he wanted to, Jessie looked at J.D. and smiled, the kind of smile one good friend gives to another. We would never know if Jessie understood why he'd gotten the new mower, but if it did nothing more than provide a place for him to sit while he did something he liked to do, then it was worth it.

Movement in the pew brought me back to the reality of the funeral. J.D. had gotten up and was heading to the door where Miz Tilly and Mr. Eli had just come in. As J.D. led them down the aisle to sit with us, Miz Tilly paused to place a white-gloved hand on Mitchell's casket and bent her head. She and Mr. Eli had asked Pastor Flemming if they could buy Mitchell's casket for him.

"We can't bury Luke, but we can help bury Mitchell," they'd said.

After their amens, Miz Tilly and Mr. Eli sat down next to Granny. Reaching for the gloved hand of her lifelong friend, Granny held it in both of hers.

With Willie Ray in jail, his wife, Annie, had called Ain't Pitty and asked if she would like to meet for coffee. Ain't Pitty had been so happy to hear from her long-ago friend that she'd smiled despite her sadness. Annie had told Ain't Pitty that she was going to sell the Feed and Seed. Apparently someone had already offered to pay cash for the building and was planning to tear it down and build a new farm-supply store where the old train depot had been. We knew who that someone was.

Pastor Flemming, looking older than his young years and once again in his dark suit, rose slowly and walked to the pulpit, placing his hands on the sides, as if to hold himself up.

"I do not want to be here today, I do not want Mitchell to be dead, and I do not want the good folks sitting in front of me to have lived through such an unimaginable nightmare. But I am, he is, and they did. The horrible events that brought us here have shattered our hearts and our minds and left many of us adrift in a sea of sorrow. I have struggled trying to think of what I could say that would help us begin to work through this tragedy. What words could possibly ease our pain and mourning for Mitchell and the others we have lost, honor their lives, and help us begin to put our lives back together? Then, last night, I remembered something my favorite Sunday-school teacher would say whenever I was lost: 'Just do what the New Testament tells you to do, Jim. Then you don't have to guess.' She was right, of course. But I also realized that New Testament scripture verses traditionally used for funerals were not adequate for a tragedy of this scale. With this much pain, this much heartbreak, and this much outrage, we need more. We need to lift up the message of the whole New Testament, not just parts of it. The twenty-seven books of Christian scripture tell us to do five things." Holding his right hand up, he counted them off. "First, they tell us to believe. Second, they tell us to be thankful. Third, they tell us to pray. Fourth, they tell us to forgive. And fifth, they tell us to act."

Picking up his Bible, Pastor Flemming started walking.

"'Believing.' It is such a simple word, isn't it? But its meaning and power have challenged human beings for almost two thousand years. For those who have accepted the gift of faith in Jesus Christ as the risen Son of the almighty God, believing in a better life beyond the one on this earth is as natural as breathing and is the lifeline we cling to, especially in times like this. But for those among us who have not yet found their way to faith, a tragedy such as this can carry the pain of a dozen burning suns, with no shade in sight. I hope you find shade and comfort within these walls and within these words."

Amens echoed softly throughout the pews as Pastor Flemming walked over in front of us.

"While it may seem unusual to be thankful at a time like this, we cannot lose sight of the many things we need to be thankful for;

otherwise, Mitchell died in vain. We are thankful we had him in our lives for as long as we did, and we are thankful for his courage and selfless sacrifice in saving the lives of these children and perhaps countless others. We are thankful for Jessie, who was in the right place at the right time and chose to help. We are thankful for the Campbell children, who made possible the apprehension of the men responsible for the horrific acts that brought us here. And we are thankful for the police and public officials, who will see that society's justice is fulfilled."

More amens followed Pastor Flemming back to the pulpit.

"Next, we must pray—as long and as often as is needed to say what is on our minds and ask for God's continued support and grace for those affected by this tragedy. Prayer lifts us up. It comforts us and gives us the power to help each other. We pray for Mitchell's soul and the souls of Luke and the other known and unknown innocent victims of this evil. We pray for relief from the anguish we are feeling over the loss of these children. And we pray for a community and a world that views childhood and the innocence of children as something to be cherished and protected by everyone."

The amens were loud now.

"As much as prayer is our power, forgiveness is our hope. However, forgiveness does not come easy. It is a word whose meaning fights against the very nature of human beings, but it is a fight that forgiveness must win. Forgiving and seeking forgiveness are as necessary to Christians as the air we breathe, and they provide the path for us to find our way through the many layers of this tragedy. We seek forgiveness for failing to protect Mitchell and the other innocent victims from these horrific crimes—for failing to acknowledge the evil that was right in front of us, and for ultimately allowing that evil to go unchecked for so long. Lord God, forgive us."

Pastor Flemming began to pace again.

"Just as we need forgiveness, we need to forgive. Forgive ourselves, forgive our neighbors, and . . . forgive the fallen men who committed these acts of evil against our children. Christian forgiveness does not eliminate the debt these men owe their victims, the families, and society. Societal laws will determine how their debt is to be repaid during their time on this earth, and at the end of their mortal lives, God will judge them according to his laws. Because we are Christians, and because we understand that at some point these men were most likely child victims of the very evil they brought into our midst, we forgive them. We need to forgive them, as much for ourselves as for them. The innocence of childhood is not lost, it's taken, and evil is not born, it's bred. Without intercession, evil will beget evil. Through God's grace, Christ interceded on our behalf, and he expects us to intercede on behalf of others who are threatened by evil, whenever, wherever, and however we can. When we fail, he forgives us, and, as hard as it may be for us to understand, he stands ready to forgive them. How can we do any less?"

The amens were whispers this time, but they were there.

With a look of determination on his face, Pastor Flemming said, "Lastly, the New Testament tells us to act, to put our beliefs to work. If we have any hope of something positive coming from this tragedy, we must act in both ordinary and extraordinary ways. As hard as it may be, we have to get back to the business of life. We have to get dressed every day. We have to drink our coffee every day. We have to go to work, school, and play, every day, just as we did before this tragedy. And because we are Christians, these events must instill a deep and long-lasting motivation in each of us to act on behalf of those who have no voice and have no choice. Act now to change the laws that allow our children to slip through our fingers into a hell on earth. Act now to be watchful over the innocent and intercede on behalf of those who cannot protect themselves, all of us, every day, every time, for every child . . . for everyone."

Walking back to the podium, Pastor Flemming picked up a different Bible.

"This was Mitchell's mother's Bible, and it held their hope for escape. Over three hundred dollars were hidden within these pages—more than enough money for Mitchell and his mother to escape the hell they were in, but they needed a safe place to go and they needed help to get there. We were too late to help them, but if we act, maybe we won't be too late for the next mother and child. All of the money found in this Bible, as well as the money confiscated from the men who committed these crimes, has gone into a special bank account to help our community start an organization whose sole purpose is to provide a sanctuary from fear and abuse. We are calling the organization Mitchell's House, the house without walls. Sheriff Coker, Judge Thorton, Doctor Anderson, and I call upon all moral people, Christian and non-Christian alike, to help by telling anyone you know or suspect is being physically or emotionally abused to reach out. Mitchell's House, the house without walls, will be there to help them."

Mitchell would love this.

Pastor Flemming went over and sat down in the mission rocker that had been placed on the altar.

"Before he died, Mitchell told me that some of the happiest moments of his life were when he was rocking on the porch with his friends. He said he hadn't known such happiness in a long time. What better way to prevent the dulling of our motivation to act than rocking chairs? Yes, folks, I said rocking chairs. Every time you sit in one, make a decision on what you will do when you get up. Make a call, give money, be a friend, report abuse, protect a child . . . Act, whenever, wherever, and however you can.

"To support the rocking-chair effort, we are tearing down the old ice house and using the wood to build as many mission rockers as we can, all with the words 'Mitchell's House' engraved on them as a reminder for our community to act. We are going to place rockers in the churches, the courthouse, the Sheriff's office, the town hall, Wilkes's, Tilly's café, the senior center, the Crossing, and anywhere else folks gather as a reminder to act on behalf of those who cannot act for themselves. Someday, maybe rocking chairs will be a symbol of a life free of pain and fear for everyone. It is a small start, but it's a start."

Standing, Pastor Flemming raised his right hand.

"We believe. We give thanks. We pray. We forgive. We act. Mitchell's life, Luke's life, and the lives of the other children are important and they deserve no less. And while their time on this earth has ended, life goes on, and it goes on in hope—hope that is grounded in our belief that these children have crossed into a new life and are now in the safe and loving care of Jesus Christ. Take comfort from knowing they are in a better place, surrounded by those who love them, and that we will see them again when it's our turn to cross over."

I'll see Mitchell again.

As Pastor Flemming asked us to stand and sing, my mind wandered outside. The rain had stopped, and though it was an end-of-summer day, the breeze coming in the window was cool and fresh. Birds were chirping, squirrels were playing under the tree next to the church, and I could see the faint beginnings of a rainbow forming above the rooflines in the distance.

I missed Mitchell. I missed his pretty face, his smile, and the way I felt when he was around. I was sad he would not have a chance to grow up and experience life like the rest of us. I missed what might have been and wondered what it would have been like to kiss him, not on the cheek but on the lips. I was sad I would never know what it was like to have him as a boyfriend and that he would never know what it was like to have a girlfriend. The idea of boyfriends and girlfriends was not as awful a thought now as it had been at the beginning of the summer. I had changed, and because of Mitchell, growing up was not as frightening anymore.

Looking at Mitchell's handkerchief, I saw something I had not noticed before. In the corner of the soft fabric was a tiny white daisy, the embroidered stitches smooth as silk and perfectly placed.

Mitchell's mother did this. They loved daisies.

If Pastor Flemming was right, and in my heart I knew he was, Mitchell was with his mother and was okay. Running my finger over and over the smooth daisy, I realized my tears were not for

Mitchell—they were for me, for all of us. We were the ones left behind.

Those around me were singing "Amazing Grace." Pastor Flemming talked a lot about grace in his sermons, but the words had never really sunk in until now. If he was right and it was the Lord's grace that made it possible for Mitchell to be safe and with his mother, then it really was amazing and I was grateful for it.

When the last stanza of the hymn had been sung, everyone filed quietly out of the church—many stopping long enough to make a donation to Mitchell's House as they left. We climbed into the Oldsmobile and, with headlights on, followed the white hearse carrying Mitchell to Hardshell Hill. He was to be buried next to his mother, in the shade of the same old oak tree we had sat under the day of the float.

Once there, most folks headed to the gravesite, but we made our way farther up the hill to sit at the foot of the big oak. We had heard all the words we wanted to hear for now. Settling down in the grass, we watched as folks gathered along the flower-covered gravesite to listen to Pastor Flemming one more time. Next to where I was sitting was the patch of daisies Mitchell had pulled flowers from to plant at his mother's grave. Looking over at her headstone, I could see they were alive and doing well.

He'd be happy about that.

I doubted I would ever see another daisy and not think about him. Pulling some of the little white flowers and their roots out of the ground, I set them in my lap.

The graveside service was short, and when it was over, folks lined up to either lay flowers on Mitchell's casket or sprinkle freshly dug dirt into his grave. Among the last in line were Sheriff Coker and the Judge, and instead of going down the hill when they were finished, they headed our way.

Clearing his throat, Sheriff Coker spoke first. "I wanted y'all to know that we would not have been able to apprehend those responsible for all of this if you all had not done what you did. We've been tryin' to catch those men for a very long time, and if we had been five minutes later, they would've been gone and we would've had a hell of a time tryin' to catch up with them again, much less prove what they did. Now, they'll never hurt innocent folks again. I thank you for that."

Stepping forward, the Judge added, "Since Mitchell's mother died two years ago, Sheriff Coker and I have been working with the state legislators in Montgomery to change the law so we can move more quickly to help folks like her and Mitchell. We are meeting with them again next week, and hopefully we can make sure something like this never happens again."

"A day late and a dollar short for Mitchell," snapped J.D., unwilling to let the two men off the hook, the anguish showing on his face.

"Yes, son, it is," replied the Judge. "We've not been able to convince the lawmakers up to now, but Mitchell's story is a powerful one and it just may help us get the law changed. Then maybe we won't be a day late and a dollar short next time."

Nodding to us, the Sheriff put his hat on and headed down the hill, but the Judge stayed on.

"I want you to know that I am very proud of all of you. You were extraordinarily brave, brave beyond your years, as was Mitchell. It's hard to lose a friend, especially like this, but don't let what happened change your lives in a way you know Mitchell would not want. He deserves better, and so do you." Putting on his hat, he added, "I hope when you all come back to Crystal Springs next summer, you'll come see me . . . uh, me and my rose garden, that is."

With a wink, he turned and went down the hill.

As the last of the folks left Hardshell Hill, we told Ain't Pitty we wanted to walk. There was going to be a gathering for a meal at her house, and we did not want to be there. Too many folks were still asking too many nosy questions, and we did not want to talk about it, especially with them. This was Mitchell's story and it was ours, not theirs.

As the last car pulled out of the driveway, quiet settled over the grave-covered hill. From where we sat, we could see the entire cemetery, old graves and new ones, generations of Crystal Springs folks here for their final rest.

"This place really is peaceful," said Eric.

"That's the whole point, isn't it?" said Sam.

"Yeah!" snapped J.D. "This place is a real hoot for someone Mitchell's age." Holding his head, he added, "It's just so unfair—so damned unfair."

There was nothing to say—he was right. What happened to Mitchell should never have happened, and there was nothing we could do to change it.

"He was only fourteen. He never had a chance to do anythin'. He never had a chance to grow up, to live his life, to see different places, to do different things, or even to know he was safe. I can't believe this is where it ends for him—not now, not like this."

"Remember what Pastor Flemming said?" I asked. "Life doesn't end here. He says life goes on. It just goes on in a different way. Mitchell's life is in heaven now."

"Right. Heaven."

"Just because you can't see it or hear it doesn't mean it's not real. Just like love—you can't see it or hear it, but you know when you have it and when you don't. Mitchell loved his momma, and she loved him. He missed her terribly. I believe he's with her now and that he's okay."

"Well, I'm not at that point yet, Nettie. I don't know if I'll ever get there."

I wasn't sure what to say. I didn't know how or why I had come to believe, but I did, and now that belief was helping to ease the pain in my heart and my head. I knew it would help J.D., too, if he could find his way there.

"Pastor Flemming said just to keep listenin' to the Lord. Just keep puttin' one foot in front of the other and keep goin', even if you're sad, and even if you think you can't. Just keep goin', keep headin' toward believin'."

"I was listenin', too, Nettie, and I didn't hear all of that. Anyway, you don't believe somethin' just because somebody says so, even Pastor Flemming."

"Well, that's true, kinda. But he said the Lord will help you know what to do if you listen with your heart. I think maybe the Lord was talking to Mitchell when he—"

"Oh, sure, Nettie! Like the Lord told Mitchell to go after the men who'd already beaten him half to death. The same men who'd done horrible things to him."

"No. That's not what I think at all. I think the Lord told Mitchell to help Li'l Bit and Sharon and his heart was listening."

Fresh tears started flowing down J.D.'s face.

"Mitchell knew what those men would do to him, and he went anyway. Where does that kind of courage come from?"

Li'l Bit moved over next to J.D. and wrapped his small arms around one of J.D.'s long legs.

"You know what I think, J.D.?"

Not waiting for an answer, Li'l Bit continued, "I think you and the others did the same thing as Mitchell. You came to help Sharon 'n' me. You knew those men could hurt you, but you came anyway. You weren't thinkin' about yourselves; you were thinkin' about us."

J.D. put one arm around Li'l Bit's shoulders and used the other one to wipe away tears.

"You think so, huh, little fella?"

"Yes, I do. That night . . . when it happened, I was prayin' really hard that y'all would find me. I was so scared runnin' across that dark field by myself. When I reached the creek, I hid under the honeysuckle bush we found. I heard Otis Pierce and Mitchell's pa hollerin' and comin' across the field after me and I watched them search the beach. They were cussin' and yellin' at each other, almost fightin'. Otis Pierce was yellin' that they needed to get goin', and Mitchell's pa was yellin' that he wasn't leavin' without me. He was so close I could smell 'im, and I was shakin' so bad the leaves around me were shakin', too, but he didn't see me. He was right in front of me, and he didn't see me. I think the Lord was protectin' me."

Li'l Bit shuddered and held tighter to J.D.

"They finally left the beach, but I stayed put 'cause I could still hear noise comin' from the ice house. Then I saw the flashlight comin' back across the field and I started cryin'. I just knew Mitchell's pa was comin' back and this time he'd find me. But then I heard your voice, and it was like cool shade washin' over me. I knew I was gonna be okay. You came lookin' for me, J.D., 'cause your heart told ya to."

"Smart heart," said J.D.

"Smart shade," said Eric, catching the eye of his best friend.

We sat for a long time, not talking, just listening to the sounds around us, watching butterflies float from bush to bush, dodging the occasional bee, and staring at Mitchell's flower-covered grave. A sad but calm peace seemed to settle over us, and the tears began to stop.

"C'mon, y'all," said J.D. "Let's go."

As the others followed J.D. down the hill, I walked over to Mitchell's grave.

I'm not ready to leave you . . . not yet.

Kneeling, I dug a hole in the soft dirt beside the grave and set the daisies I had picked down in it. Covering the roots with dirt, I patted it down until the flowers stayed upright. I didn't want the daisies to die or be thrown away with the cut flowers. I wanted them to stay with Mitchell and find a way to take root and grow like his momma's.

Brushing the dirt off my hands, I wiped away the last tears.

"I hope you're happy to be with your momma again, Mitchell. I miss you a lot. I wanted more time with you, more summers. I wanted to watch you grow up and fly helicopters, and I wanted to grow up with you. I'm tryin' to do what you said—tryin' to keep the good memories close and the bad ones put away. And I'm tryin' to choose happy. It's hard, but I'm tryin'."

"C'mon, Nettie," called Sam. "It's time."

The clouds had cleared, and the sun felt warm against my face.

"I'll never forget you, Mitchell. Don't you forget me."

Giving him a little wave, I made my way down to where the others were waiting in the shade. Glancing back, I could not see the daisies I had just planted, but I knew they were there, and in my heart I knew they would grow.

"Life goes on."

J.D. looked up the hill one last time and then turned for the road.

"You're right, Nettie, it does. And so will we. C'mon, y'all. Let's go swimmin'."

Acknowledgments

While writing a novel is a solitary endeavor, it is never completed in isolation. Many people play essential roles in making a story greater than the sum of its parts. To that end, I wish to thank:

- Buddy, Cindy, Eric, Sandra, and Sharon for allowing me to model characters after their wonderful childhood selves,
- Claudia, whose heartfelt support in John David's absence was an important and meaningful connection for all of us,
- Friends who took the time to read earlier versions and offer comment and encouragement,
- Dave Allen Photography whose body of extraordinary work is where I found the cover *The Wiregrass* was meant to have,
- John Burns, for his beautiful illustrations, and
- Merrissa Hill, of Portrait Lady Photography, for working her magic on the author picture.

Hugs and thanks to my children, Michael, Sarah, and Cindy for their love and support, and a special thank you to my husband and best friend, Jeff. How blessed am I to have such a wonderful life's partner. He supported every facet of writing this novel; listening, reading, traveling, and helping edit the manuscript too many times to count.

Last but not least, thanks to SheWritesPress, a paradigm-changing publishing company, and the extraordinary staff I was privileged to work with:
- Annie Tucker, developmental and copy editor
- Cait Levin, project director and self-proclaimed organizer of messes
- Brooke Warner, visionary publisher

Recipes

Granny's Divinity

Ingredients:
2 c. sugar
½ c. white corn syrup
½ c. cold water
Few grains of salt
2 egg whites, room temperature
1 tsp. pure vanilla
½–1 c. chopped pecans (depending on how much you like nuts)

You will also need plenty of time and patience (on the front end), speed (on the back end), and a low-humidity day.

Directions:
Place sugar, syrup, water, and salt in a heavy saucepan and heat over low heat. Stir until sugar is dissolved, then cook without stirring until the mixture reaches 260°F on a candy thermometer or until a small amount of mixture forms a hard ball when dropped into very cold water.

While syrup is cooking, beat egg whites until stiff peaks form. Once the sugar mixture reaches 260°F, wipe the crystals from the pouring edge of the pan and gently pour a small stream of syrup into the egg whites. Once you start pouring, do not stop. Beat constantly on high while pouring, and continue to beat until mixture loses its sheen and forms soft peaks (approximately 10 minutes). Fold in vanilla and nuts.

Using one spoon to dip the mixture and another spoon to slide it off, quickly drop the divinity onto waxed paper (forming a peak). Allow candy to cool. You may also turn out the mixture into a shallow, oiled pan and cut into 1-inch squares when firm. If the candy becomes too stiff, add a few drops of hot water. Yields about 1 lb.

Ain't Pitty's Hush Puppies

Ingredients:
3/4 c. fresh cornmeal
1/3 c. all-purpose flour
1/2 generous c. finely diced onion
1 tsp. salt
1/2 tsp. sugar
1 finely diced hot pepper (choose your degree of hotness!). You may also add a few drops of hot sauce, if desired.
1 egg, beaten
1/2 c. buttermilk
Peanut oil

Directions:
Combine cornmeal, flour, onion, salt, sugar, hot pepper, egg, and buttermilk. Stir well and let set 15 minutes. Make sure all ingredients are wet (if they are too dry, add a little more buttermilk). Drop mixture by the spoonful into a cast-iron skillet filled with about 1 inch hot peanut oil (medium-high heat) and cook about 3–4 minutes, browning on all sides. Remove and drain on paper towels. Yields 10–12 hush puppies.

Miz Tilly's Fried Chicken

Ingredients:
3 c. thick buttermilk
2½ tsp. salt, divided
1 large whole chicken (washed and cut up)

Peanut oil
1¼ c. all-purpose flour
2 eggs (beaten)
2 tsp. ground black pepper
1½ tsp. paprika
½ tsp. garlic powder
1 tsp. sugar

Directions:

Mix buttermilk and 1 tsp. salt and pour over chicken parts. Cover and refrigerate at least 1 hour (or overnight, if possible).

Fill a deep cast-iron skillet with 1–1½ inches of peanut oil and place over medium-high heat.

Mix the flour, remaining salt, pepper, paprika, garlic powder, and sugar in a brown paper bag and shake. Drain excess buttermilk from individual chicken parts, dip in the beaten egg, and place in the paper bag three pieces at a time and shake. Place chicken parts in hot oil, making sure they are not touching. Fry about 15 minutes, until golden brown and cooked through (adjust heat as needed). When chicken is done, drain on paper towels.

Book Group Discussion Questions for *The Wiregrass*

1. What do landmarks on the road from Virginia to Alabama reveal about Nettie?

2. What characteristics of the Wiregrass region are most relevant to the story?

3. How would you describe the relationship between Nettie and Sam? Between J.D. and Eric?

4. Why do you think Ain't Pitty, Uncle Ben, and Granny let the cussins have the freedom they do?

5. What makes Mitchell different from other abused and sexually violated children?

6. What role does secrecy play throughout the story?

7. How does faith develop in the characters?

8. How does the concept of grace evolve throughout the story?

9. What does Hardshell Hill symbolize?

10. How does the concept of family change from beginning to end?

11. How do battles between good and evil play out throughout the story?

12. Examine the use of laughter and tears in moving the story forward.

About the Author

Merrissa Hill

Pam Webber is an author and nationally certified nurse practitioner and award-winning university level nursing educator. She has published numerous articles, and co-authored four editions of a nursing textbook. Pam resides in Virginia's Northern Shenandoah Valley with her husband, Jeff. *The Wiregrass* is her first novel.

SELECTED TITLES FROM SHE WRITES PRESS

She Writes Press is an independent publishing company
founded to serve women writers everywhere.
Visit us at www.shewritespress.com.

Fire & Water by Betsy Graziani Fasbinder. $16.95, 978-1-938314-14-8.
Kate Murphy has always played by the rules—but when she meets
charismatic artist Jake Bloom, she's forced to navigate the treacher-
ous territory of passionate love, friendship, and family devotion.

Bittersweet Manor by Tory McCagg. $16.95, 978-1-938314-56-8. A
chronicle of three generations of love, manipulation, entitlement,
and disappointed expectations in an upper-middle class New Eng-
land family.

Watchdogs by Patricia Watts. $16.95, 978-1-938314-34-6. When
journalist Julia Wilkes returns to the town where her career got its
start, she is forced to face some old ghosts—and some new enemies.

Water On the Moon by Jean P. Moore. $16.95, 978-1-938314-61-2.
When her home is destroyed in a freak accident, Lidia Raven, a divorced mother of two, is plunged into a mystery that involves her
entire family.

Beautiful Garbage by Jill DiDonato. $16.95, 978-1-938314-01-8.
Talented but troubled young artist Jodi Plum leaves suburbia for the
excitement of the city—and is soon swept up in the sexual politics
and downtown art scene of 1980s New York.

Cleans Up Nicely by Linda Dahl. $16.95, 978-1-938314-38-4. The
story of one gifted young woman's path from self-destruction to
self-knowledge, set in mid-1970s Manhattan.